BUMPING *into* YOU

BUMPING into YOU

JESS JEFFERIES

JUST ADD INK PUBLISHING

Paperback ISBN: 979-8-9873301-3-5
E-book ISBN: 979-8-9873301-2-8

Printed by IngramSpark in the United States of America.

First printing, 2024.

Library of Congress Control Number: 2024911349

Just Add Ink Publishing
Murfreesboro, TN
JustAddInkPublishing@gmail.com

Front cover design by Melody Jeffries
Interior design by Christina Crosland

Content Warning

Hello Readers,

Before you jump into *Bumping into You*, I wanted to offer a few content warnings. Unlike book one in this series, this is an open door romantic comedy, which means there are explicit scenes on page. This book also deals with grief and the loss of a parent due to cancer (past). If any of these are too difficult for you to read, please know your mental health is important to me, so it's okay. If you are good with the above, then happy reading!

Jess Jefferies

Also by Jess Jefferies:

Unlucky in Love Series

Thirteen-Year Crush

Bumping into You

To the friends who become family, I couldn't do this life without you.

And to the ones who always push yourself too hard trying to be enough—Let this be your reminder that it's okay. YOU are enough.

BUMPING *into* YOU

CHAPTER 1
Gwen

"Will you just stop and sit for a minute?" Bradley walks toward my office desk. "We need to talk."

I look up from my checklist, then return to counting the vases for the centerpieces. "I've told you about this event and how particular these clients are. Can't you give me like thirty minutes first?"

Bradley lets out a heavy sigh before mumbling, "I've given you more than that for the last two years."

I whip around to face him. "What's that supposed to mean?" I question.

Shaking his head, Bradley stands and puts his hands in his jean pockets. "It means I'm done waiting, Gwen. I think it's past time for us to break up."

"What?" I sputter. "What are you saying?" My legs go weak, and I grab hold of the chair closest to me to help steady myself.

I picture the wedding vision board I had created for us. We had been talking about wedding plans for months, and I had thought he was about to propose. The board is filled with all of our favorite things and little memories of our relationship over the past two years. There's his parents' church where his parents always dreamed of him getting married, roses of all colors as they're my favorite flower, a cake made by my best friend Holly because there is no one else I'd rather have make my wedding cake, a beautiful wedding dress that would be perfect for a church wedding, and so much more. Everything is on it, down to the color of the invitations and tablecloths.

I never doubted that one day we'd get married. We've been together long enough and even moved in with each other six months ago. Marriage is the natural next step for us. Why is he wanting to break up out of the blue?

"You're a beautiful person, and I loved you," Bradley continues, "but I can't keep being second. We were supposed to be a team, partners, but all you care about, all you talk about anymore is this business."

"How long have you felt this way?" I ask, heat rising in my cheeks. "How long have you been planning to break up with me?"

"A few months now," he admits. "Not to break up. That's been more recent, but a few months of giving you a chance to make us a priority."

"You gave me a few months to make us a priority, and you didn't have the decency to communicate this with me?" My lips pinch together as I shake my head. "How can I fix something I don't even know is broken, or breaking?" My shock morphs into anger. "I started Whimsy and Wonder Events by Gwen from scratch, Bradley. This business is my baby. I can't just abandon it. What do you expect me to do? If I fail, this business fails. Then where does that put us?" I stare at him, my brows raised in question and my heart racing at the implications.

"That's not the point, Gwen," he says, his voice cracking as he avoids eye contact with me. "You gave up on us when you put this business first. We could have been a team, but it was always about you, your business, your future. It was never about us. When was there supposed to be time for us?"

"Okay, I get it. You've made it clear you hate my job."

"No, Gwen, I don't hate your job. In fact, I've always been supportive of you and your business. I was even proud of you, but I hate the woman you've become. You're not the same Gwen I started dating. I'm fed up with being second to your work. I'm tired of you running out at all hours to fix this emergency or meet with a new client. How many times did you leave our dates early with some work excuse? How many times did you cancel our plans only to never reschedule them?"

"Well, you always said you were okay and you understood," I reply, heartbroken and confused. "That you'd always support my career choice."

"Yeah, I didn't tell you how I was feeling, Gwen." He turns his body away from me. "I was too embarrassed to admit that you cared more about your job than about me."

"That's not true. I cared about you a lot," I snap back.

"Really? Then tell me, what did we do for our two-year anniversary? Hmm?"

"I . . ." I scramble through my brain trying to recall. "You went to go visit your parents. You told me your parents needed help with some house project."

"Yeah, I made up that story because every time I suggested some way to celebrate, you had something else going on. What was I supposed to do? Was I supposed to tell you it broke my heart?"

"You were supposed to communicate with me."

"Gwen, you scheduled a three-day wedding over our anniversary weekend and were so excited because of the exposure this would get your business. I made up the story about my parents needing help with a project so you wouldn't feel bad. But did you ever try and make it up? No, you never said a damn thing, and that was it for me.

I stopped caring, stopped trying. And now here we are." Sighing, he turned to me. "Yes, I kept things from you, and I feel bad about it and want to come clean. But a lot of this is on you. I sank down to that level because you made me feel less than. You stopped being fun; you stopped trying to be an *us*. I didn't need a pretty face, a roommate. I needed a companion. We just aren't right for each other."

"You don't just get to decide this for us both. You finally open up to me, and it's to tell me it's over. The past two years are just done, finished, no chance to work on it together? I can't believe you're so self-centered that you've made this all about you," I bite out, hurt that he's ending our two-year relationship over me being a little busy.

His head snaps up at my statement, hurt emanating from his eyes. The sight gives me pause.

"Bye, Gwen," he says as he backs away slowly. "I'll have my things moved out by the end of this weekend." Then he turns to leave.

"But . . . wait, Bradley . . . I didn't mean . . ." I trail off as he looks back at me, his eyes full of sorrow, before shaking his head and walking out the door.

The weight of what just happened hits me, and I collapse into a chair. Two years of my life gone, wasted on someone who couldn't even bring himself to communicate his feelings with me. I could have adjusted things. I could have fixed it.

I wipe away the tears that begin falling down my cheeks. I'm a strong, independent woman, and I don't need a man who isn't going to communicate with me, who isn't going to put in the effort to make us work.

Forget him. I'm just going to put all my energy into my business and reap the rewards of it—that'll show him. I'll make sure nothing ever gets overlooked again. Whimsy and Wonder Events by Gwen will be more successful than ever, and then Bradley will understand why I've had to work so much.

EIGHT MONTHS
Later . . .

CHAPTER 2
Niall

I open my locker at the firehouse and take off my gear.

Mitchell, a fellow recruit I started at the firehouse with, takes his coat off next to me. "Did I hear that you're going to be off for the next week and a half?" he asks.

"You heard right," I say.

Johnny sits next to us and pulls a homemade cookie out of a Tupperware. "Want one?" he asks us.

I nod, and Mitchell doesn't hesitate to grab one.

Johnny hands me a cookie. "What has you takin' off for so long?" he asks.

I put the whole cookie in my mouth then dig out the wedding invitation I'd received a few months ago, which had been stuffed in my locker. "This is one of the reasons I'm heading to Miami tomorrow."

Mitchell takes the invitation from me and reads it aloud.

HOLLY PALMER
and
GREGORY KENTON

REQUEST THE PLEASURE OF YOUR COMPANY
AT THE CEREMONY OF THEIR WEDDING.

—— JULY ——

FRIDAY   **14**   5 O'CLOCK

—— 2023 ——

REGAL VOYAGE CRUISE LINES
CRUISE DETAILS ATTACHED.

"Who are Gregory and Holly?" asks Johnny, eating another cookie.

"Greg is an old college mate of mine, and Holly is his grade-school sweetheart that he's finally marrying," I reply.

"That's nice," says Johnny. "I'd dated my gal since high school before finally marrying her after we graduated."

I laugh. "Greg wishes he was so lucky. He'd been pining after this lass for years. Thirteen to be exact. About a year and a half ago, they finally got together."

"Damn, that's a long time," says Brianna, who had just walked into the locker room.

"So, are you hoping to find your girl on this cruise then?" Mitchell teases.

"God knows it's about time you find one," Johnny adds.

"Nothing like that," I say. "Greg asked me to be one of his groomsmen. I couldn't deny my mate's request. Plus, another college mate of ours, Trent, will be there too. I'm looking forward to seeing them again. It's been too long."

"College?" asks Mitchell. "Do you mean the fire academy in New York?"

"I actually went to Boston University and met Trent and Greg there," I say. "I graduated with a degree in business, but found out quickly after graduation that the nine-to-five desk job wasn't for me."

"I get it," says Johnny. "I'd be too restless sitting around all day."

"Exactly," I say. "I was just staring at a bunch of spreadsheets. I needed action, adventure, a job that gave me purpose."

"So you joined the academy," Brianna says.

"I did. Not even six months after graduating, I'd quit my job and signed up for the FDNY Fire Academy. Eighteen weeks later, I was a fireman."

"And now you're getting all the adventure you wanted, right?" asks Johnny, slapping me on the shoulder.

"Don't get me wrong," I say, "I know being a firefighter isn't all bells and whistles. It's stressful, not only the toll it takes on the body but also the mind. But it makes me happy."

All three of my coworkers nod in agreement.

"Helping people," I say, "making a difference one life at a time, that's what really makes it worth it."

"Your mom would be proud of you," says Johnny.

"Thanks." I look at the ground, hoping they'll take the hint that I don't want to talk about her. It's been one year since I lost her, but it still feels like a fresh wound.

Growing up, it was just me and my mam. We were inseparable. It's why I stayed close to home for college and live in the Boston area to this day. When my mam was in her twenties, she met my dad in Ireland, fell in love, and followed him back to the States, his home country. She left Ireland and came to Boston with nothing but a bag on her back. After she and my dad got married, they moved into my childhood home, and she and I have lived in the same house ever since, even after my dad left. Thinking about her absence still leaves me feeling empty.

"I agree," says Captain Frank, entering the locker room. "Your mom would be proud of you. I know it's hard not having your mom around anymore. Anyone can tell you've been different this past year. Your mom would want you to get your spirit back. She'd want you to go on this vacation."

A lump forms in my throat. Captain Frank's been a father figure to me since I started at this firehouse. I don't know what it is about him, but it seems like he naturally falls into that position for most of the crew. They have all become *mo thaeghlach*, or my family, to me since my mam got sick.

They stepped in to help with Mam whenever they could or cover my shifts when she got worse. Mam and I always had a homemade meal from someone in the crew, which helped to make me feel like I wasn't alone in everything.

I push the lump in my throat back down. Changing the subject from my mam, I say, "I don't know if I'd call a wedding a vacation."

"You'll love it!" says Brianna. "Paul and I went on a cruise last summer, and it was a blast."

"Yeah," I say, "from the sound of the wedding itinerary, it'll be a *craic*-filled, jam-packed week, so I will definitely be doing a lot."

"I'll bet all the women will be falling all over you with your Irish accent," says Mitchell.

"I still can't believe the Boston accent hasn't worn on you after all these years," says Brianna.

"Ha," I shrug, "with how strong my mam's accent was and how she made sure we were always surrounded by other Irish families here, I'm not surprised in the least."

My mam had flourished in the large Irish community in the Boston area. I grew up fully immersed in the community, and even though I've only gone to Ireland once to visit my grandparents, I've never lacked for learning about my roots. My mam was proud of her Irish heritage and instilled that love deep into me. Growing up in the States didn't remove my Irish accent.

"And he's definitely not complaining about all the ladies it brings him," says Mitchell, elbowing me in the ribs.

"Not as many as you would think," I reply. "Anyway, I'm not the relationship type. Sure, I've dated, but I've never wanted to settle down."

Before she died, my mam had been on me for years about settling down and giving her grandchildren, but that just wasn't the life I wanted. I had no desire to be a father—a husband—not after my father left my mam to raise me all on her own. But before my mam passed, I'd made a promise to her. I can still remember a delicate wisp of hair poking out from her headscarf, her frame draped in loose-fitting clothes. She looked so vulnerable, a drastic contrast to the resilient and strong woman I grew up with before she had cancer.

"*A chroí*," Mam had said, "I want you to promise me something."

"Anything," I replied, coming to sit down next to her on the couch and taking her trembling hand in mine. She'd been in treatments for a while, and they made her tired and frail.

"Don't just say that. You have to really promise me. Soon I might not be here, and I don't like to think of you by yourself."

"Mam, don't say that. You're getting your treatments; the doctor says they're working."

"Hush, *a chroí*, and listen to me. I don't like the thought of you being alone in this world. I want you to promise me that when I'm gone, you won't stay alone," she said softly.

"I won't be, Mam. I have my friends and coworkers—"

"That's not what I mean," she cut me off. "I'm not going to tell you not to mourn me, but there better damn well be a limit. One year, *a chroí*, that's all I will allow. After that, I want you to really try. Try and find a *cailín deas*, someone who makes you happy, who fights for you, and laughs with you, and makes it so you no longer feel alone."

"Mam—"

"I'm not done," she continued. "I want you to put yourself out there, date someone for a while, really try. You've never been one for long relationships, and that breaks my heart."

"I'm not the relationship type."

"Don't be an eejit. You're the most loving and caring lad. I should know because I raised you up right. Now promise me you'll put your all into forging a relationship with someone who deserves the kind, sweet lad I raised."

Patting the top of her hand, I gave her a sad smile. "I promise, Mam."

"One year," she emphasizes. "I mean it. One year from me passing and you better be trying to find someone."

"I will do my best to keep that promise," I say, squeezing her hand.

"That's a good lad, *buachaill maith*. Now help me lie down. I'm feeling a bit tired."

My deadline for keeping that promise is up, and even though it's hard to move on, I won't disrespect the memory of my mam by disregarding her last wishes.

"Well, you never know," says Johnny, bringing me back to the conversation. "Just don't miss out on a good time or keep yourself from having a little fun if it bumps into you."

"I won't," I say. *I can't. My year's up, and I promised Mam.*

"Good," says Captain Frank. "You need to get rid of the black cloud that's been hanging over you." Captain Franks turns to look at the rest of the crew. "Now stop this lollygagging. You've been working for the past twenty-four hours. Everyone get home and get some sleep, and I'll see you back here in forty-eight hours. Except you, Niall. You have a nice time on that cruise."

CHAPTER 3
Gwen

It's finally happening. I never thought this day would come. My best friend, Holly, and my brother, Greg, are getting married. I am over the moon for both of them!

Holly asked both me and her younger sister Margot to be her bridesmaids. I also get the honor of helping her plan the event. Sure, the cruise has its own wedding coordinator, Courtney, who I've chatted with a few times, but I need to make sure everything is just right for Holly and Greg. Never has there been two people who deserve to have a perfect day more than them. I'm not going to leave their wedding to some stranger. I'll be managing it—the most important event of my career.

They won't have to worry about anything because I'm always prepared for the craziest or most random things to go wrong at any event. Weddings in particular seem to always need some of the most outlandish fixes.

Groomsmen shave off the groom's eyebrow the night before the wedding? Well, I have a fix for that.

Bride loses her something blue? I'm prepared for that.

I pull out my emergency bag and triple-check everything is packed and ready to go for the wedding. I'll make sure everything goes off without a hitch.

My thoughts slip back to the wedding I had planned for Bradley and me.

Ugh, Bradley, why do I let that man take up space in my brain? *Well, Gwen, maybe it has something to do with the fact that you had your perfect wedding all planned out, and instead of him proposing to you, he dumped you.*

It's been eight months since our breakup, and I can't help but think that if Bradley hadn't broken up with me, I would've been close to walking down the aisle now.

Forget him. I put the rest of my clothes in my suitcase. *You have a thriving business, and he couldn't even stand by you as you made it successful.*

It was all about him and his needs.

Ugh, why are men so frustrating? Who needs them anyway?

I have been just fine without Bradley, happily spending my time building my business up. I've even been able to hire more people to help with the influx of events we get asked to do.

Plus, it's not like he was right. I don't work all the time. I put other people before my work sometimes. I get out and do things.

I just went to that event-planning conference in Florida last month, and I somewhat regularly see Holly, Greg, and Trent. Okay, I mean I guess I don't see them all the time, and I mostly see Holly when I stop by her bakery to make sure an order for an upcoming event is good to go, but they understand. They, unlike Bradley, know how important my event-planning business is and how busy it keeps me.

I sigh, zipping up my suitcase. With Greg and Holly getting married, the dynamic of our friend group won't be the same. I'm starting to realize how quiet my own company can be.

Music rings on my phone, and I dig through my purse to find it. That ringtone can only mean one person is calling.

"Hi, G," says Holly cheerily from the other line.

"Hi, Hols, you have everything packed up that you need?" I ask.

"Of course."

"And the lists I sent you and Greg, did you go over them?"

"Yes, Greg and I both checked our lists twice. I'm just ready and excited to be so close to the wedding date now! A few more days and we'll be on the cruise, hanging out, relaxing, drinking mocktails by the pool."

"But you have everything you need for the wedding—your dress, the rings, your vows?"

"Yes, Gwen, we have everything," she says. "Stop worrying so much, you are supposed to be having fun on this trip. Remember, Courtney is supposed to be taking over most things so you can relax. You've been working so hard lately, throwing yourself into your work more than ever. We haven't really seen you in months, and you seem different lately, not as spunky as you normally are. We want you to use this cruise to spend time with us as friends and get back to your old self."

"I know. I will," I say. *Once I know everything is all set and perfect for the wedding itinerary and the wedding rehearsal, of course.* "I'll let you know once I get to the hotel, and you text me once you land in Miami, okay?"

"Sounds good. See you soon," Holly says before hanging up.

Glancing at my to-do list, I check off the last item after slipping my passport into my purse. *Everything's all set for my flight to Miami tomorrow. Now, time for a bubble bath.*

CHAPTER 4
Niall

Pulling into my hotel in Miami, I see a long line at the valet. Realizing it may take a moment, I take out my phone and shoot off a text to Greg, letting him know I made it to the hotel. Just as I hit send, this beautiful lass opens my passenger door.

"Umm, you've got a lot of stuff in the front," she says as she looks around at the things strewn about the front seat of my rental.

My dress bag and suitcase lie haphazardly in the back-seat, and the clothes I'd changed out of are thrown on the ground. In the front seat is my half-empty backpack with some of its items strewn on the seat and the floor. I'd been in a rush when I left the airport, and then I thought I'd left my passport at home. Luckily, I'd found it in my backpack when I managed to rummage through it at a stoplight. So yeah, my rental is a little messy. But why does this valet care? Don't they just get paid to drive? Besides, most of this stuff will come into the hotel with me.

"I guess I do have a lot of stuff," I say, eyeing her curiously.

As she catches my Irish accent, her head snaps up. It happens so often I almost don't notice people's reactions anymore. Except I notice hers because she sucks in a breath of air, making a cute little noise in the back of her throat.

"Okay, so do I sit in the back then?" she asks, bending in to look at the backseat. As she leans closer, the sweet scent of strawberries and cream floods my senses.

"What? Sit in the back?"

Narrowing her eyes and sighing, she says slowly, "Yes, where am I supposed to sit back here?"

I shake my head. "Umm, you don't? You sit in my seat and take my keys?"

It has to be this lass's first day on the job. But even so, what kind of valet asks if they sit in the back? Don't they always come round to the driver's side to take your name and information? Did I miss a sign somewhere? Maybe I'm not in the right place, and she can't pick up my car here.

Her gaze flicks upward before she says, "What are you talking about? I drive your car? That's ridiculous. I've never driven the rideshares I've booked before. Is this new?" She's still leaning halfway in my car, and as she shakes her head, the intoxicating scent of strawberries and cream once again fills my senses.

It takes me a moment to realize what she's said. Rideshare? She thinks I'm her rideshare driver. She most definitely is not the valet then. Though, to be fair, her outfit does look a bit similar to what you'd expect a valet to be wearing. She is dressed in black slacks, a button-down shirt, and a vest with coffee mugs on it. If I'd paid more attention to her clothes, those coffee mugs would've told me she definitely wasn't the valet. But man does that outfit look class on her. The pants hug her lean figure, and the vest and partially unbuttoned shirt accentuate her—

No, not going there. Concentrate.

Glancing out the window, I see a bloke with a button-down shirt and bowtie finishing up with the car in front of me. He must be the valet.

"I believe you're mistaken. I am not your rideshare driver. I'm waiting for the valet." I motion toward the bloke with the bowtie. As realization dawns in her starburst eyes, my cheek quirks.

"Well, that's not embarrassing at all," she says. "Sorry for barging into your car, er . . ."

"Niall," I offer.

"Right, Niall."

Just then, a car identical to my rental pulls up across the drive. "Oh, that must be my rideshare," she says, gesturing to it. "Well, I'll just be going. I'm sure the actual valet will be with you shortly." As she pulls herself back out of my car, she hits her head on the top of the door frame. The pink on her cheeks brightens to match the red hues in her hair.

She gives a small nod before she shuts the door, then she turns and rubs the back of her head. She glances back at me before sliding into her rideshare.

The scent of strawberries and cream stays behind, the only reminder of the *beore*, the beautiful lass who just rode out of sight.

A light knock on my door alerts me to the actual valet. I roll down the window and give my name and information before unloading my items. And the bloke doesn't even ask about all the stuff I have in the back. A bellman helps carry my belongings as I head inside.

I chuckle at the misunderstanding as my stomach twists. An image of the fair lass passes through my mind. Her fitted clothes showing off her lean figure, her intoxicating scent. Shaking it off, I check in with the front desk to get my room key then make my way to the elevators.

CHAPTER 5
Gwen

After closing the door to my rideshare, I lean my head against the back of the seat. What is wrong with me today?

I'd slept through my alarm this morning, and now I'm running behind schedule. It's unlike me to be late for anything, but I'd been tossing and turning all night, and I barely managed three hours of sleep.

Thankfully, my "oh, shit" alarm woke me up.

But I hadn't had time to go through all my checklists or—most importantly—grab a coffee before catching my flight.

I'm thankful that I arrived at the hotel the day before the cruise sets off and had the time to check my emergency bag. I found out that I only have one bottle of Dramamine, my sewing kit is missing the black thread, my first aid kit only has Advil instead of both Advil and Tylenol, the thermometer stopped working, and I only have two bags of tissues. It's unacceptable.

Have I ever not had something I needed in my emergency bag for an event? Never. Not once. And I especially can't be missing anything for this event.

It's the one event that I would never want to mess up or have something go wrong. Not that I ever want any event to go wrong, but this one is just more special than any other event.

I normally don't accept events this far away from home. It's harder to keep organized this far, but when your best friend forever is marrying your older brother, you must make an exception.

The couple is nauseatingly sweet, but I am super happy for them.

How could I not be? My best friend will soon be my sister-in-law. What more could I ask for?

My own happily ever after?

Ha. No, thanks to Bradley.

You'd think after being together for two years—yep, two years!—that he'd be used to how much I have to work. Boy, how wrong I was on that.

Do I work a lot? Yes. But even though Bradley thought I worked too much, I have done quite well for myself. Whimsy and Wonder Events by Gwen is now the biggest event-planning business in Chessie Valley, Tennessee, and is becoming a leading contender in Middle Tennessee. You don't get to this level of success at the age of twenty-five without putting in hours of work and living and breathing the business.

I mean it's not like I try to be a workaholic. I own my own business for Pete's sake. How was I supposed to know he wasn't happy?

Did he ever say anything? No. Of course not, because why should a guy try to communicate? Not when it's easier to just leave me out of the blue.

Ugh. I'm better off without him anyway. I don't have time for a relationship in my life. Not when my business is picking up steam. All those hard hours working and marketing and getting my name out there are finally paying off.

No worries, Gwen. You'll pull this wedding off without a hitch. A quick rideshare drive to Target and I'll have everything I need. Then I'll get back to the hotel and double-check all my lists, every one of them.

What a day. And to add to it, I had that super embarrassing run-in with the deliciously sexy Irish man with the heart-stopping accent.

I mean come on, who sounds like that? Okay, well, just about everyone Holly and I met on our spring break trip to Ireland years ago, but still, we're not in Ireland, are we?

And why didn't I check my app or notice that my rideshare driver should have been female? I look at the dash where my actual driver, Miss Trudy, has her name and information posted. I should have noticed the man's car had none of that. I'm just off-kilter today.

Would I have preferred handsome Niall to be my rideshare driver just so I could hear him talk in that sexy accent? Yes. Yes, I would have.

Do I need distractions like this before the most special event of my career? No.

I need zero distractions.

Nada, none.

Zip.

Irish accents have always been my Achilles' heel. Holly practically had to drag me onto the plane to come back home after our week in Ireland. Plus, Niall was just too messy. Who has things strewn all over like that? What is he, in college?

"Here we are," says Miss Trudy cheerily as she pulls over in front of Target. "Hope you find everything you need!"

"Thank you," I say as I give her five stars on the app and a nice-size tip for not trying to get me to engage in small talk. Normally, I don't mind the occasional small talk, but to be honest, I'm a bit embarrassed after the whole wrong-car, sexy-Irish-man thing and need a breather—and an extra strong cup of coffee.

By the time I've walked around the store, downed a coffee from Starbucks, and found about half the items I need, my phone rings.

"Hi, Hols," I answer brightly.

"Hi, G, I can't wait to see you tonight. Did your flight go alright?"

"Yes . . ."

"Oh no, what happened?" Holly asks, hearing the hesitancy in my voice.

I laugh at how in sync we are sometimes. Of course she'd know something is up. It doesn't matter that Holly and I haven't hung out as much as we used to. She can still read me like a book.

"Nothing wrong with the flight and nothing big, just had a super weird moment when I mistook someone for my rideshare."

"Tell me more," she said earnestly.

I spent the next few minutes regaling her with my most recent vexing moment and the man with the Irish accent.

"The whole thing was so irritating. Even if he did have a sexy Irish accent," I finish.

"An Irish accent!" she squeals. "It's meant to be! So did you think he was cute?"

Ugh, of course she wants to know if I was attracted to him. She's been wanting me to get back out there ever since Bradley. I blush at her statement, the image of Niall passing through my mind and making my heart race as I recall his rugged good looks and the pierce of his sky-blue eyes. Thank goodness Holly can't see me now.

"Umm . . ." I start.

"You did, didn't you! Oh my gosh, G, what if this was your meet cute?"

I can picture Holly grinning, mischief sparkling in her eyes. She loves romance books and thinks everything could be a meet cute. It would be funny and I'd play along if this wasn't the seven hundredth time she's asked me that in the last month.

"Okay, don't get all crazy on me, Hols. Meet cutes only happen in Hallmark movies. They don't happen in real life and certainly not to someone like me. Plus, we're going on a cruise tomorrow. I seriously doubt I'll ever see him again." I laugh, placing my hand on my fluttering stomach.

I must have eaten something funny; that's what's causing this. I make a mental note to pick up some Tums too, just in case. I don't need anything else to go wrong. And I definitely don't need Holly to get it in her head that Murphy's Law is out to get me on this trip.

She chimes in over my thoughts, "G, I don't want you being a workaholic on the cruise. It's as much a vacation for you as it is for the rest of us. Once we're on the ship, the wedding coordinator will take over, and you can just sit back and relax. In a few hours, we will be on the cruise, and I can't wait for all of us to do the escape room, hit the spa, and just spend time together!"

"Okay, okay, I won't be a workaholic," I say, crossing my fingers. There is no way I will let the wedding coordinator be in charge of making sure Holly and Greg get their happily ever after. I will make sure that everything goes off without a hitch.

I wake up the next morning to anxiety hitting me and making me think that I've forgotten something important. I get up and double-check all my lists and unpack and repack everything I brought. Nothing is missing, and I breathe a bit easier.

After brewing a much-needed cup of coffee and then downing it almost as fast as it brewed, I push myself through a thirty-minute yoga routine to help me wake up. By the end of my routine, I am lightly sweating and feeling better about the day. After taking a shower, I dress and dry my hair, opting for a slight wavy look this morning. I'm sure the breeze from the deck of the cruise ship will make my natural wavy hair have a mind of its own, so no use wasting time straightening it.

Throwing a bead necklace over a simple white shirt and sage green jumpsuit, I finally feel like I can conquer the world.

Well, I will once I get another cup of coffee, or two, in me.

Walking down to the hotel's breakfast buffet, I make a beeline straight to the coffee. I pour myself a nice strong cup; no milk or sugar for me. No, thank you.

Yes, this is my third cup this morning, but can you blame me? It's most definitely needed.

I grab a bagel and cream cheese before finding a booth to sit and enjoy the last few moments of calm before things start ramping up for the day. Leisurely drinking my coffee and glancing around the open space, I see Holly and Greg. Thank goodness; I have a million things I need to discuss with them.

CHAPTER 6
Niall

Eating breakfast at the hotel's buffet, I can't help but think this cruise could be a turning point for me. Since my mam's passing, I haven't felt up to doing much. It's been mostly work and then staring at the walls of my childhood home. How was I supposed to figure out what to do next? I hadn't prepared myself enough for her passing. Even with all her treatments, it was still too sudden. I wanted—no, needed—more time with her. Without her, I'd been feeling so lost.

Lately, though, I've been forcing myself to be more like me again. The happy-go-lucky lad who is always up for a *craic* time and a fun adventure. This cruise is just the thing I need to enjoy some time away from home and live a little, while supporting my friend as he marries the woman of his dreams.

An image of the fair lass from the valet line crosses through my mind and I shake my head. No denying she was beautiful. That encounter is already bringing a smile to my mind.

I finish the last bite of my breakfast when Greg walks in.

"Hey, mate!" I stand and clasp Greg in a hug.

"Hi, man, I'm so glad you could make it."

"Where's the infamous Holly?"

"We just ran into my sister Gwen," Greg replies. "Holly is with her going over some last-minute things before Gwen heads out to the ship to check in with the wedding coordinator onboard. Holly will be over in a few."

"I can't wait to meet her."

"You're going to love her, but listen." Greg sits down and leans closer. "While it's just the two of us, I've actually been thinking and was hoping you could help me with something."

"I'm listening," I lean in a bit closer because Greg is all but whispering.

"I know you haven't met her yet, but Gwen could use some of your energy in her life right now. She's had a rough past few months, a bad breakup and whatnot, and has been working herself to the bone. And she's been helping us plan the wedding. She's supposed to let the cruise's wedding planner take over so she can enjoy herself. But if I know my sister, that's not going to happen. Anyway, Holly is worried that Gwen will be all work and no play on the cruise. So, I was thinking you could help with that."

"How am I to help with this, exactly?" I ask, not quite sure what he's asking of me.

"Well, you know, spend time with her, become friends and let your Niall energy rub off on her. Help bring her spunky side out again, and let her actually have some fun on this cruise. We don't want our wedding to be her only focus. We want this cruise to be more about having some friends together for a fun vacation," Greg finishes, sitting back in his chair.

"And you think me spending time with Gwen will help?"

"Yeah, back in college, you were the life of the party, getting us to do all sorts of fun things we'd never have done if we hadn't met you."

It's been about three years since I've seen Greg in person. He knows about my mam's passing, but he doesn't know that since then, I haven't been the same Sully he remembers. Sure, I still go out and have a bit of *craic*, but it feels shallow and pointless. I'm not sure that I would bring that "Sully energy" Greg is talking about. "I don't know about this, Greg."

"Come on, man! I really need your help. Gwen won't listen to any of us, and with the wedding days away, she will only tell me not to worry about anything, that everything is fine, and for me to just focus on Holly." Greg rolls his eyes in frustration at his sister.

"Well, she sounds interesting. . . ." I say.

"She's a super fun person, and if she wasn't in this funk, I think you two would really hit it off. But obviously, she's my sister, so, like, keep it PG, please." Greg gives me his best big-brother warning glare.

I laugh at his expression. "I'm sure I can handle that."

"So you'll do it?"

I have been wanting to feel like myself again. And making sure someone else is having fun is a good way to make sure I live a little too. Plus, my mam always told me focusing on helping others is the best way to heal your soul. Maybe this could be good for me. "I'll give it a lash."

"Great!"

"But no promises. I don't know anything about your sister," I add.

"Thank you so much, Sully!" A wide smile spreads across Greg's face. "Oh, and remember, don't tell Gwen I suggested it though." He motions toward the breakfast buffet. "I'm going to grab a bite."

As he fills up his plate, a woman joins him and gives him a kiss on the cheek. It must be Holly.

They both come back to my table, and I stand to greet Holly, giving her a big hug. "You must be the beautiful Holly that Greg won't shut up about."

"Aww you're so sweet," says Holly.

"Look at the glowing bride-to-be!" I say. "You got a good one, Greg."

"I know I did," Greg says, smiling ear to ear.

"Your accent is so much more prominent in person than on the phone," says Holly.

"Yeah, I've always had my Irish accent. The prominent Irish community in Boston was my mam's home away from home, since Ireland was so far away. And because of that, I've grown up surrounded by people with strong Irish accents. My mam would roll over in her grave if I ever lost this accent."

"Well, you better hang on to it then," says Holly.

"I plan on it."

"Did everything go alright with your arrival?" Holly asks.

"It did. Got in around noon yesterday and was able to get a good night's sleep."

Holly eyes me curiously, then nods. "We got in kind of late last night, but I'm so used to getting up at the break of dawn that instead of sleeping in, we decided to head on down for breakfast."

"When we're done eating," says Greg, "we should ride over to the ship together."

"*Cúla búla*, sounds good," I say.

CHAPTER 7
Gwen

On the cruise ship, I reach the boarding agent in record time due to my priority boarding. Being an event planner has its perks. The agent scans my passport, takes an updated picture, and asks, "Anything change from your submitted health screening answers?"

"Nope," I answer.

He nods and motions for me to pass. "Up the stairs to your right. Have a great trip!"

"Thank you," I say as I walk by.

I love walking onto the ship. It has a red carpet and greeters to welcome me aboard; just another reason why I love to cruise with Regal Voyage Cruise Lines. They go above and beyond to make guests feel like royalty. Not one for pictures, I skip the photographers. Plus, with a wedding in a few days, there will be plenty of pictures to last me the next few years.

Looking around the Grand Promenade, my pulse slows as I take a deep breath. It's almost time. My brother and my best friend are getting married. This is going to be the greatest cruise and wedding.

A ping from my phone breaks me out of my calm.

MOM

> I don't want to make you nervous, but we ran into some traffic and we're running a bit behind.

What the hell?! Seriously, why couldn't they just listen to me and get here yesterday? I love my mom and dad, but for Pete's sake, it's not every day your only son gets married to his childhood crush—someone who has been like a daughter to them for years. You'd think they would want to make sure they were here early!

GWEN

How far away are you?

MOM

I don't know, like 5 hours away?

Five hours? Let me think. Okay, there are about six hours left before the set cruise departure time. That's cutting it a bit close for my taste, but if they don't make any stops until they get here, it should work out.

GWEN

Ok, you can still get here in time. Just don't stop for anything, not even a fast bathroom break. You cannot miss this cruise!

MOM

We aren't going to miss the cruise. We didn't mean to make you nervous. I was just telling you so you wouldn't freak out when we weren't there as early as you thought we'd be.

Too late for not making me nervous. Ugh, if they don't make it, I just . . . nope, no, not going there. Mom and Dad will make it. They have to.

GWEN

I know mom, sorry. I'll see you in a few hours. Love you!

MOM

Love you two honey.

I shake my head and roll my shoulders back. Right. *Focus, Gwen.* I take some deep breaths, in for four, hold, out for four. *Ok, find Courtney and go over the plan. Nothing can go wrong when you plan for everything.* And I am a pro at planning.

It doesn't take me very long to find Courtney at our designated meeting place next to the clock tower on the Grand Promenade.

"Hi, Courtney?" I ask, glancing at her name badge.

"You must be Gwen. So lovely to meet you face-to-face," says Courtney.

"Same," I say. I've spent the last five months coordinating with Courtney over the phone about aspects of the wedding that involved the cruise ship. As annoying as it's been to have to work with another wedding planner, it has been useful to talk to someone who knows the ins and outs of the cruise. And at least she hasn't had to be told things twice. But now that I am here, I can take over the cruise details and not have to rely so heavily on Courtney. "Right, so let's go over the itinerary," I tell Courtney.

"If you don't mind, I'd like to go over the guest list. I'm a bit confused about who will be participating in which event."

"Okay, sure. Holly and Greg will be participating in everything, except for the port at Curaçao night when I've planned a special dinner for them at the hibachi grill. Then, obviously after the wedding, they'll be on the start of their honeymoon and doing their own thing."

"Great," says Courtney, checking a box on her tablet. "Then I have Mr. and Mrs. Palmer and Mr. and Mrs. Kenton."

"Right, the bride's and groom's parents."

"Now, I don't see them on many of the activities at all. Is that correct?" asks Courtney.

I nod. "Yes, they said they'd not be doing many of the activities because they, and I quote them on this, 'don't want to slow us down and keep us from any fun.'"

Courtney laughs at that. "Sounds just like something my parents would say."

"As part of the wedding party, there's myself, Trent, and Margot, Holly's younger sister."

"And we have one other guest in the wedding party, a Mr. O'Sullivan."

"Yes, Sully, as my brother calls him. He's the other groomsman," I confirm. "Holly's other sister, Vivian, will be joining us too. She has a friend, Tammy, joining her who is not part of the wedding party. Vivian and Tammy will be participating in most of the events but not all."

"Right, I see Vivian is only in a few of the items. Okay, then we have Gillian and Miles, with a five-year-old Magnolia, who is to be the flower girl, correct?"

"Yes," I sigh heavily. I have a million things I need to look over and want to get this guest list over with. "You don't really need to worry too much about all this, Courtney. I can handle the itinerary and who is supposed to be where and when."

Courtney types on her tablet, then looks up at me. "I'm sure you're more than capable of handling everything, but I'd love to be filled in just in case."

"Right, just in case," I say.

"So, the flower girl?" continues Courtney.

"Maggie, as she prefers to be called, is the sweetest girl. I have her signed up for the kid's club as well. Gillian is Greg and my sister. She and Miles, her husband, are treating this trip as a babymoon before they welcome baby number two in a few months. They will mostly be spending time together as a family."

"How perfect! I'm sure Maggie will have a wonderful time at kid's club. Let your sister and brother-in-law know that there is an adult-only pool up at the front of the boat if they want some quiet time."

"Of course," I nod. "And that should be everyone."

"Actually, there is one more," says Courtney.

"What?" I ask.

"Vivian reached out to me earlier, and her plus one, Tammy, brought a plus one."

"A plus one for the plus one? Who does that?" I ask.

"It's Tammy's fiancé, I believe."

I sigh in frustration. Why can't people just plan ahead? Why do people have to do things last minute like this? Don't they know it messes with people's plans? "Well, that certainly would've been great to know beforehand."

"You'd be surprised at how many people add a friend or two to their cruises. It's a fun place to be," says Courtney.

"Is there any problem with the additional plus one?" I ask Courtney.

"No, we've already taken care of it. Except I'm not sure if the fiancé will be going to any of the wedding events?"

"Well, since I just found out about him, I'm not sure either. For now, let's add him to only the activities that Vivian and Tammy are attending. That won't be an issue, will it?" Internally, I'm seething at how Vivian and Tammy could do this when I confirmed with Vivian a week ago about her plus one—just one plus one, I might add. These complicated last-minute changes could all be avoided if people just communicated.

"Nope, another person won't be an issue. I'll make a few adjustments. Just have Vivian or Tammy contact guest services when they get onboard, and we will get the fiancé added."

"Thanks," I say. "Oh, and something else I should mention: my parents will be checking in a little later than we planned."

"Is everything alright?"

"Yes, they hit some traffic but should make it right before the ship sets out."

"Do you know where they are? Maybe I can offer an alternate route to help them make up some time?" Courtney suggests.

"Don't worry about it. I've got it handled."

"Alrighty then, looks like everything is in order. Each person will get a notification in their app for the preselected shows, activities, and port excursions."

"Perfect." I look down at my list. "Now, could you show me where the wedding will take place? I've seen pictures online, but it's just better if I see it in person."

"Of course," says, Courtney. "Right this way."

Over the next four hours, I tour all the locations for the wedding and related events, go over all the details, and confirm each and every activity Holly and Greg picked out for the cruise. My list is checked off for the day.

"You all have a fun-packed nine nights ahead of you," says Courtney as we wrap things up. "If anything comes up, don't hesitate to reach out to me." She hands me her card, gives a little wave, and heads off.

Looking down at my phone, I notice it's just under two hours until the ship is set to depart. My parents are still not here yet.

I need a drink. Just as the thought hits me, my stomach growls. Maybe I'll get some food first. Alcohol on an empty stomach is never a good idea.

In the elevator, I press the button for the sixteenth floor to head up to the Duke's Diner for a quick bite to eat. I check my itinerary. We have dinner in the main dining room tonight at seven o'clock with the whole group, but I'll meet up with just the wedding party at the Imperial Bar for some drinks around three o'clock. I better eat now before three o'clock rolls around or I'm needed somewhere else.

I grab a plate of food and fill my coffee mug before finding an empty table with a view facing out to the ocean.

My phone pings and I glance down, hoping to see an update from Mom, but it's Vivian.

VIVIAN

Hi G, you know how I brought a friend, Tammy, as my plus one for the wedding?

GWEN

Yes. . .

I know where this is going.

VIVIAN

Ok, well don't be mad, but she bought a last-minute ticket for her fiancé and he will be joining us too. Just for the activities I signed up for. They have their own table so we don't need to change any of that. I just wanted you to know.

GWEN

No worries, Courtney already filled me in on this addition.

VIVIAN

Ok, great! I hope it's not too much of a problem.

GWEN

We'll make it work. The three of you need to go talk to a guest service agent and they will get you set up.

Of course you will, I think and then, after counting to ten to calm my mind, I text her a thumbs up and take a sip of my coffee. *Thank goodness for coffee.*

After putting down my phone, I turn to the ocean. I don't know what it is, but just seeing the ocean brings me a sense of calm. The chaos of the past few months, with Bradley breaking up with me, me planning a wedding for my best friend, my business taking off . . . there's been a lot weighing on me. Most of it good, but the stress of it all caused a tightness in my chest.

Being here now, staring at the ocean, it feels like I can breathe again, that everything will be okay. I take a sip of coffee, close my eyes, and let out a deep breath.

"Well, this must be fate," says an accented voice I couldn't forget if I tried. "Alright there, not-my-valet?"

My eyes shoot open, glancing at a pair of piercing blue eyes. McHottie. What are the odds that I'd see the not-my-rideshare driver again? Why in the world is he on this same cruise?

"What are you doing here?" I bite out, setting my cup back on the table.

"Cruising." He shrugs, setting his plate of food across from me like he doesn't have a care in the world. Oh, to be so lucky.

"Obviously, but why are you setting your things at my table? What if I'm saving it for someone?"

His eyes glint with mischief as a dimple appears next to the smirk he's sporting. I don't have time for this guy's flirtatious ways. There is too much happening today.

"Are you waiting for someone?"

"Well, no . . . but you didn't know that."

"No harm done then, and seeing as there isn't another open table," waving his hands around as if showing me the space, "and we already know each other, I think you can find it in your heart, Rose, for me to join you for lunch." Raising his eyebrows, he waits for my answer.

I roll my eyes and give a brief, almost imperceptible nod. He takes the seat across from me.

Adjusting in my seat, I look out to the ocean and take several breaths. In for four beats, pause, out for four beats, pause, and repeat. I'm not going to let McHottie spoil the calm that has finally washed over me. Even though his presence causes my calm to slip ever so slightly.

I try to avoid looking at him as he takes a bite of his burger. It's like a flipping sexy hamburger commercial up in here. Eating a burger should not look so sensual. Why does he have to look so good doing it?

"What're the odds that both of us are on the same cruise?" McHottie asks, bringing me back to this odd little luncheon.

I swallow a bite of salad before answering. "Considering it's a cruise port town and roughly six to seven thousand people can be on this ship, I'd say it's high chances we both ended up here."

"Fair enough," he says, relaxing back in his seat and tilting his head as if he is studying me.

Sighing, I ask, "What?"

"Nothing, just trying to figure you out."

I perk up in suspicion. "Why?"

"Why not? We seem to keep meeting up, and with a ten-day cruise ahead of us, I just figure we'll be seeing a lot of each other over the next few days."

"Who's to say we will see each other again at all?" I ask, waving my arms around us. "As you can see, there are literally thousands of people on this ship. We may never meet again.”

“Ah, well now, second time’s the charm.”

“It’s ‘third time’s the charm,’ not second,” I say.

“I guess I’m just optimistic that a *beore* such as yourself wouldn’t mind getting to know a nice guy like myself.”

Sitting up a little straighter in my seat, my ears pinken at what he’d just said. “I’m sorry, did you just call me a boar and then basically ask if we could hang out?”

“No, no, that’s not it at all.” His eyes go wide. “I was merely saying you’re lovely to look at.”

“I’m lovely to look at?” I ask, brows furrowing as I curl my hands into a fist in my lap. There’s nothing more annoying to my inner feminist than someone wanting to be around me for just my looks. “I’m sorry. . . .”

“No apology necessary,” he says mischievously.

“I’m not apologizing to you, um . . .” I can’t remember his name.

“Niall,” he offers.

“Niall,” I snap, “I was saying I find it a bit offensive that you’d only want to get to know me because I’m lovely to look at. Is that all you think women are good for? To be nice to look at?” I start gathering my items in preparation to leave, then remember that the staff on the ship take care of bussing the tables.

Ugh, this guy. Just because McHottie is, well . . . hot, doesn’t mean that I only want to catch someone’s attention for my looks.

“I’m more than just a pretty face,” I say, putting my tray back down and standing to leave.

“For the love of . . .” Niall starts, and then mumbles to himself before saying, “It’s not just your looks, though you haven't given me much in the way of conversation to give me reason to believe you have a class personality."

My ears redden at his comment. "Just because I don't want to talk to strangers doesn't mean I have a bad personality. For your information, I have a great personality and am a super fun person to be around." And with that, I fling my bag over my shoulder and walk away, leaving my lunch half-eaten on the table.

CHAPTER 8
Niall

Well, that could have gone better. I watch Rose walk out of Duke's. I haven't been off my game that long, have I? I mean it's not like I've been on many dates, but I typically catch the occasional eye when I'm out with my crew at the bar. I mean, who can resist a dimple and Irish accent? Well, obviously she can. She's beautiful as ever but prickly as a thorn. Rose is a fitting name for her.

Maybe she was right. Maybe we won't run into each other on this cruise. I'll be doing things with the wedding party most of the time anyway and helping Greg with his request, so I don't know why I even bothered to strike up a conversation with her.

Because there is something about her that calls to me.

I realize this is the first time in a long time someone has had that effect on me. I think back to the promise I made my mam and wonder if Rose could be the one to help me fulfill it.

Yes, she's beautiful, but there's something hiding beneath that rough exterior she keeps up when we interact that pulls me in, something about her that makes it fun to flirt with and tease her. Maybe I won't write her off just yet.

Taking another bite of my burger, I get my phone out and text Greg.

Setting my phone down, I finish up my lunch. It'll be good to see the guys and get to know Holly better. I'm happy for Greg. He's about to marry the woman of his dreams—which also happens to be the only thing my mam wanted for me before she passed.

When my mam got sick, I stepped up. I was there for her, driving her around to her appointments, hiring a caregiver for her when I was on a twenty-four-hour shift with the firehouse, and doing everything in my power to ensure she was able to still be as active as possible in the community.

We'd definitely had to scale back on what all we did; she just didn't have the energy for much. But we made time for music nights at the community center and picnics on the beach.

And now she's gone.

Sadness floods through me. I want to fulfill this promise to her. I want to try and find someone I can be with, someone who makes me genuinely happy like she wanted. It's the last way I can show her that I am always there for her. I promised her to look for that person a year after her passing, but it's so hard. How can I care for someone when they could just leave so unexpectedly? I couldn't bring myself to put my heart out there just for the potential to lose them someday like I lost my mam. And now that it's time to keep that promise, it looks like I won't be able to. Sorry, Mam.

Shaking my head to clear away the thought, I stand and leave for the Imperial SkyDeck to hang out until I meet up with the others.

Located at the front of the ship, the Imperial SkyDeck is an adult-only lounge with a pool, a bar, and a small restaurant. After making a right hames of things with Rose, I am ready for a drink. A pick-me-up of sorts.

The circular bar is full of people, but I manage to snag a seat just as an elderly couple get up. As a firefighter, situational awareness is a big part of my job. I tend to carry my keen observation skills into my normal life, and I enjoy relaxing and observing people and their surroundings. Due to the wall of alcohol in the center of the bar, I can only see to my left and right, but I can still hear those on the other side.

A group of college kids are trying out the drink of the day, the Bahama Mama. An older bloke is sipping on what appears to be a glass of whiskey. A couple who looks to be in their mid-forties are debating about some excursion they are going on at the first port. Chuckling to myself, I hear the husband going on and on about how they never just relax on their cruises and it's always go-go-go with the missis. He looks wrecked, and we haven't even left the port yet.

Poor bloke.

As I sip on my Blue Hawaiian, I continue to listen to the different groups around the bar as I wait for my own group to arrive.

A voice catches my ear; my heart races and my eyes go wide. I can't say for sure, but considering the giving out I'd just had at Duke's, I am sure I'm listening to Rose.

I fiddle with the edge of my napkin. I'm suddenly restless, not wanting to make my presence known, especially after our last conversation. But something about her tone has me leaning in to hear better. She doesn't sound like the same fierce and in-control Rose from earlier. There's a nervous edge to her voice. Something is off. Where is the confident, take-charge woman from lunch?

CHAPTER 9
Gwen

I'm a jumble of emotions as I make my way to the Imperial SkyDeck. Niall is still throwing me off, and I don't have time for whatever he wants with all the things I need to do for the wedding. Trying to calm myself, I grab a drink before sitting at the bar.

As I'm mid-sip on my Miami Vice, a tall figure stops by my table.

"Gwen?" he asks.

I cough on my drink, sputtering all over the bar. It can't be. But it is. The man standing in front of me is no other than Bradley.

"Fancy meeting you here," he says.

My head whips up, taking him in. He looks just as good as he did the last time I saw him when he left my office eight months ago.

I just blink at him. This cannot be real life; this can't be happening. It's like I've short-circuited, and I can't compute what my eyes are trying to tell my brain. Bradley is on the same cruise. The cruise that Holly and Greg are about to get married on. A cruise that is going to last over a week. My brain is screaming at me to do something, anything. *Say something, Gwen!*

"Yes, small world," I say, my voice shaking slightly. What the heck is he doing here? On this exact cruise, what are the odds of this even happening?

"What's it been, about a year?" asks Bradley.

I lean back a bit, trying to distance myself from Bradley, my shoulders stiff as I force a smile on my face.

"Who's counting?" I say, dryly. I am not prepared for this little reunion. I can't even wrap my head around how Bradley is on this cruise too. "What are you doing here?"

"At the bar?"

"On this cruise." I say with more than a little heat in my voice.

"Oh, um, I'm here with . . ." Bradley looks around, then says, "Here she is." He gestures toward a woman coming our way with a drink in each hand.

She gives him a peck on the cheek. "Here, Bradley Boo," she says, handing him a drink.

"Gwen," says Bradley, "this is my . . . uh, fiancée."

His WHAT?! My ears ring. I can't be hearing him correctly. It's not possible. Not after we'd been together for years. It doesn't make sense. How is he engaged to someone else when we haven't even been broken up a year? The blood drains from my face. I feel panicked.

"It's so nice to put a face to the name," says the fiancée, offering me a smile. "I've heard a lot about you." She is showing way more skin than I'd ever feel comfortable showing, practically walking around in just her swimsuit, not a care in the world. Who is this person? And how did she end up engaged to Bradley so soon after our breakup?

"What about you?" asks Bradley. "Here with anyone?"

"Of course," I say. I can't let Bradley think that he was right—that I'm too much of a workaholic to be in a relationship. He can't think that he's the only one who has moved on from our relationship. "I'm here with my boyfriend," I blurt.

"Well, I'm happy for you," says Bradley.

"Thank you," I say. "We're very happy together."

"We'd love to meet him," says the fiancée. "Maybe we could get drinks together sometime?"

"Oh, that won't be necessary," says Bradley.

Sensing how uncomfortable it makes Bradley to talk about me being in a relationship, I push it a step further. "We'd love to," I say.

"Great!" says Tammy.

What have I done? Where am I going to get a boyfriend on this cruise? Now, I'm just going to look even more pathetic to Bradley when he finds out the truth. I look around trying to find some escape out of the hole I just dug for myself.

And then, across the bar, I lock eyes with McHottie.

I don't even think. I jump up from my seat and walk over to Niall. Grabbing his arm, I say in a sharp whisper, "Come with me. I need your help with something."

"What?" Niall says. "Is everything okay?"

"Sort of. I just need your help." I'm practically begging him with my eyes. To my utter surprise, he puts his half-finished drink on the bar and stands.

"Okay," he says.

I jump slightly at how quickly he stood. I'm shocked again, but this time by his willingness to help me after the tongue-lashing I'd given him in Duke's Diner. When I return to my place at the bar, I don't hesitate before saying to Bradley, "This is my boyfriend, Niall."

Niall blinks twice then leans in and plants a quick peck on my cheek, jumping right in on my little charade. *Well, that was unexpected.*

"I was looking for you, *mo ghrá*," Niall says.

My what? What did he say? I don't care. I'm just so thankful he's playing along that I could cry. The shock on Bradley's face after he takes in Niall makes the risk I took worth it.

I reach over and take Niall's hand in mine; my body zings from the contact. Electricity shoots through me, making me come alive. I glance quickly down at our hands and then back up into his eyes. I know mine are full of relief but his convey something different that I can't quite place.

"Well, that's great to hear," says Bradley. Bradley and Niall are about the same height, but Niall's dark hair contrasts with Bradley's blonde hair. And Niall is much broader in the shoulders. And his arms, wow, his arms! I could definitely . . . *Snap out of it, Gwen!*

"Niall, this is Bradley and his fiancée," I say, adding emphasis on *fiancée* because I still can't wrap my head around it.

Niall reaches out his free hand to greet them. "Nice to meet you. You're an old friend of my girl, then?"

Shock courses through me. He's playing along flawlessly. He's not going to make me look like a fool in front of Bradley.

Niall's blasé comment catches Bradley off guard. He responds, "Surely she's told you about me before?"

Niall shrugs, like he hasn't a care in the world who this man is. "'Fraid not. Sorry, should she have?"

"I just thought . . . that after two years together—"

"Is that an Irish accent?" asks the fiancée, butting in. "Are you Irish?"

"Sure am," says Niall, flashing that amazing smile. "Have been since the day my mam birthed me."

"So, what brings you two on the cruise?" I ask, trying to be as nonchalant as possible.

"Tammy's here for a friend," says Bradley, gesturing toward his fiancée. "I'm just an extra plus one for her."

Why does the name Tammy sound so familiar?

"Yeah," says Tammy, "I thought, 'Why waste a perfectly good trip?'" She grabs Bradley's arm. Seeing her touch him makes me want to throw up. "And we're here for a wedding. So romantic, right? So, I thought Bradley should join me. Then I won't be all alone in my room."

"Wait," I say, suddenly looking between Tammy and Bradley. "Tammy, are you friends with a Vivian?"

"Why yes, I am."

"A Vivian Palmer?"

"Yes!" exclaims Tammy. "She and I have been friends since we started working at the same company years ago."

"Well, that makes so much more sense then." I look at Bradley. "You're the fiancé."

"Yeah, that's what I literally just explained," Bradley says.

Bradley is the unexpected plus one Vivian's Tammy brought with her. That means he's going to be around this whole week.

There is no getting rid of him.

None.

What the hell am I going to do? Especially now that I've dragged Niall into this fake boyfriend bit that I thought was going to last all of five minutes?

Internally, I groan. Why, oh, why do embarrassing things have to keep happening around McHottie? First the rideshare, then the heated ending to our conversation at Duke's Diner, and now this with Bradley—when will it end?

Then, to my relief, Niall jumps in. "Well, as lovely as this has been, we're supposed to be meeting up with a few other people. Don't want to be late. Right, *mo ghrá*?" Niall squeezes lightly on my hand that is still clasping his.

I finally look up at him, wonder in my eyes. This man, who has no reason to be kind and helpful to me after how rude I've been to him, has rushed in like a knight in shining armor. Realizing he asked me a question, I nod, before looking back over at Bradley and Tammy. "Of course, yes, the others. I must have lost track of time."

Bradley furrows his brows at my statement. "That doesn't seem like you to lose track of time."

"Well, I must have changed in the last eight months. Seems like we've both been busy that way," I snap, a fire raging through me now that I've got my bearings and a little help from McHottie. The shock of seeing Bradley, much less of finding out who Tammy is, has me heated.

But Niall's presence is giving me courage. Not that I need a man to feel confident, but seeing as this is the first time Bradley and I have spoken since he moved out of my apartment eight months ago . . .

"I guess we will be seeing a lot of each other," says Tammy, "since we're going to the same wedding and all."

"Right, I guess so," says Bradley. "We're heading out anyway. See you around." Placing his hand on Tammy's back, the two stand and leave. I stay there watching them until they've walked out of the Imperial Bar area.

CHAPTER 10
Niall

Did Tammy just say they were all here for a wedding? It can't be the same wedding, can it?

Before I can put much more into that thought, Rose drops my hand. "Thanks for going along with that."

"Don't be worrying yourself," I say. "Helping people, it's ingrained in me. My job and all." I feel hollow at the lack of contact with my Rose.

My Rose?

Since when did I start thinking of her as mine?

Since her touch caused a chemical reaction.

Rose eyes me curiously. "Right, and what would your job be?" she asks.

"I'm a firefighter."

"Well, you definitely saved me," she laughs, the sound sweet like the soft tinkling of Christmas bells. "I appreciate what you did for me there, for playing along." She picks up her frozen drink and takes a long sip.

"You looked like you needed it. I'm guessing he's the ex?"

She glares at me but there is no passion behind it, no fire in her eyes. She sighs. "Yes, we dated for two years. He broke it off about eight months ago."

"Wow. What happened?" I sit in the empty seat next to her.

"It's really none of your business," she says angrily, but then her facial features sag.

"Okay, fair's fair." I signal the bartender and order another Blue Hawaiian. We sit in silence watching the bloke make my drink. Only once I've taken a sip of the frozen blue concoction do I speak up again.

"So," I ask, wanting to get more details about this wedding. "What brings you on this cruise? Obviously not the fascinating couple that just left here?"

Her mouth quirks up in a half smile, and I swear my tongue goes bone dry. I'd actually managed to get a smile out of Rose. Be still my heart.

"No, I am definitely not here because of them," she huffs out gently. "I'm actually here . . ." but she trails off and looks past me.

A woman calls, "Gwen!"

"Sully!" I hear, and now I turn too.

Greg and Holly come around the corner.

Wait. . . . Did Holly say *Gwen?*

I glance over at the *beore* I've bumped into multiple times now. Is she Greg's Gwen?

Before I can ask a question or even know what hits me, I'm wrapped in a big hug from Greg. It's as if we didn't eat breakfast together this morning, but seeing as how I haven't seen him in about three years, I wrap him back in a hug.

Next to me, Rose, or maybe Gwen, is attacked by Holly.

"Holly!" Rose squeals, clasping Holly's hands. "I'm glad you made it on the cruise."

"We're finally here." Holly smiles. "And it's almost wedding time."

"I know," says Rose, "and I've made sure everything is in order."

"This is going to be the best friend's trip-then-wedding we've ever had!" Holly says.

"It's the only friend's trip-then-wedding we've ever had," Greg replies.

Rose chuckles, her mood vastly improving and hopefully pushing thoughts of her ex and his fiancée to the curb, right where they belong.

"Come here, Gwennie," says Greg, letting go of me and wrapping Rose up in a big hug.

"Why do you insist on calling me Gwennie? We're not kids anymore." She laughs. I catch a glimpse of Rose's face and her smile is illuminating.

"It's just a habit, a hard one to break," says Greg. "You will always be Gwennie to me. And I see you've met Sully." Greg steps back and pats me on the back.

"Yes?" Rose says, furrowing her brows as her eyes narrow at me.

I, catching her confusion, say, "Though I don't believe we've properly introduced ourselves yet. Niall O'Sullivan. 'Sully' to my mates."

"Of course you are," she transforms her face and plasters a smile on it then reaches out her hand to shake mine. "Gwendolyn Kenton. 'Gwen' for short and Greg's sister."

So Rose *is* Gwen then. Greg's request to spend time with his sister just got a lot easier.

"Hey, not just his sister," pipes up Holly, pretending to be affronted, "but also my best friend for, like, forever, my partner in crime, a bridesmaid, and our wedding coordinator. Seriously, Niall, if you have any questions about what's going on this trip, this one right here is your girl."

My girl? I could get used to that.

"Good to know," I say, grinning at Gwen.

Gwen claps her hands together. "Right, so when are Trent and Margot supposed to be here?"

"Right now," says Trent, walking through the door behind me with Margot.

Gwen jumps, startled at their sudden appearance, but then she turns and gives Trent a big hug like she hasn't seen him in years.

"Hi, Trent," Gwen says, then laughs as he picks her up and spins her around. Trent may be built like a linebacker, but he's all teddy bear.

"And where is the beautiful blushing bride?" asks Trent after he sets Gwen back down.

Gwen and I lock eyes as she steadies herself. I catch myself frowning slightly at the show of familiarity between her and Trent.

Margot and Holly barely release their hug before Holly is being spun around by Trent just as he'd done with Gwen. I smile seeing my friends so happy.

"I got the teddy-bear twirl as well when Trent found me on the Promenade," laughs Margot. "We almost knocked down an old lady!"

Trent chuckles and shrugs, "What can I say? I missed you all."

"You just saw most of us this morning," laughs Holly.

"So?" Trent asks, a boyish grin on his face.

"What," I say, "I don't get a . . . what did you call it? Oh, teddy-bear hug?"

"Sully!" Trent says, noticing me next to Greg. "Come here, dude. How long's it been?" We share a quick brotherly embrace.

"Too long, mate," I admit, shaking my head.

"When are we going to convince you to join us all in Tennessee?" asks Trent. "You're the only one that's not there."

I shake my head in response. This isn't the first time he's asked me this.

"Well," says Holly, "we've got lots of time to catch up on the cruise. I'm so glad everyone could make it. Greg and I really appreciate it."

"Of course," Gwen and I say at the same time.

"I wouldn't miss it for anything," says Margot.

"You couldn't pay me to stay away," says Trent, grinning again.

Tears gleam in Holly's eyes, and Greg brushes them away lightly before giving her a quick kiss.

My pulse races slightly at the reminder of my lips on Gwen's cheek not too long ago. A light touch, a quick peck as I pretended to be her boyfriend. I glance over at her only to find her looking at me, offering a slight smile that quickly morphs into a glare.

CHAPTER 11
Gwen

I just want to crawl in a hole and hide until the wedding day. Why does Sully have to be Niall?

Now I will most definitely see him the entire cruise. And why did I spill my past failure of a relationship to Niall? What is wrong with me? Why does the world hate me?

I was cool sharing personal information with some random stranger that I thought I'd barely ever see again on the cruise, much less see at all after. But to find out that Niall is Sully, Greg's best friend from college?

Oh.

My.

Gosh.

I pretended he was my boyfriend when Bradley showed up. . . Oh crap, what am I going to do about that? There is no way I can just hole up in my room and avoid any chance of seeing Bradley and his perfect, beautiful fiancée, Tammy. He must love Tammy to be marrying her. She must not be just a pretty face. And soon they'll find out I don't have a boyfriend at all because I have no idea how I'm going to convince them that Niall and I are together now that we'll be seeing each other much, much more than I thought.

My cheeks heat and my heart races in my chest. What am I going to do? Then I realize that there are three sets of eyes staring at me. Curiosity in Greg's eyes, concern in Holly's, and something I can't quite place in Niall's.

"How small of a world is it," says Holly, sipping a drink at the bar and looking between Niall and me, "that you two would meet without knowing who each other is?"

"The world is feeling pretty small right now," I mutter under my breath.

"What was that?" asks Margot.

"Nothing," I snap.

"We are all going to have such a great time together," says Holly. "I can't wait for all the fun things we've got planned!"

"What's on the agenda for tonight?" Greg asks me.

"Well," I say, "we have dinner reservations at seven o'clock, but otherwise, tonight is kind of a free night. Get settled into your rooms, eat dinner, and then get a good rest because we've got lots of fun things going on tomorrow after breakfast in the main dining. It's a day at sea so there will be tons of activities onboard, and Holly and Greg wanted us to try out a bunch of different things."

"When I was boarding, I heard the announcement that our rooms are ready," offers Margot.

I nod, having heard the same announcement before the run-in with Bradley.

"I, for one," says Trent, pointing to the bar, "would like to try another one of these yummy drinks."

The others nod in agreement.

Having already had a drink and then roped Niall into my past, I really just want to run and hide until I can gain some composure. I get a bottle of water and take a few sips before excusing myself.

"I need to check in with Becca to make sure she has the corporate event for tomorrow all set. Then I think I'm going to go check out the rooms, make sure everything looks good, and put my feet up for a bit. Meet you all at dinner. Our parents and other siblings will be joining us for dinner tonight as well," I announce.

"Are you sure, G?" asks Holly. "We'd love for you to stay with us."

"I'm sure." My voice rises in one of those infamous "I'm fine" moments like Ross from *Friends*. You know, the one where he finds out about Rachel and Joey and swears he's fine?

Yeah, that's me right now.

Just call me Ross because I am totally not fine.

In fact, I am the opposite of fine. I'm freaking the flip out.

"I'll catch up with you all later," I say, clearing my throat and excusing myself from the group.

Mom and Dad. Ugh, with everything that happened this afternoon, I didn't even get a chance to check in with them.

I better have a message from them that they are safely on this boat. I pull out my phone as I walk out of the Imperial Bar and head toward the elevators. No message. So I send one.

GWEN

Please tell me you've made it and are already on the cruise ship. We are set to depart in less than an hour.

MOM

Oh honey, I'm so sorry I didn't message you sooner. Yes, we are checking in with the boarding agent now. We were in such a rush when we got here that we didn't think to give you a heads up. Sorry if we worried you!

GWEN

All good. I'm just happy you all arrived in time. I'm heading to my room for a bit, but I'll see you at dinner.

I smile and shake my head as Mom sends me a thumbs up. I love my parents, but they just may be the death of me one day. Thankfully, everything worked out this time, but I might not be as lucky if there is another mishap.

CHAPTER 12
Niall

After a drink with the group, I promise everyone I won't be late for dinner and head to my room. My mind is still reeling from the revelation that Rose is Gwendolyn.

Greg's little sister.

I never could have imagined this. I was hoping for a chance to get to know her, to have a good time on the cruise, and now it's like the odds are in my favor because she and I will be together all week for the wedding festivities.

The room is nice and roomy with a king-size bed, a little sitting area with a couch, and a balcony view of the ocean. The cruise ship left port shortly after Gwen left the group. I open the balcony and take a step outside, looking at the shore fading off into the distance.

A sharp intake of breath causes me to freeze on the spot.

It can't be.

Gwen's eyes are wide with shock as she sits in a chair on my balcony. Well . . . our balcony.

I chuckle. Of course our rooms are connected. It fits; it must be fate.

"Hi, Rose," I say.

"What are you doing on my balcony?" she sputters.

"Pretty sure this is our balcony, seeing as how I just came from my room." I point to the side.

She leans forward to peer around me, as if looking to see if I'm lying.

"Why is this happening?" she asks before laying her head back against her chair. She looks wrecked.

"My guess is that the group of us are all next to each other, seeing as how we're all here for the same wedding." I take the seat across from her.

Gwen rolls her eyes. "That's not what I meant. Seeing as I'm the one who coordinated everyone's rooms, I know the wedding party is rooming close together. I arranged to share a balcony with Margot, but of course that got messed up. And now I guess I'll be sharing a balcony with you instead. How do you keep showing up? And don't you dare say because you are here for my brother's wedding. Obviously, I know that already. I mean, I didn't know you were Sully. But seriously, why do you keep showing up?"

"Maybe it's not me who keeps showing up, but you who keeps getting to the places first."

"That is literally the same thing," she says.

"I beg to differ, Rose. If you didn't go to the places you've gone, then I wouldn't have shown up where you were."

Sighing heavily at my comment, she lifts her eyes to the sky. "And for that matter, why do you keep calling me Rose? I have a name, which you, of course, now know."

"You're right, I probably shouldn't be calling you Rose anymore. It's just that I didn't know your real name and I needed something to call you since we kept running into each other, didn't I? Now, I'll call you Gwendolyn, though Rose does suit you nicely."

"How does Rose suit me?" she asks, her forehead wrinkled.

"Well, your beauty is so captivating that when you enter a room, it's impossible for people not to take notice.

And before you say anything, it's not all about you being pretty, but also, your hair looks red when the light hits it and you're a bit prickly on the outside. All qualities of a stunning rose."

She glances over her shoulder at me, rolling her eyes.

"Riddle me this," I say. "If it's not you causing us to run into each other so often, then what were you in so much of a rush for last night that you hopped into my car?"

"I did not hop in your car," she says, though a touch of pink trickles up her cheeks to her ears. "Plus, I wasn't the one who almost gave my keys to a total stranger."

"True, though your outfit was so like that of the valets that I'll admit, I was briefly confused."

"I was not dressed like a valet!" she exclaims.

"I'm just stating my opinion." I shrug.

"Well, you're wrong."

"It's an opinion. How can that be wrong?" I question, leaning forward in my chair.

"Because . . . it just is."

I raise my brow at that and ask, "Are you always this argumentative on vacation?"

"I'm not argumentative. I'm just stating a fact," she says matter-of-factly. "And I'm not on vacation." She leans back in her chair and stretches her legs out, her hair blowing in the wind.

It mesmerizes me, and I can't help but stare at her. Our eyes meet briefly, and I catch a glimpse of the golden flakes in hers, glistening from the sunset. She quickly looks away.

Get a grip, it's just a little flirting. I clear my throat before continuing, "Fair enough, Gwendolyn."

Gwen's phone pings. Looking down, she types out a message before saying, "And no one calls me Gwendolyn, I'm Gwen. . . . Just Gwen. And can we be done with this conversation? I'm getting a headache and already had enough stress from Bradley and my mom and dad."

She slumps a little in her chair, putting her feet up on a makeshift lounge chair across from her. She looks out at the ocean, rubbing her brow.

I study her for a bit. Do I really stress her out that much? I can't get a read on her. First, we had that cute little incident in the car, but then she ate my head off at Duke's Diner for saying she was beautiful. And what's wrong with saying that, by the way? But then she seemed so grateful to me when I played along with her in front of Bradley and Tammy. And when we held hands, it felt like time slowed down and the world seemed to fade away, taking all its chaos with it. We were hand in hand, in our own private existence. She had to have felt that too. And now? Now, I have no idea what she feels toward me.

But it doesn't matter. I'm unexplainedly drawn to her. I want to bring back the smile that I've so rarely glimpsed.

"What happened with your folks?" I ask.

She studies me before answering, "They almost missed the cruise."

"Wow, the groom's parents missing the cruise, what a nightmare. No wonder you have a headache."

"I mean I would have figured out a way to get them here, but it wouldn't have been until our first port day." She sits up a little straighter in her chair, her eyes piercing me with her earnest sincerity. "I don't want anything to go wrong this week for this wedding. Holly is my best friend, and she's been through so much. She deserves the perfect wedding. And I love my brother. I wouldn't want anything to ruin their celebrations. I have to make sure this cruise is perfect," she says. Wiping tears from her eyes, she continues, "Thankfully, Mom and Dad listened to me and booked it here after they passed the traffic. They were literally the last two people to board the cruise. That's what the text I just received from my mom said. And she was laughing about it. Can you believe that?"

"Sounds like all's well then, right?" I ask.

She nods. "For now." She stands and leans against the rail, looking out at the ocean, then adds, "It's beautiful, you know? I forget sometimes how much I love the ocean."

"Ah, it is," I say, joining her. "I used to enjoy going to the beach in Boston with my mam. Not as warm as the Caribbean, mind you, but still, it's a beautiful sight to see."

"Used to? You don't go anymore?"

"Well, err . . . you see, my mam passed away about a year ago. And I haven't been able to bring myself to go to the Boston beach without her." I scratch at my neck. I wasn't planning on talking about any of this, but for some reason, I felt like opening up to her. Memories of the year-round picnics I had at the beach with my mam stream through me. She loved feeling the breeze and watching the waves roll in and out. A sadness blooms within my chest at the memory.

"Oh, I'm sorry," says Gwen.

"No need to be sorry, it's all good. She would have loved the cruise, but she never really cared to leave Boston."

"I've never been to Boston."

"No?"

"Nope, I've been so busy building up my business that I've only been on work trips, and none have been in the Boston area, though I've always wanted to go."

Studying Gwen, I see how tired she is. She's running herself ragged. Maybe Greg was right, and I can help her bring a little *craic* and a lot less stress into this week.

At a quarter to seven, I leave my room. I don't want to be late to dinner, and this cruise ship is huge. Gwen had left the balcony earlier, so I hadn't asked if she wanted to go together.

The main dining room is at the back of the ship and is full of people talking to their tablemates, waiters bringing drinks and taking orders. There's a soft din of noise as I am led to our table. Our group is so big we get our own little corner of the restaurant. With windows lining us on one side, it's actually quite cozy.

"Oh, Niall, how nice to see you again." Mrs. Kenton stands to wrap me in a hug. The Kentons have always been nice to me. They came up to Boston a few times during college, so I got to know them well, having been in the dorm room next to Greg and Trent since our freshman year. I haven't seen the Kentons in years, but whenever they visited Greg in college, they always made me feel like one of their own. Mrs. Kenton reminds me so much of my mam. I hold onto her a little longer than normal. It's been a while since I've gotten a mother's hug, and I didn't realize how much I missed it. A ping of sorrow hits me hard at the thought, but I brush it off and give her a big smile.

"It's lovely to see you again as well," I say as she moves aside for her husband.

"I was sorry to hear about your mom," says Mr. Kenton, giving me a squeeze on the shoulder.

"We're always here for you if you need anything," says Mrs. Kenton.

Realizing I've started to feel melancholy, I plaster a smile on my face and brush off their concern. "No worries. My mam wouldn't have wanted me sulking around in sadness. She's always been one to celebrate those who've gone, but I thank you for your kind words."

As I turn to take my seat, Holly introduces me to the older couple sitting next to her. "Mom, Dad, this is Niall, or Sully, as Greg and Trent refer to him. He's our other groomsman. Niall, this is my mom and dad."

"Pleasure," I say as I tip my head in their direction, taking a seat next to Greg. Gwen walks in alongside a small family.

"Grams and Papa!" exclaims a little lassie.

"This is our granddaughter, Maggie," says Mrs. Kenton. Maggie runs right up to her grandparents, overflowing with joy. They sweep her up in a big hug.

"And this is our daughter Gillian," says Mr. Kenton, "and her husband Miles."

"Nice to meet you all," I say.

We all adjust our seats some, and before I know it, Gwen is situated between me and the others. Holly's other sister, Vivian, soon joins us and sits just to the side of Gillian. The two must know each other already from their animated conversation that starts the second she sits down.

The Kentons regale us with their road-trip experience. Traffic from multiple car accidents, an unexpected detour, and a flat tire practically kept them from making the boat. Luckily, as Gwen already explained to me, they made it just before the cruise stopped letting people board.

As we finish dinner, some of the group heads out while the others sit and catch up. Vivian jumps up excitedly and rushes over to embrace another woman. It isn't until they break apart and a crowd of people passes that I notice who it is. Tammy.

Instinctively, I reach over and place my hand on Gwen's forearm. My touch shocks her, and she snaps her head in my direction only to see Tammy and Bradley standing off to the side waiting to be seated.

Gwen grips my hand roughly. "Help," she whispers to me. "I can't handle another run-in with them today. I just need time to process that he is here and he's engaged. Not to mention," she gestures to the rest of the wedding party, "I'm not sure who knows my ex will also be around for the wedding, and I don't want this dinner to turn into something it shouldn't."

I nod. I can imagine Greg would not take kindly to seeing his little sister's ex. Then I stand and say, loud enough for the rest of the group to hear, "If you're done eating, Gwen, would you mind walking me to my room and going through the wedding agenda and the next few days of plans, since I haven't been caught up to speed on everything yet?"

"Of course," Gwen says, jumping out of her seat and almost knocking her chair over.

"See," says Holly, "I told you she was your girl."

I smile and then gesture for Gwen to head out first. We say our goodbyes and manage to take a wide route out of the dining room without catching Vivian, Tammy, or Bradley's attention.

"I still can't believe he is Tammy's plus one," she says, shaking her head.

I eye her curiously. "What do you mean?"

"Vivian, instead of bringing a date for her plus one, brought a friend, Tammy. Which by itself wouldn't have been an issue. But then earlier today, I found out that Tammy also brought a plus one."

"Bradley, right?"

"Yes, Bradley!"

I process that information for a minute. "So if Vivian is the bride's sister, and Tammy is her guest, and Bradley is Tammy's guest, then that would mean—"

"That would mean," says Gwen, "that I'll be seeing my ex and his fiancée on this cruise way more than I had originally hoped."

"Well," I say, "that is going to make things a bit more interesting now, isn't it?"

CHAPTER 13
Gwen

The gentle rocking of the ship helps me fall asleep. But the past two days have been too full of unplanned events for my liking, and my sleep is restless.

Hours later, bright light from the late morning sun streams in through the glass. Sitting up in bed, I wish I had closed the blinds last night. All I want is to go back to sleep. But there's no point. I know I won't sleep much anyway. Besides, I need to look over today's schedule. At least the ocean view is beautiful, a consolation prize.

I start a pot of coffee before sliding open the door to the balcony and sitting in one of the lounge chairs. It's so relaxing and peaceful, a slight hum coming from the people on higher levels going about their day. The light shines off the sea as the ship continues on its course. Everything is as it should be.

Opening up my cruise app, I look over our agenda for the day. I know it by heart, but it never hurts to double-check.

Today is a day at sea. We are all pretty much on our own to have some time getting acquainted with the ship, except for our two o'clock reservation for the rock-climbing wall. This will be for the bigger group.

All of us are listed on the reservation as expected. Holly, Greg, Trent, Margot, Niall, Miles, Gillian, Vivian, and myself. Check!

I love when I can cross something off a to-do list. For my personal agenda, I've planned to attend the ten-thirty yoga class. I click my phone off, then go inside to quickly dress in yoga pants and a sports bra and toss my hair up in a ponytail.

My coffee is finally ready, and I gulp down one cup then grab another. I walk out to the balcony and watch the waves.

It's a new day.

Everyone made it onto the ship, and even though there have been some more-than-stressful instances, with each breath of ocean air, the stress dissipates like the waves as they break and settle.

Yoga is everything I needed. There's something about it that awakens my body and mind in a calming silence. Lately, I've had to miss my regular classes back home. But I vow right here and now that when I get back, I will make time for these classes.

Even if that means having to schedule them in like a client meeting.

I can't help but leave the class with a giant grin on my face, my yoga mat in its holder and my bag strapped over my shoulder.

I hit the Noble's Café and order a superfood green smoothie. It's perfect. Taking another sip as I turn around, a chirp sounds on my phone, and I glance down to see a notification from the onboard messaging feature in the cruise app.

DAD

> Hi, honey, this is actually mom. I can't figure out how to use this app on my phone, so I'm just using Dad's phone. Anyway, your dad is feeling a bit seasick. Anything you know that could help?

Poor Dad. I weave my way through the small crowd as I exit Noble's Café.

I'm just about to hit send on a reply to my mom when I round the corner and bump right into someone. The lid pops off my drink and green smoothie spills everywhere.

"Oh no, I'm so sorry," I say as I set my things down and quickly grab my small towel from my bag to try and clean up the poor person who was unfortunate enough to have me run into them.

When I look up, I freeze.

Oh.

My.

Goodness.

It's Niall.

McHottie strikes again.

How do we keep bumping into each other?

What's left of my green smoothie is slowly dripping down his shirtless chest. I wipe the napkin quickly over his abs. My hands tense slightly as I stroke over Niall's chiseled form. He has an amazing six-pack. "I'm so sorry," I say, unable to stop wiping his chest. Damn, Niall is hot.

"No worries," says Niall.

"I wasn't paying attention to where I was going, and I was dealing with a situation. . . ." I trail off as his warm hands move over mine.

"It's okay, I think you got it all," says Niall huskily.

I stop short as I look at my hand covered under his, pressed against his hard abs. I can feel redness flood my face.

His shirt is slung over his perfectly broad shoulders. Shoulders that are glistening slightly, just as his chest and abs were probably glistening before I spilled my drink.

Heaven help me, he's just come from a workout, and I have been standing here dumbstruck, running my hands all over his chest. I will not be attracted to this man. Even if I do refer to him as McHottie in my head. *You do not have time for this, Gwen.*

"Good morning, Gwendolyn," he says, clearly amused by the situation.

A shiver runs through me at his use of my first name. "Morning," I say, trying to keep my composure but failing miserably. My cheeks feel like they're on fire.

The smile on his face crinkles his eyes as he watches me intently. "I just came from a run and didn't expect to have . . . What is this? A smoothie? Spilled on me by a lovely lass."

My stomach flips at his comment. No, bad stomach. Bad.

"Again with the comments on my looks? Can't a girl just . . . be, without being objectified?" I stand one hand on my hip as my eyes shoot daggers at him.

I mean, yes, I was ogling him first, but I'm not going to *tell him* that he's hot. He just makes me feel confused. I don't want to be attracted to him. I don't have time for this. I have a wedding to pull off.

Niall looks dumbstruck, like I've completely stunned him. His eyes widen at my words, and all traces of the smile vanish from his face. "I never meant to offend you, Gwendolyn."

Maybe I've gone too far this time. And now that I know Niall a little, I really wasn't that offended.

Words fail me as I see the only thing that could make this moment worse—Bradley and Tammy coming toward us.

"No, no, no, not again," I whisper, frustrated at my dumb luck. I should have just stayed on my balcony this morning and done yoga in solitude. Then I'd only chance bumping into Niall, not Niall, Bradley, and practically-perfect-in-every-way, my-hand-is-too-heavy-from-the-diamond-in-my-engagement-ring Tammy.

My sudden change in demeanor has to be giving Niall whiplash because he's suddenly on high alert. "What, what is it?"

I move slightly so he is blocking me from view. "I know I just practically yelled at you, and I spilled my drink all over you, but I would be forever in your debt if you'd just play along . . . again," I say, peering up at him, my eyes wide as I silently plead with him for the second time in less than twenty-four hours, *Pretend to be my boyfriend.*

"Oh em gee," Tammy squeals, "Bradley Boo, look who it is!"

It takes Niall practically one point two seconds before he becomes all charm and smoothness. It oozes off him in waves, not unlike the green smoothie that was dripping off him a few moments ago. "Why, look who it is, *mo ghrá.* Fancy bumping into you two here."

Thank you, Niall!

"Hi," I say forcefully. Seeing Bradley and Tammy together cuts. *I'm a strong, independent, intelligent woman. What Bradley thinks of me doesn't matter anymore. I am better off without him.* I try to regain my confidence. Bradley still looks great.

But not as good as Mr. McHottie, whose body I now know much more about. Wait, what? I shake myself from my internal dialog to focus back on the conversation happening around me.

". . . planned for later this afternoon," says Niall. "It should be a grand start to the activities on the cruise."

I'd clearly zoned out and missed part of the conversation.

"Oh, how fun," Tammy exclaims. "I'm not a fan of sports, but Bradley Boo was so excited when he'd found out this ship had it, he insisted we sign up. Maybe we'll see you both there!"

"Sounds great," I choke out, not registering what I'm responding to. I lean in close to Niall, slipping my arm through his and wrapping it around his back.

"We should compare times," says Bradley. "Make it a competition."

"May the best couple win," offers Niall cheerily as he places his arm over my shoulders. "Anyhow, we best be off. Got to get washed up. I'm afraid I'm a bit too sweaty to take this one to a proper lunch."

Tammy's eyes roam slowly over Niall, his shirt still hanging over his shoulder. I have to fight the urge to gouge her eyes out. I place my other hand on his chest and lean up to give him a quick peck on the cheek.

What the heck has come over me?

After a nod from Bradley and a wave from Tammy, we are alone again. I step back from Niall, taking a proper breath for the first time since seeing Bradley and Tammy.

"Well, that was some *craic*," says Niall.

"What do you mean 'crack'? Like, 'on crack'? Not exactly how I would have described it, but thank you. I owe you one, or I guess two now." I huff out a feeble laugh, then take a sip of what's left of my smoothie. That's twice now Niall has helped me out of a pickle. I'm going to owe him forever if it keeps up at this rate.

"Not a problem," says Niall. "And *craic* means fun in Irish. Anyway, I'm going to wash the rest of this off," he gestures to his chest. "I guess I'll see you at lunch." Niall waves and heads to the elevators.

This ship is getting smaller and smaller by the minute. And now that I know I'll keep bumping into Bradley and Tammy with Niall around, what am I going to do? Of course, they're inevitably all going to show up to some of the same wedding activities. *How are you going to pull off this fake boyfriend thing, Gwen?*

This is going to be the absolute worst.

I can't keep asking Niall to pretend to be my boyfriend, right?

Or can I? Maybe he wouldn't mind helping me out for the rest of the cruise. A crazy idea begins to form, but I'm interrupted by a chirp from my phone.

DAD

> Hi, honey, I don't mean to bother you again but did you have something for Dad. He hasn't left the bathroom and is looking a little green.

I had completely forgotten about my mom's text.

GWEN

> Sorry, yes. On my way. Got caught up with something, but I'm heading back to my room now and will bring over the Dramamine asap!

DAD

> Thank you so much, oh dear, Dad needs me. Just knock when you get here and I'll let you in.

Thankfully, I have a plethora of Dramamine in my emergency bag. I'll deal with this first, and then I think I will go chat with Niall.

After all, I know which room is his.

CHAPTER 14
Niall

A sharp rapping on the door catches my attention. I turn the shower off and grab my towel from the hook. Who'd be coming to my door?

After rushing to somewhat dry my hair with the towel, I wrap the towel around my waist and step out of the bathroom. The rapping starts up again, but it's not coming from the hallway door. It's coming from the connecting room. Having met with Gwen on the balcony yesterday, I know for a fact that door leads to her room. She did say she had a situation earlier; I hope nothing's gone wrong. My concern that something might actually be wrong has me going against my good sense and heading to open the door in just my towel.

I quickly unlock the door and pull it open in front of me, hoping to somewhat block me from view. At the same time, Gwen's hand reaches forward to knock again. She fumbles at the lack of door, but then pushes her way into the room, eyes down on the floor. Immediately, I can tell something is wrong. From the short time I've known her, I've learned she's not one to avoid eye contact.

"Oh good, you're here," she says, looking out my balcony door. "I wasn't sure since you didn't answer right away."

I'm momentarily stunned at her sudden entrance into my room while I'm still in my towel *and nothing else*. Then,

I close the door connecting our rooms while reaching my other hand down to hold where the towel barely comes together. The towels here are much smaller than the bath towels I have at home. Gwen paces back and forth in the sitting room area, still not having looked at me.

"Want to share what you're on about over there?" I ask. "Is the situation from earlier going okay?"

She stops pacing and turns around to face me. "Yes, everything is—" Her piercing eyes take me in, roaming over my body. Finally, her eyes meet mine and she audibly gulps. "You're naked."

I chuckle softly, raising my eyebrow at her. "You don't say? Actually, I wouldn't call it naked. I do have this lovely towel." I motion with my free hand.

Her eyes briefly jump down to the barely-there towel and back up to my face. "Umm . . . the towels aren't that big."

"No, no, they're not." Her heated gaze causes things in me to stir. Trying to think about anything other than being practically naked in her presence, I adjust how I'm standing so she can hopefully not tell that I'm clearly attracted to her.

Get a grip, man.

"Why are you standing there in a towel?" she asks, her voice raising to mouselike levels of squeakiness.

"Well, you see, I was in the shower when I heard an urgent knock, so I quickly grabbed a towel and answered. And, well, here we are, standing in my room, me in this towel, and you over there."

"Right," she nods, and continues to nod, like a bobble-head. It's like she doesn't know what to do with herself. Do I really make her feel that uncomfortable? I run my hand through my hair, water droplets falling as I do.

"So about your situation?" I ask.

"Just forget it, forget I said anything. I can't believe I thought it was a good idea. I don't know what has gotten into me." She walks toward our adjoining door.

"What was a good idea?" I reach out and grab her arm softly with my free hand, the other still securely holding onto the towel. She stumbles and falls against my chest. I shouldn't be noticing how right she feels against me. How perfectly we fit together. I try my hardest to rein in my thoughts as I right her.

"Gwendolyn, please look at me."

"I can't. Not when you're like, well, like that," she waves her hands blindly in my direction, clearly avoiding looking anywhere in my vicinity.

"Would it help if I put on something with a bit more coverage? Would you talk to me then?"

She nods, still avoiding eye contact.

"Okay, then turn around and don't move."

She turns to face the hallway door.

I move slowly toward my pile of clothes on the couch, making sure she won't bolt to her room. Taking another quick glance to make sure she's not looking either; I drop the towel. Her presence and my nakedness do nothing to help my attraction for her. I press against myself to calm things down, then slip on some boxers and grab a pair of joggers from off the couch.

"Okay, I'm decent. you can turn around."

She turns, and her cheeks go red. "You said you were decent!" she exclaims.

"I am. I put on some pants," I say in confusion.

"But not a shirt."

Reaching behind me, I grab an exercise top off the side table and throw it on. "Better?"

"Yes, thank you."

"You're welcome. So, what's the story? Does it have something to do with the situation you were on about when we ran into each other earlier?"

"Huh? Oh, that. It was nothing," she waves me off. "Dad's just sick."

"What? Is he okay?" I ask, instantly brought back to my mom in her hospital bed, hooked up to way too many machines. The memory makes my pulse race as my worry for Mr. Kenton increases.

"Oh, yeah, I gave him some Dramamine that I had in my emergency bag, so he'll feel better soon."

Okay, so he's not sick, just seasick. I study her for a moment. Clearly something is weighing on her, but if not her dad, then what?

"How can you stand having your things all over the place like this?" Her hands wave around the living room area.

I survey my room and realize it is a bit messy, clothes scattered over the couch and dresser, shoes wherever I kicked them off. But it's not like I was expecting company.

"You didn't come here to talk about the cleanliness of my room, did you?" I ask, kicking a few of my clothes under the bed.

"Well, no. . . ."

"Grand. So, what brings you to my room?"

She stiffens for a moment before rolling her shoulders back. Her captivating beauty may catch the occasional eye, but it's her spunk that draws me in.

"Okay, I'm just going to say it. This might sound crazy. Actually, I know this is crazy. But it's the only way. I mean, I don't want you to feel obligated to say yes. You can say no."

Her rambling is making me confused. "Just ask, Rose," I say, knowing my use of the nickname will snap her out of whatever this is.

"Fine," she looks to the ceiling before rushing out, "I'd like to propose that we pretend to date for the duration of this cruise. Now that I know I'll be seeing Bradley much, much more than I thought, I can't let him find out that I lied about being in a relationship. It will make me look like a total loser. I know there really isn't a reason for you to agree to this proposition, but I need your help and I already tangled you in my web of lies. Twice." She lets out a deep breath.

I can tell it's not easy for her to ask me this. Shifting on my feet, I think through her proposal. If we date—err, pretend to date—then we'll be spending even more time together on the cruise, which is what I've wanted, isn't it? I've been drawn to her since the first time I saw her in my rental car. And now, I'll have a reason to be with her as much as possible. We'll have a better chance of getting to know each other. And she'll get to know the real me, not the me that is always slipping up and saying the wrong thing.

Fake dating would also be a very convenient way to keep the favor I'd promised Greg. I won't have to put in much effort to convince Gwen to spend time with me. Not to mention, I'd be helping Gwen out of a stitch.

And most importantly, I'd be putting myself out there, like my mam wanted.

A smile stretches across my face at the memory of my mam. *I'm going to keep my promise, mam, just like you wanted me to.*

Fake dating Gwen sounds like a good thing all around. Although, I do need her to clarify a few things. "Before I agree to anything," I say, "I need to know what the deal is with you and Bradley, like what would I be getting myself into per se?"

Gwen sighs, and after moving a hat off the corner, she lowers herself onto my bed. She's quiet for so long that I don't think she's going to tell me anything, but then she looks up at me before finally speaking. The sadness in her eyes is gut-wrenching.

"I guess it's fair that you know some of it," she says, "if I'm asking you to fake date me and all that."

I nod, encouraging her to go on.

"After two years of dating, living together for part of that time, Bradley broke up with me. I was completely blindsided. One minute, I thought we were going to get married and that he was going to propose soon, and the next, he broke up with me."

"Feck," I swear.

"He said it was because I put my work before him. But it's not that I chose it over him. It's that I started my own business from scratch. I had to make it a priority or else it would have failed. Funny thing is, our relationship ended up failing instead."

She stands up and, with more energy in her voice, continues, "Being blindsided like that crushed me. That's why I put so much effort into making sure every event I put on is perfect, that I don't miss any details, because I am determined not to be blindsided again."

The fiery personality that I am so attracted to is coming out once again. It's seeing her this way that has me agreeing to her crazy proposal. That and the thought that my mam would love to see me with someone like Gwen. "I'm game," I say.

"You . . . what? You are?" she asks, her shoulders relaxing slightly.

"Of course. Let's give it a lash, can't hurt."

"Give it a what?" Her nose wrinkling at my words.

"A lash, er, a try. Let's try. Can't do worse than we've been doing, right?"

"Okay. Right. Then we need to come up with a plan, some rules. I don't want to be winging this," she says as she gestures between the two of us, "around Bradley and Tammy."

Nodding, I sit down on one side of the couch. I move a piece of old toast off a side table and grab the complimentary notepad and pen that were lying beneath it. "Okay, what are the rules?"

Gwen walks over to the couch and looks at it. I glance over and quickly reach to pull the other articles of clothing into a pile and place them on the side table before she sits opposite me.

"Seriously?" she says, motioning to the pile of clothing.

I shrug. "I haven't really settled in yet."

Gwen takes a seat on the couch next to me. "Rule one: none of our friends can know we are in a pretend relationship. To them, it will just be like we've become good friends."

"Why don't you want them to know? You don't think they'd understand and play along?" I ask, honestly confused at this request.

"I mean . . . I'm sure they would, but it's . . . it's just too embarrassing. I just can't deal with them knowing this. Please, can we just keep it a secret?"

I can understand how Gwen could be embarrassed by this, not that I think she should be. And if I'm not telling Gwen about Greg's request, it's only fair that I not tell Greg about Gwen's request. "We can keep it a secret," I say.

"Thank you," Gwen continues. "Also, I don't want to hamper your style. I know you're on vacation. So feel free to do whatever you planned on doing or to spend time with any woman you want during the cruise, just don't let Bradley or Tammy see you with anyone else."

"Not to worry. I came on this cruise for Greg and Holly, not to hook up with random women." I scribble the first rule on the pad of paper, then say, "Rule two: you have to go on a few dates with me, just the two of us—as a fake couple, of course."

"I don't have time for that," Gwen protests. "This cruise and wedding are important. Nothing can go wrong."

But I can't take no for an answer. Time alone together would not only show Greg I'm fulfilling his favor but would also give me the opportunity to secure my promise to my mam. It's my chance to genuinely try to make a connection with someone. We have to go on these dates. I can't fail my mam.

"I hear you. I do," I say, "but it's important that you have a little *craic* while we are on the cruise. It shouldn't be all work and no play. This is your brother and best friend's wedding, after all. You're a guest as much as the wedding planner."

"True, but mainly I'm the wedding planner. Who else is going to make sure everything is perfect?"

"This rule is a deal-breaker for me."

"Why is it a deal-breaker? What's it to you?" asks Gwen, tilting her head.

"Let's just say, you have your reasons, and I have mine. And one of mine is that we spend time together as a fake couple. If you can't agree to this, then we don't have a deal." I stare into her gorgeous hazel eyes, silently begging her to agree to my request.

Sighing heavily, she says, "Fine, we can go on a few dates. It will help our cover in case we run into Bradley and Tammy anyway."

Nodding, I jot down the second rule: *Go on some dates, just the two of us, as a fake couple.*

"Rule three," she glares at me then catches herself, shaking her head as she says, "I promise to not be too mean to you."

"What if I like your spunky side?" I ask.

She grins but quickly hides it, raising her eyebrow at me. "Well, I'm not perfect so I'm sure that side will come out plenty. I'll be busy with the wedding and cruise itinerary, and even in the short time I've known you, you've already distracted me too much. I just promise I will try to not act like I hate your guts while you're pretending to be my boyfriend."

"Ah, so I distract you then," I say, a grin spreading across my face.

"No, ugh, you like riling me up, don't you? Okay, rule four: you can't rile me up."

"Hey, a boyfriend would tease his girlfriend."

"Fine, you can only do it when you are acting like my boyfriend. Otherwise, you have to try and be nice too."

"Oh, I'll be nice to you, no worries there."

"Right. Well . . . we're not really going to be dating, only pretending."

I can see the insecurity in her eyes. It's taking a lot from her to ask me for this favor. What she doesn't understand is that any bloke in his right mind would jump at the chance to be with her. She's snarky, tough, fiery, and drop-dead gorgeous.

"Grand. Any other rules? Because I'm not counting your rule three and four."

"Fine, don't add them. I have just one more then. When we're around Bradley, we need to sell our relationship."

"Okay, do you want to give me more details?"

"Um, it's not necessarily a requirement, it's just that . . ."

"Spit it out, Rose. We haven't got all day. I'd still like to catch lunch before it's time for dinner." My eyes curl up with mischief because I think I know where she's going with this. And my mind has been playing it on loop since she first asked me to fake date her.

"Well, it's just, you know, Bradley can't find out we're fake dating, so we have to . . ."

"Make it look real?" I offer.

"Exactly."

"So, what are you thinking? How real do you want it to look?"

"I mean handholding, being close to each other in public, hugs . . ."

"Kissing?" I question, heat pulsing straight through me at the thought of kissing her.

"Umm . . . only if absolutely necessary?"

I nod. "Okay, the final rule, rule number three, is when fake dating, PDA is acceptable but kissing is only allowed if necessary."

"Right," she nods.

"*Cúla búla.*" I stand, reaching my hand out to her. She stands and takes my hand and shakes it to seal the deal.

"I should probably . . ." she looks over to the door connecting our two rooms.

"Yeah, sounds good. See you around, fake girlfriend," I say, though I don't let go of our handshake.

"Right. . . ." she says slowly, then, looking down and seeing our hands together, she lets go quickly, grabs the paper with the rules, and turns to walk back to her room. "I'm going to hold onto this. With how messy your room is, I can't leave it up to you not to misplace it."

I hear the lock of her door click and chuckle to myself. *Well, this afternoon definitely took a turn. This is going to be the* craic.

CHAPTER 15
Gwen

"Hey, there!" says a female voice I unfortunately recognize all too well now.

Tammy. No. No. No. Tammy and Bradley must be rock climbing too.

Oh shit, I didn't have time to warn Holly or Greg that Bradley and his fiancée are on this cruise.

I was really hoping I could keep the rest of the wedding party from seeing them so soon. Honestly, I was hoping that the agreement Niall and I made this morning wouldn't ever come into effect with my friends around.

But I am not that lucky.

Nope.

Not even close. Because as I walk into the rock-climbing area, sure enough, Bradley and Tammy are signing their waivers on the little pads.

My body sputters to a stop. And when I say sputters to a stop, it's like the comical screeching-of-tires, frozen-in-time, heart-in-my-chest kind of sputter.

It wouldn't have been so bad, but my untimely stop causes everyone in the group behind me to topple forward in what is probably the most comical slow-motion game of human dominoes ever seen.

Before I can register what's happening, we are all in a pile on the ground.

"G, what in the—" starts Holly.

"Miles, you're on my arm," says Gillian.

"Gwennie, seriously why'd you stop?" asks Greg.

Margot and Trent chime in with their own complaints.

There's only one person who didn't need an explanation but instead knew why I'd frozen mid-step. A Mr. McHottie. Niall extracts himself from the pile and easily lifts me to my feet, pulling me close to him in what I hope is both just a friendly way, but also a boyfriend-ish way, considering the two groups.

"You okay?" he asks me, making my heart jump into my throat.

"Oh em gee," exclaims Tammy in her four-inch wedge heels, showing off her perfectly light-pink toenails, and looking like a barbie in her short shorts and lacy white shirt. "Are you okay? That looked like it hurt." She makes her way over to our group, who are all still trying to untangle limbs and right themselves.

I groan and lean my head against Niall for a second, trying to gain composure.

"Hi, Tammy," I say, plastering the most fake-but-trying-not-to-seem-like-I-am-losing-my-shit-internally smile I can muster. "How awesome that you were able to join us."

"I know, right? I was just telling Bradley that I had a feeling we'd get here before you all. I have a sixth sense for these types of things. Don't I, Bradley Boo?"

Rolling my eyes, I hold my plastered smile on my face. Bradley Boo doesn't seem as happy at seeing us all together as Tammy did, and from the look on his face as he looks over my shoulder to Niall, he doesn't like how close Niall is holding on to me.

Not that he should care. He's the one who dumped me.

"You don't say," Niall replies to Tammy, sensing I am not in the mood to deal with her Barbie-esque personality.

"Tammy!" exclaims Vivian, rushing over to give Tammy a hug after extracting herself from the domino pile. "I was hoping you'd be able to join us this afternoon."

"Oh my gosh, Vivi, yay," says Tammy. "I'm so excited we were able to get in the same time with you!"

Motioning to the rest of the group, Vivian says, "Tammy, this is the rest of the group. Everyone, this is Tammy, my friend and coworker, and my plus one to the wedding."

"Hi, ya'll," says Tammy sweetly.

"Hi," they chorus back to her.

"And this," says Tammy, pulling Bradley to her side, "is my fiancé, Bradley."

Margot's eyes go wide. Trent's mouth falls open, Greg looks like he could rip something in half, and Bradley looks like he wants to be anywhere but here.

I echo Bradley's sentiment, wishing I could melt into the floor and disappear rather than go through this moment. Niall's touch at my back is the only thing keeping me from sprinting away. We made a deal, and if he's going to stick to it, so can I.

"Bradley?" says Holly.

"Hi, Holly," Bradley says.

She looks from Niall to me, then back to Bradley and Tammy, and I can see the tirade of questions forming in her mind. But I know Holly. She won't cause a scene here. Though I'll definitely hear about it later.

But the same cannot be said for Greg.

"What are you doing here?" asks Greg.

"Do you guys know each other?" asks Vivian.

"We sure do," says Trent.

The rest of the group stares at us with a mixture of confusion and horror.

"Congratulations to you both on your engagement," says Bradley, nodding toward Holly and Greg.

"Thank you," says Holly sweetly.

But Greg holds a heated gaze. "Seriously," he says, "why are you here?"

"I thought you guys knew I would be here?" Bradley says, placing his hand around Tammy's waist. "Vivian, didn't they say it was okay if Tammy brought me?"

"I did," says Vivian.

"What are you guys talking about?" asks Greg, only getting angrier. "Why would we ever be okay with Gwen's ex being on our wedding cruise?"

"Gwen's ex?" says Miles incredulously. Gillian swats him on the arm, then leans in and whispers something to him. I know exactly what she is saying because his eyes glance at me then to Bradley.

"Oh," says Vivian, "I had no idea. Is this going to be a problem?"

"No—" start Holly and I.

"Yes," say Trent and Greg in unison.

"I'm sorry if I caused any trouble," says Tammy. "I just knew that Vivi would be busy a lot with the wedding party events, and I didn't want to be lonely. I didn't think it would be an issue to bring him."

"It's not that you brought someone," answers Trent tersely. "It's the person that you brought."

The tension going around the group is palpable. It's almost too much for me. I lean in a little toward Niall, unable to take my eyes off the scene in front of me, my cheeks hurting from the forced smile I've kept pasted on my face.

"It's fine," Holly says. "We did say that Tammy could bring her fiancé. Right, Greg?"

"Yeah," says Greg, "but we didn't know that it would be *him*."

Holly places a hand on Greg's arm and pats it softly, giving Greg a stern look. "Vivian, it will be fine; Tammy and Bradley, we are happy to have you join us on the cruise."

Ah, yes, ever the placating bride.

"Thank you," says Bradley.

With another stern look from Holly, Trent finally nods. "The more the merrier, I guess."

Greg excuses himself from the group. "I need a breather," he says.

At that comment, I seem to snap back to reality. *Okay, Gwen, you can do this.* Clapping my hands together, I say, "Alright, now that we've had this little reunion, how about we get an instructor over here?" I wave to one of the rock-climbing instructors. "We're ready to sign the rest of the waivers and get to rock climbing," I tell him.

Holly eyes me, and I try to give her an expression that I'm doing fine.

"Okay," says the instructor, "I'm Chadwick, and I'll be helping you out today. Who still needs to sign a waiver?"

After the waivers are signed, we follow Chadwick to the rock-climbing wall.

"Thank you all for coming," says Chadwick. "We're going to have a great race! We'll get you all harnessed, and then we will set you up next to the others. We can have three people going at the same time. First to the top wins, and best time in each group will race each other for a final overall winner. Alright, any questions?"

Our friend group from Tennessee has been rock climbing a few times in downtown Nashville back home, and we have always had a blast. No wonder Greg and Holly added this event to the itinerary.

First up are Niall, Trent, and Greg.

"Have you ever rock climbed before?" I ask Niall as he gets a final check from Chadwick.

"I have," Niall replies, a slight smirk on his face.

"Well, I hope so," says Margot. "Trent and Greg are pretty good. It'll be tough to beat them."

I nod in agreement.

"I'm not too worried," says Niall.

Margot and I step back to watch the guys race up the wall. Niall wasn't lying. He's definitely done this before. He manages to beat Greg and Trent, but just barely.

We're all clapping as they rappel down and get unhooked from the harnesses.

Margot, Holly, and I are up next. I'm ready for this and am bouncing from foot to foot waiting for our start.

Greg gives Holly a kiss as she gets her final check from Chadwick. "Good luck," says Greg.

"She's going to need it," says Margot, grinning.

It's over almost as soon as it starts. I manage to reach the top right before Margot, and I'm so excited that my foot slips a bit and I bump into the wall before rappelling down to the ground.

Once unharnessed, I step back with the guys as we watch Miles and Gillian get ready to start their climb.

"You're okay," a soft voice says from beside me. I startle but glance over and see it's Niall.

"Yes, why wouldn't I be?" I reply. "I won."

"But you hit the wall after ringing the bell. It looked like it hurt."

"I'm okay. Might get a little bruise later, but nothing to worry about."

Niall nods, standing close to me and rubbing my arm.

"Go, Gillian," Greg yells, as we watch she and her husband start up the wall.

"You got this, Miles," calls Holly.

All and all, they're making decent time—not enough to beat my time or Niall's, but still decent enough. Miles reaches the top first and rings the bell, then he and Gillian rappel down together.

Vivian, Tammy, and Bradley are up next. Unsurprisingly, Bradley scorches them, beating the girls to the top while they barely made it halfway up. He was always great at sports, and Vivian and Tammy don't seem upset as they chat, slowly making their way down the wall.

"Alright, gang," says Chadwick, "we have four winners from the first rounds. Niall, Gwen, Miles, and Bradley."

"I'll sit out," says Miles quickly. "While it was fun and all, this is not my kind of sport."

"Alright," says Chadwick, clapping his hands together. "Looks like we will have Niall, Gwen, and Bradley racing to the top to see who becomes the final winner."

Oh no, I wasn't paying enough attention to the winners to put together that it would be us three competing against each other at the end. This is going to be a disaster.

"Sounds great," says Bradley.

"Let's do this," says Niall, his eyes filling with fierce determination.

"This should be fun," I mutter.

"You got this, G," says Holly encouragingly.

Chadwick checks our harnesses, and we line up on the rock wall with Niall to my right and Bradley to my left. *What have I done to deserve this torture?*

I brace myself and try to clear my head, focusing only on the wall. And we're off.

"I'll wave to you from the top," says Bradley.

"Not a chance," replies Niall. They take off up the wall quickly. I try to ignore the little quips they're throwing back and forth. We're all keeping fairly good pace. The guys are leading ahead of me by just a hair.

Before I know it, the torture is over, and Niall rings his bell.

"The view from up here is great," he teases Bradley.

Bradley only shakes his head and mutters under his breath.

"Behave," I scold Niall.

He turns and gives me a sheepish smirk. "Sorry, *mo ghrá*, I was fighting for your honor."

I smack his arm as he repels down next to me.

"The best time of the group was Niall," Chadwick tells our group. "It was close but Niall finished a few seconds before Bradley."

"Great job, Niall," I say, giving him a hug.

"Now," says Holly, "how about we head back toward the lounge for some drinks?"

Bradley glances over at me and Niall again, a flash of annoyance in his eyes. I know that look. It's been aimed at me many times over the years.

Vivian comes up beside me and whispers, "I'm so sorry, Gwen. If I would've known, I wouldn't have asked if it was okay he came."

"It's okay," I say, offering her a smile. "It was all a misunderstanding. I'm going to be fine."

"You sure?"

"Yes, I'm not the first woman in the world who's had to be around her ex."

"That's the truth," says Vivian, giving me a squeeze on the arm. "I'm sure you'll be seeing each other here and there with the wedding activities, but we're going to sit this one out to give you some space."

"Thanks," I say, "I appreciate that."

"Holly," says Vivian, "drinks sound great, but Bradley, Tammy, and I are going to head over to the pool."

Holly nods. "We'll catch up with you all later."

"Stay cool at the pool," says Trent.

I watch Vivian, Bradley, and Tammy head in the direction of the pool. I breathe a sigh of relief when they are finally out of sight.

"Gwennie, you okay?" asks Greg.

Gillian gives me a hug. "Let me know if you need to talk," she says.

"I'm really fine," I tell my siblings.

But no one seems to buy that. Everyone knows I did not take the breakup well. I'd thought he was close to proposing. Not on the verge of dumping me.

I'd been completely blindsided.

They all probably think I am freaking out at seeing Bradley at rock climbing. What they don't know is . . . I'd already run into him two other times, so I am fresh out of the freaking-out stage. I'd just hoped I could keep it from all of them, because now they'll be focusing on me being around Bradley. And I can't have that.

Not when this cruise is about Holly and Greg.

I take a deep, calming, centering breath before turning to the group and laying everything out to them.

"Yes, that was Bradley. Tammy is his fiancée and Vivian's plus one for the wedding." I hold my hand up at Holly, Margot, and Gillian's expressions, all three on the verge of either trying to mother me or sharing some sentiment about their ill will toward Bradley. "Before you say anything, yes,

I was shocked when I first found out. No, this isn't the first time I've run into them on this trip."

"What?" says Margot. "How many times have you seen each other?"

"It doesn't matter," I say. "You all just need to know that I'm not going to fall apart. And most importantly," I look around at the group expectantly with my sternest look, "I will not have this week be about me. I can be an adult and deal with the fact that Bradley and his . . . fiancée"—I internally cringe at the word coming out of my mouth—"are on this cruise too. But this cruise is not about me. It's about celebrating Holly and Greg. I hope you all will respect that I don't want to be the center of attention. It is my job as best friend and event planner to make this week all about the soon-to-be newlyweds. Everyone understand?"

Stunned expressions are on everyone's faces, but they all nod in agreement.

Everyone except Niall. He is looking at me with a lopsided grin, his eyes twinkling at my speech.

Clapping my hands together, I say, "Alright, we've climbed a wall, we escaped the domino collapse, I'd say we are more than deserving of a round of drinks. Everyone ready?"

"Miles and I are actually going to head out," says Gillian, "to spend time with Maggie."

"Give our niece a hug for us," says Greg.

Holly, Margot, and I walk arm in arm into the elevator. The guys hang back chatting before following a ways behind us.

"Why didn't you tell us about Bradley?" Holly asks.

"It wasn't a big deal, honestly," I reply.

"Seriously?" says Margot. "How can you say that?"

"I didn't want to worry you all," I say, "or take any of the light away from Holly and Greg." I squeeze my best friend's arm. "Was I freaked out at first? Yes. Was I furious that he is engaged to Malibu Barbie? Yes. But I realized this afternoon after running into them the second time that I am better off without Bradley holding me back. I want someone who is going to support my work and perfectionist nature."

"I'm all for you standing on your own two feet and going after your dreams," says Holly. "I mean, a year and a half ago I was miserable, but look at me now."

"I'm just happy that you aren't freaking out," says Margot.

"Just so you know," says Holly, "if you are freaking out and you're trying to hide it, I will be furious with you."

"Same," says Margot.

"I promise I'm okay," I say. "After my epiphany of sorts this afternoon, and I think everything will be just fine." I'm not going to tell them that the epiphany is lying to my ex and pretending to be in a relationship with Niall. No one needs to know that except Niall and me.

I smile as I think about Niall agreeing to fake date me this morning. I still can't get the image of him dripping wet in that too small of towel out of my head. I think it will be forever seared into my brain.

CHAPTER 16
Niall

"Dude, I can't believe Gwen's ex is on the ship," says Trent as he sits next to Greg and me at the bar. "Let alone Tammy, his fiancée. I hope we aren't going to be seeing that much more of him."

"Seriously," says Greg, "he was such a dick to her in the end. I can't believe I liked the guy at first."

Gwen had already told me the basics of her and Bradley's relationship, but I can't let Trent and Greg know that. I don't want them questioning why she would have opened up to me so soon and potentially blow our fake-dating cover. "So, what happened with them?" I ask.

"They dated for years, then one day he decided he didn't like her working so much and called it quits," offers Greg. "At least, that's all she was willing to tell us." He shrugs and glances over to his sister, who is linked with the girls, one on either side. Worry lines Greg's features.

"She's been a mess for months," says Trent. "Hasn't been quite the same since. Throwing herself into her job even more than before. She's more reserved now. It's like her natural vigor seemed to dim."

"Wow," I say, "he must have done a number on her then." I wonder what she was like before. I bet she was a force to be reckoned with, a firecracker.

I look toward the bar where the girls are sitting. In the interactions I've had with her the past couple days, she's seemed pretty spunky to me. Maybe she is finally getting over the breakup.

Getting out of her wedding-planning work mode is good for her. Another reminder that it was good I added those one-on-one dates to our rules.

"Yeah," says Trent, "I bet she's freaking out right now knowing Bradley is here, and with the wedding too, you know she's stressed trying to make everything perfect."

"I'm glad I asked you for that favor. Now more than ever," says Greg, grinning at me. "Who knew she'd also need you to help her avoid her ex?"

"What favor?" asks Trent, looking between the two of us.

"Well," says Greg, "even before I knew about Bradley, I just wanted Gwen to have fun on the cruise, not stress so much about the wedding, you know? Niall was always the one back in college who could get us out of our heads, so I was hoping he'd do the same for Gwen. You know, help her bring out her spunky side again."

"Hmm . . ." says Trent. "Does Holly know about this?"

"Well, no," says Greg sheepishly.

"Seriously, dude?" says Trent.

I just shrug. It's not my place to get in between Greg and his fiancée.

"I know," says Greg. "I should probably tell her, but I'm not sure how she would take it, and Gwen really needs this."

"And if Gwen finds out about this . . ." Trent trails off.

"I know, I know," says Greg.

"She won't find out," I say.

"Not unless you tell her, Trent," Greg says. "Plus, this is only to help her, so there's really no downside."

"I'm not convinced it's a good idea," says Trent. "But I'll go along with it, and if it comes back to bite you two in the butts, I hold the right to say 'I told you so.'"

"Sounds good, man," Greg says.

Trent nods then says, "This cruise keeps getting more and more interesting." He claps me on the back. "It's good to have you back, Niall."

"I know," I reply, "I wish it hadn't been so long since we got together. I was so busy helping Mam her last year. It was hard to get away, and then after . . . well, it definitely won't be so long between visits going forward," I finish, plastering a smile on my face.

Mam's cancer had caught me off guard. I guess that's normal, because who expects to get cancer?

When I'd first heard the news that she'd been diagnosed with stage four breast cancer, I didn't hesitate. I'd known what I had to do. I immediately notified my landlord and moved back in with Mam.

Back into my childhood home.

It was a rough adjustment. Nothing in the house had changed since I'd moved out, so it was like taking a step back in time. But instead of games of basketball in the driveway with friends and riding my bike around the neighborhood until all hours of the night, my new reality was days on at the firehouse, taking Mam to her cancer treatments on my days off, and sleeping in the bed from my youth.

I got Mam a nurse who'd come stay with her on my working days. Between all her medical bills, doctor's appointments, cancer treatments, and the nurse, the bills were overwhelming. Even though Mam had her retirement money and I made a decent living, we still had to be tight with our money. I wanted to make sure it would last as long as she needed it to.

I'd thought Mam was starting to improve, but then one day, she woke up feeling worse. I took her to the hospital, and the next day she was gone.

Just like that, the only family I'd ever had was gone. Vanished from the earth. Nothing more than a culmination of memories.

For the past twelve months since she passed, I've still been living in my childhood home. I don't know what I want to do or where I want to go. I feel lost. I've been a shadow of myself since her passing. The memory of my promise to her only intensified as the year-long deadline loomed nearer and nearer.

Now, among these friends who I haven't seen in way too long, I'm finally starting to feel like myself again. Add in Gwen, and I'm actually looking forward to spending time with someone, seeing where things could go.

How is it that one person, whose natural reaction to me is to glare and give me snarky comebacks, makes me feel like this? Like I'm going to be able to live up to the promise I made my mam.

It was way too easy for me to agree to her scheme this morning. I found myself craving more time with her. Craving those moments when her glare would ease up, and a slight smile would cross her face, lighting up everything around her.

"Sorry about your mom," says Greg after pausing to allow me to be with my thoughts. "I can't even imagine what you've gone through."

"It's fine now, really," I reply, trying to brush off the feeling of melancholy settling within me.

Trent clasps my shoulder. "I'm sure that's not true."

"It's all good," I say, turning and facing the girls as they walk toward us.

"What's not true?" asks Holly, before leaning into Greg and giving him a kiss on the cheek.

"Yeah, what's up with you? Miss us already?" says Margot, taking the seat opposite Trent.

"Nothing much," I say, "just shooting the breeze." I take a sip of my drink and smile at the group. Gwen catches my attention; her eyes bore into me, causing my pulse to race and my smile to shift from a simple smile to one of joy.

We head up to the Duke's Diner for an early dinner and load up our plates before finding a table for all six of us toward the back of the ship. We watch people playing Putt-Putt golf and others on the basketball course. There's nothing but blue ocean as far as the eye can see behind that.

Soon, we're chatting away about our lives, families, and careers. "Trent," says Holly, "tell us about your latest adventures of managing the marina."

"Managing the crazy boaters is more like it," says Trent. "The boats are fine; they don't cause problems. However, the boat renters . . . now they're a whole different kind of group. Dude, I tell you, it's never a dull moment. And with all the new marketing Greg has been doing, we're getting more and more people from all walks of life."

Laughing, I say, "I'll have to come visit sometime, and you'll have to show me around."

"That would be a ton of fun," says Greg. "We could take out one of the double-decker pontoons we have."

"That sounds grand."

"It's so much fun, isn't it, Gwen?" adds Holly.

"Definitely," Gwen agrees.

Finishing our food, we remind each other of the water show later that evening, then pile into the elevator to go our separate ways.

After a few floors, it's just Gwen and me, the others having gotten off earlier to do their own things.

"Ladies first," I say, gesturing to Gwen.

"Thank you." Stepping out of the elevator, she pauses, waiting for me before we continue the walk to our rooms.

"You really should come to Chessie Valley sometime," she says. "I know the guys would like having you around more."

"Are the guys the only ones who'd like my company?" I tease.

Rolling her eyes at me, she says, "Well, I'm sure the others would like to see you too. And my parents, as annoying as that is. Mom and Dad can't stop talking about how charming you are."

"You don't think so?"

"I mean, you're not the worst to be around." She bumps into me lightly.

I bump her back then say, "Wow, that was probably one of the nicest things you've said about me, Rose. We should document this moment or put it on a billboard." I hold up my hands, arching them across the wall. "Rose says I'm not the worst to be around."

She laughs, amusement dancing in her eyes. Her laugh is so sweet and sincere, like a wave spilling into my heart, gently cresting and breaking softly toward the shore. It's like this *beore* was hand-picked by my mam.

Unable to help myself, I reach out and pull her into a hug, grateful to spend time with her, if even just for a short time. It's helping me move past my sadness and feel alive again.

"What . . ." says Gwen, muffled against my chest.

"See you tonight?"

"Tonight?" asks Gwen. "Oh, the water show, right. Yeah, see you then."

I nod and pull her away from me, still holding onto her arms. Leaning in gently, I kiss her check before turning and walking into my room.

CHAPTER 17
Gwen

Niall kissed my cheek.

No biggie, right? Wrong.

Why did he do that? It's clearly against the rules of our agreement. Bradley and Tammy weren't even around.

Was my saying something nice to him that much of a shock? No, that can't be it. He was just being nice. Right?

I'm still reeling from the kiss as I work on my to-do list. I try to reach Becca but am unsuccessful. Then, I message Courtney.

GWEN

> Hi Courtney, I just wanted to check in and make sure everything is still on track for the reception. Remember, we want to have a dance floor with the tables surrounding it on three sides.

COURTNEY

> Just checked my notes and that's how it appears to me. All good on my end, I was just about to head to talk to the chef and make sure he has everything for the menu.

GWEN

> No worries. I have a few minutes to talk to him.

I set my phone down with a huff. I guess I can let her check on this one aspect of the wedding. I try to focus on checking the order of events for the reception and wedding ceremony, but I'm unable to get the kiss off my mind and can't focus. Instead, I order in some room service and try to take my mind off Niall.

When it's time for the water show, I still haven't been successful. I touch the spot on my cheek where Niall kissed me, gather my things, and make my way down to the outdoor theater.

Margot is already in her seat in the first row, right next to the water. I scan my regal pass with the cruise staff and join her. I remove the towel on my seat before sitting down.

"You okay?" asks Margot. "You look a bit flushed."

"I'm fine," I say, trying to stop the pink from rising to my cheeks.

Mom and Dad, the Palmers, and our siblings all arrive along with Holly, Trent, and Vivian. Looking at the wedding itinerary, I notice that Bradley and Tammy aren't listed to attend this event. I breathe a sigh of relief.

Niall is the last to arrive. My stomach does a happy dance at the sight of him, but I quickly quelch that feeling.

Greg, who is sitting next to me, notices Niall arrive. "Oh, here," says Greg, motioning to Niall. "Why don't you sit here?" Greg stands from his own seat. "Everyone can scoot down, right?"

Before I can protest, everyone is standing and moving over a seat, making room for Niall to sit next to me.

"Hi, Rose," says Niall as the show begins.

"Hi, Sully," I reply. I can't handle the barrage of emotions that come over me every time we are near each other.

I try to distract myself by focusing on the setup of the outdoor theater. As an event planner, I'm always looking for new ideas. There are lots of lights of varying colors that change along with the short movie clips playing on the large screens on either side of the theater. The show is a musical mashup of movie soundtracks. But neither the setup nor the show is helping me ignore the feelings coursing through me.

Finally, I can't take it any longer. I lean over to Niall and say, "You broke the rules."

"What?" he says over the sounds of music and water.

"You kissed me," I say a bit louder.

Gillian glances over at us. I give her a quick smile letting her know that everything is fine. Then I lower my voice to an almost imperceptible volume and whisper into Niall's ear, "That's against the rules."

"I shouldn't have," says Niall. "You're right."

The music gets louder, and more swimmers make their way into the pool. My frustration with my own lack of control over my emotions soon subsides as I watch the performers dance.

Not only do they dance in the water as a shelf raises and lowers, but they dive from varying heights. Each dive splashes us with more and more water. There's a reason for the towels, for sure. I catch myself laughing as I use Niall as a shield. Laughing himself, Niall tries unsuccessfully to block me and himself from getting wet.

It doesn't work, and we both continue to get spattered with water. All of us do. I can hear Maggie giggling and clapping along to the music. She is loving the show and all the water.

When the performers are dancing up by the diving boards, I notice Niall looking at me. He has a goofy smile on his face, and his eyes shine with happiness. A warm, fuzzy feeling settles in my stomach. I give him a little grin, then quickly compose myself and clear my face.

I've been enjoying the show, and even though I got annoyed with him about the kiss, he's been so sweet trying to shield us from the water. But I can't let him know how he affects me. How my insides flutter with nerves and I keep flashing back to him half naked, wrapped in a barely-there towel.

As the performers bow, the whole crowd gives a standing ovation. The show was magnificent. The performers were so talented not only on the ground dancing but in the water with their acrobatics.

Our group makes its way through the boardwalk, the summer heat quickly drying our damp clothes. I grab Niall's arm to hold him back a bit. "I'm sorry for being annoyed with you," I say. "I just can't seem to rein in my emotions when I'm around you."

"No need to apologize," he says. "You're correct. The kiss was against our rules. I let my emotions get the better of me too. How about this? Next time I kiss you, I'll ask your permission first." His eyes crinkling, he gently tucks a loose strand of hair out of my face, thumb grazing my cheek. Then, he turns and follows the others up the stairs.

It takes me a few seconds to realize what he said, and once it hits, I gasp, staring incredulously after him. Is he planning on kissing me again?

I swear I could hear him chuckle to himself.

The group makes a pit stop at the ice cream shop further up the boardwalk. I stand back and take a few deep breaths, trying to calm the butterflies in my stomach before

I have to be around Niall again. By the time I catch up with everyone, they are sitting at the multicolored tables outside the ice cream shop waiting for me.

"Get lost?" Trent asks me.

"Where did you go?" asks Holly, staring intently at me. "Are you getting stressed about the wedding?"

I chance a glance at Niall, and, sure enough, he's looking at me, his eyebrows raised as if questioning me.

Get a grip, Gwen.

I smile at the group. "Nothing's wrong, and I'm not worried about the wedding planning. Everything is all taken care of. I just needed a minute. Now, are we just going to sit here, or are we getting some ice cream?"

I don't even wait for them to join me as I walk right into the ice cream shop to look at the different flavors.

The others trickle in a few at a time while the rest of the group holds our tables.

My phone pings with a message from Becca before I've ordered.

BECCA

> Sorry I missed your call. I believe everything is set for the Fieldman and Steiner luncheon tomorrow. Are there any last-minute things you want me to look over?

"Auntie Gwen, look at the ice cream I picked out!" Maggie tugs at my shirt.

"Hold on, Maggie, I just need to take care of this real fast," I say. My attention is on my phone as I think through everything that will be needed to take care of this plated lunch for 200 people.

GWEN

> Has all the silverware been polished and the extras packed? You know how people tend to drop their utensils.

"Auntie Gwen, look at my ice cream," Maggie tugs again. "One moment."

"Auntie Gwen!" Maggie persists.

I put my phone away and turn to look at Maggie's ice cream. Maggie, of course, picked the chocolate flavor and added gummy bears, sprinkles, chocolate sauce, and whipped cream.

"Maggie, that looks so yummy!" I exclaim.

"Yes, it's going to be scrumptious, even though it's a little melted because you took forever to look," she says.

Feeling a little bad, I watch as she skips out the door back to the table. I chuckle at her use of "scrumptious," such a big word for a little girl. She's always trying to sound like a little adult.

I order a scoop of chocolate in a waffle cone, topped with whipped cream and salted caramel sauce, and head to the tables and take the only open seat—next to Niall.

"That show was such a delight," says Mom. Dad nods in agreement.

"It's a good thing they provided towels," adds Margot. "The cruise staff wasn't kidding when they said we'd get wet."

"Luckily, my hair is almost dry now," says Vivian.

Laughing, we all eat our ice cream. Being too short to reach the ground, Maggie kicks her feet back and forth. She looks like the happiest five-year-old in the world.

Grinning, I take another bite. The warm summer weather is making fast work of melting our ice cream. I'm starting to regret getting a cone, but only a little, because how could I regret a waffle cone?

"You have a little . . ." Holly says, making a motion that I have ice cream on my face.

Swiping where I think she's referring to, I ask, "Did I get it?"

"Definitely not," says Greg, then laughs.

I try again but to no avail. After my second miss, Niall reaches over and wipes the drip of ice cream clean with his thumb.

Everything would have been fine; I could have handled the reaction my body felt when he touched my face. But then, catching me completely off guard, he licks the ice cream off his finger.

"Mmm . . . Tastes good," he says, like him licking ice cream off his thumb wouldn't cause my stomach to flutter with anticipation.

Lucky finger. I can think of a couple places I'd like him to lick.

Wait?! What the heck am I thinking?

Not too many hours ago, I got annoyed with him for kissing me on the cheek, and now this is where my mind goes, to places I'd like him to lick. Um no. *Get it together, Gwen.* It has to be the heat; it's making me delirious. Right? Or the lack of sleep. Yep, that's what it is.

Did no one else realize Niall practically licked ice cream off me?

Niall is grinning his charming, sexy grin at me as he takes another lick of his cone.

CHAPTER 18
Niall

Maybe I'm flirting too much, but I can't help it. I love seeing Gwen's cheeks turn red as I catch her off guard. The look on her face when I licked the ice cream off my thumb was perfect. Her eyes were wide, expression full of shock and want. I know she's attracted to me. That was clear when she realized I was in a towel earlier.

Regardless of the deal I made with her and the one with Greg, thoughts of her have been running through my mind since the moment she bumped her head in my car and her strawberries-and-cream scent caused my body to react to her in a way that no one has made me feel in a long time.

After ice cream, everyone talks about ending the night with the late-night karaoke at the Hurdy-Gurdy bar. A few people bow out, already having made plans, and others say they'll see how the night goes.

A while later, after arriving at the Hurdy-Gurdy, it ends up just being Gwen, Greg, Holly, Trent, Margot, and me. After watching a few other people sing, some good and some completely horrendous, the girls are up. They've picked "Super Troopers" from *Mamma Mia!*

I can tell at once they've done this before, and I smile as they pose facing the audience.

"This is their song," says Greg, chuckling.

"Why's that?" I ask, curious for as much information about Gwen as I can get.

"Well," says Trent, "they've been singing ABBA since they were kids, and after *Mamma Mia!* came out and they saw Meryl Streep and her friends dancing to this song, they made it their mission to learn the dance."

"You're in for a treat," says Greg, before cheering loudly for the girls.

The music starts, and, in the most hilariously choreographed dance, they begin their karaoke version of "Super Troopers."

None of them miss a single move, with Gwen taking the lead and Holly and Margot as the backups. The crowd sings, whoops, and hollers during their performance.

My stomach does a flip. If only Gwen really felt that I could be the person who makes her happy, just like the lines she's singing now. As they finish the song on a "you . . ." and point toward Greg, Trent, and me, I can't help but beam at Gwen.

Greg, Trent, and I stand and cheer the loudest. Gwen is all smiles until she starts walking off the stage. She tenses for a split second. I don't think anyone else notices, but no one else is watching her as intensely as I am either.

Scanning the room, I notice Bradley, Tammy, and Vivian in the crowd. They must have decided to join us after all. Vivian and Tammy are standing and clapping along with the crowd, but Bradley is staring at our little group, dread etched across his face.

"Wow," says Greg, patting me on the arm. "Your Sully energy must be working. I haven't seen Gwen have that much fun in a while. She must be feeling more like herself already."

As the girls join us back at the table, Greg embraces Holly.

"That was awesome," says Trent.

I grin at Gwen as she comes and picks up her piña colada.

"Gwen, that was so great!" says Margot. "I never thought we'd get you to take the lead again."

Gwen beams at her friends and shrugs. "Just felt like time, I guess."

Vivian, Tammy, and Bradley join our group. "We made it," says Vivian, pulling a chair out next to her sister. "I was glad we caught your *Mamma Mia!* performance."

"It looked so fun," says Tammy, "that I signed Bradley and I up for a duet."

Everyone nods politely, and then there is a beat of silence before Margot says, "I want to do another song. Come sing with me, Trent."

"Alright, but there's only one song I'll do," says Trent, then laughs.

"Ha," says Margot, "I already knew you'd say that, and I put us on the list." She grabs Trent's arm and drags him toward the stage.

Trent doesn't miss a beat as the piano chords start, and he sings "Don't Stop Believin'" by Journey. Margot catches the chorus, and they're off. Playing air guitar, hopping up and down, and walking around the stage as if they own it. Not as choreographed as the girls were, but clearly this is another regular for the group.

Catching Gwen's eyes, I notice she seems a little down. Her smile says happy, but her eyes are far, far away from this bar.

"Let's do a duet," I whisper in her ear.

"Do you sing?" she asks.

"In my shower, mostly. But I've done karaoke with the guys before, back in college."

She wrinkles her nose but then slowly nods in agreement.

"*Cúla búla*, I'll get us signed up." I hop up quickly before she has a chance to change her mind.

When I sit back down, Gwen leans over and asks, "So what song are we singing?"

"It's a surprise."

"Hmm. . . . How do you know I'll know it?"

"Everyone knows it. You will be fine. I promise," I hold out my pinky to her.

Looking at me like I've lost my mind, she loops her pinky with mine, and we shake on it. "You better not let me make a fool of myself up there."

"No worries, I'll always have your back," I say. "Plus, you're too cute to ever appear foolish."

She wrinkles her nose again as Trent and Margot make their way back to the table.

Next, Bradley and Tammy are up.

"This should be interesting," adds Greg.

"Yep," agrees Trent.

"Gwen," says Holly, "we can head out if being around Bradley is making you uncomfortable."

"I'm fine," says Gwen. "I'm here to have fun and spend time with my friends. I'm not going to let Bradley ruin that."

"Good for you," says Margot.

"I'm so sorry again," says Vivian, "for the misunderstanding."

"Don't worry about it," says Gwen. "Though, I hope he sounds like a goose when he sings," she adds with complete sincerity.

There's a moment of stunned silence, then we all burst into laughter, getting a few looks from the people around us. I guess we are about to see for ourselves.

Tammy is grinning at the crowd like she's Miss America. Bradley is the complete and utter opposite. Glancing briefly in the direction of our little group, he looks as if this is the last place on earth he wants to be. When the music begins, Bradley and Tammy sing "Don't Go Breaking My Heart" by Elton John and Kiki Dee.

Tammy immediately gets into it, bopping and leaning into Bradley at each of her lines. Tammy, bless her heart, is giving it her all.

I cringe a little at their performance. It's a little much, but somehow endearing. Bradley, unfortunately for Gwen, seems to have a decent tone. Though his demeanor onstage definitely does not come off as endearing. The man looks like he has stage fright.

I almost feel bad for the bloke. He clearly doesn't want to be up there, and it's clear he only is because Tammy is having the time of her life.

As they finish their song, Bradley practically runs off the stage, followed by a smiling Tammy. There is a smattering of applause from the crowd and a whistle from Vivian, who, bless her, is so supportive of her friend.

Two more singers and another group go before it's Gwen and my turn to sing. I signal to her with a tilt of my head.

"Go get them, Sully!" cheers Greg.

"Woohoo, didn't think we'd get you up there," says Trent. "We haven't heard you since college, Sul!"

I wave them off, chuckling. It really has been too long; this is going to be the *craic*.

Eyeing me with trepidation, Gwen takes the mic and follows me onto the stage. The DJ announces our song, and at that, Gwen's eyebrows almost go into her hairline. Surprise at my choice colors her face.

"You got this," I mouth to her as the music intro starts. I just have to hope she'll start singing at her part as I belt out my best John Travolta version of "You're the One that

I Want" from *Grease*. Never one to do things halfway, I get into the moves, channeling my inner Danny Zuko.

Gwen is laughing, surprised at my performance. And bless her, she doesn't miss a beat. Clearly a *Grease* fan herself, she immediately embodies the not-so-sweet-anymore Sandy. Even going so far as to push me back with her foot on my chest.

A radiant sparkle in her eyes, a buoyant energy enveloping her, she becomes this fearless, sexy version of herself, and it's like I'm getting to see the real Gwen. Dancing around the stage, we are so in sync. It's like we've practiced before. By the end of the song, we are laughing, dancing, and having the time of our lives. I give her a hug after spinning her around as the song ends. The crowd is going crazy. Our friends whoop and holler for us too. Taking Gwen's hand in mine, my fingers tingling at her touch, I lead her in an over-the-top bow onstage.

As we make our way off the stage, I notice Bradley and Tammy leaving the karaoke bar. Looks like Bradley might not have enjoyed the performance as much as everyone else.

"Okay," says Holly, "that was seriously the best thing I've seen all day!"

"Totally agree," adds Margot.

"Did you all practice that?" asks Greg, eyeing me curiously, a smile on his face.

"Nope," says Gwen. "And Niall, you didn't tell me you could sing or dance. That was so much fun!"

Trent clasps me on the shoulder. "It was fun to watch too. Just like the old days."

"Sure was grand," I say, grinning at them all. Being up there with Gwen, dancing and having fun, that . . . that is exactly what I want with her, for us.

CHAPTER 19
Gwen

I wake up to the late morning light coming in from my balcony. There's something to be said about seeing the ocean when you first open your eyes. You just don't get that same view in the landlocked state of Tennessee. Nothing bad on Tennessee. It has some gorgeous views, but the ocean is exactly what I've needed lately.

After making a ridiculously strong cup of coffee, I sit back in my bed with my legs curled up in my blankets as I sip, watching as the waves roll across the water. Finally, I get up, stretch, and throw on my running shorts and sports bra. I find the running track, wanting to get a long run in today. Nothing better than running with a nice breeze from the ship and the ocean view all around the boat.

My brain is so full of conflicting thoughts and emotions that I need a good hard run to clear it and figure out . . . well, everything. The wedding in a few days, Tammy and Bradley on the cruise, trying to have fun and not only work on this cruise, and Niall, literally everything about Niall. . . .

Turning at the bow of the ship, I follow the path back down toward the aft, my feet pounding out the familiar rhythm, a cadence that is both invigorating as much as it is calming.

I didn't realize until I was singing karaoke last night how much I missed feeling like myself. As much as I hate to admit it, with Niall, I feel like the old me again. Full of life and a feeling of giddiness. And it feels good. Really good. He brings out a side of me that's been missing.

He's been so kind to me. And to top it off, he has a history with the guys that makes it feel like he's been a part of our group for years. I mean, I guess he has with Greg and Trent, but he fits in so easily with all of us. And when I get out of my own head, I find that I can have fun and enjoy his company too.

Like that duet we did . . . damn.

When he started singing, my heart practically jumped out of my body. And then when he began dancing, it shattered any lingering annoyance and fear I had of being around him and letting him in. He's so goofy and adorable, but damn, the look in his eyes when he picked me up and spun me around at the end of the song was intense. My skin prickled the rest of the night, the lingering warmth from his touch staying with me long after we left the Hurdy-Gurdy.

"Morning," I say as I move around an older couple walking the path.

"Good morning," they call back after me as I continue to run ahead of them.

If I'm being honest with myself, I think it was the feeling of someone looking out for me that made me sleep so soundly last night. When Niall noticed that Bradley and Tammy were at the Hurdy-Gurdy, he did what I never thought possible. He made me forget all about them.

Just as I'm thinking about Niall, he, Greg, and Trent appear beside me.

"Hey, Gwennie," says Greg.

"Hi, guys," I say, frustrated they popped up just as I am finding my rhythm running.

"We haven't seen you on the track yet," says Trent.

"Nope, I went to yoga yesterday," I answer.

"Didn't want to go today?" Niall asks, the guys all easily keeping pace with me.

"Couples yoga today," I reply.

"Well," says Greg, "don't let that stop you. Niall would love to go with you. Right, Niall?"

"Um, yeah," says Niall.

I narrow my eyes at Greg. What is he thinking suggesting Niall and I go to couples yoga together?

My mind jumps back to Niall shirtless outside the gym as I wiped the spilled green smoothie off him. I need to change the subject before I lose myself in this memory. "Don't forget this afternoon we have the cupcake decorating class with everyone."

"Thank you," says Greg, "for adding the cupcake class to the itinerary. I know it will make Holly so happy."

"Of course," I say. "It'll be fun for all of us."

"As long as you and Holly don't make a giant mess," says Trent, "like you did baking at the cabin."

We laugh at the memory, then run in silence for a while.

"As much fun as this is to run with you three," I say as we round the corner at the back of the ship, "it's feeling a little crowded."

"Right, well, we'll get out of your hair," says Trent.

"See you around, Gwennie," says Greg.

Trent and Greg speed up a bit, but Niall calls after them, "I'll catch up in a minute, need to ask Gwen something."

The guys wave at him so he knows they heard him, and Niall settles in next to me. He quietly keeps pace with me before saying, "So about the cupcake decorating class, I was thinking maybe we could pair up."

"Pair up?"

"Yeah, I looked into it, and it requires groups of two."

I glance over at him; he's grinning at me like the Cheshire cat with a secret.

"Yes, I know that. But don't you think it will be weird if we pair up together in front of everyone?"

"Well, you mentioned that everyone would be attending the cupcake decorating class, right?"

"Yes. . . ."

"Does that mean Bradley and Tammy will be there?"

After looking at the itinerary this morning, I know they will be. "Yeah, they will."

"So wouldn't it make sense that we are working together, since they think we are supposed to be dating?"

"Yes, but I don't want anyone else thinking something is going on between us."

"I don't think they will," says Niall.

"And why is that?"

"After karaoke at the Hurdy-Gurdy last night, no one said anything to me. And if they didn't say anything about it last night, I doubt they will over cupcake decorating."

"True. It does make sense for us to be partners with Bradley and Tammy being there. I guess you're right."

Niall's grin grows slightly, and his eyes seem to sparkle with amusement. "Did you just say I was right?"

I try to glare at him. "No."

"Well then," says Niall, a mischievous twinkle in his eyes, "I guess it's settled. At the cupcake decorating class, we will put on the best show."

We run in silence for a few more minutes. But I'm getting nervous about Greg and Trent getting curious about Niall and I spending so much alone time together. I don't need them getting in the middle of our pretend relationship and messing things up. "You should probably catch up with the guys," I say. "I don't want them getting suspicious of us."

"Right," says Niall. "I don't want to stir up suspicions. See you in class." Niall waves and takes off in a sprint to catch up with the guys.

I try to keep my same rhythmic pace, but watching Niall's butt as he runs throws it off and ruins my whole plan to clear my head during this run.

CHAPTER 20
Niall

When I knock on the door adjoining Gwen's and my rooms, I wait for a beat before Gwen opens it. She looks beautiful in a yellow skirt and a white shirt tied in a knot, giving off a brief view of her stomach. My hand itches to reach out, to touch her, to pull her close to me so I can feel the softness of her. Just the thought of touching her causes my body to react.

Taking control of where my mind is going, I say, "You look perfect."

She instantly blushes, a light pink brightening her sun-kissed skin.

"Well, you don't look so bad yourself," she replies, her eyes roaming over me.

I feel the grin breaking out across my face at her attention. "Since I'll be your cupcake decorating partner, I thought we'd walk there together."

Nodding, she slips her phone into her pocket and slides her sea pass lanyard around her neck. Not wanting anyone to be suspicious if they see us leaving the same room together, I step back into my room and close our adjoining door. With our friends having rooms right next to ours, it would be way too easy to run into the others.

Gwen and I meet in the hallway, then we make our way to the class. I can feel my nerves running, no, rampaging around inside me. *What the feck is going on with me? We're just walking together, and my insides are going crazy.*

I smile when I notice Bradley and Tammy are in the class. I'm happy my excuse is confirmed. Time to play boyfriend.

After we meet up with the others, we partner up for the class.

"Sully," says Trent, "want to be partners?"

Greg shakes his head at Trent and motions toward Gwen.

"Oh, right," says Trent.

"I was actually thinking the same as Greg," I tell Trent. "With these two here," I motion slightly toward Tammy and Bradley, "maybe this would be a sound time for me to hang out with Gwen. Let some of my Sully energy help them not ruin the class for her."

"Dude, good call," says Trent. "Hey, Margot, want to be partners? I promise I'll let you eat your fair share of the icing."

"Ha," says Margot, "someone's got to keep an eye on you, or we're not going to have any icing at all. Right, Gwen?"

Gwen is typing intently on her phone.

"Right, Gwen?" Margot repeats.

"Hmm?" Gwen asks, not looking up from her phone.

"You would have heard me if you weren't stuck with your nose in your phone," says Margot.

"Sorry," says Gwen. "I was just checking in with work. I'm all yours now. What's going on?" She puts her phone in her pocket.

"It was nothing," says Margot, already heading to her cupcake station.

Our cupcake stations are equipped with ingredients to make our own frosting, colored dye, and a whole array of decorating pieces. I am clueless to the differences between them all.

"Thank you for this," Gwen says. "It was so thoughtful of you to think about Bradley and Tammy being in this class and suggesting we be partners."

"No worries," I say genuinely. "That's what fake boyfriends are for."

Patting my arm, she says, "Right, and now I can show Bradley how much better off I am without him."

"You sure are," I reply quietly, watching her smile and a lightness ease into her.

Holly stops by our station. "You two ready for some fun?" she asks.

"Of course," I reply happily.

"She just wants to show off how amazing her decorating skills are," Gwen teases. "Ten bucks says Holly's decorations are better than the instructor's."

"Oh no, I'm not touching that bet," I say. "I've heard all about Holly's baking prowess from Greg."

"Stop it, you guys," says Holly, feigning embarrassment as she turns and walks back over to her station with Greg.

Nancy, a sweet older lady, is the instructor of the class. She walks us through how to make the icing base.

I'd say we did a fairly decent job. Vivian and Tammy were supposed to be partners, but with Bradley, the three of them are sharing a workstation. Glancing over at them, it looks like they've managed to make icing soup, so while the instructor helps them thicken their icing, Gwen and I separate ours into multiple smaller bowls so we can mix in the colors.

"What colors are you thinking?" she asks me while eyeing Bradley and Tammy.

"Red, for sure," I say.

Quirking her eyebrow at me, she says, "For all the fires you put out?"

"For the red of the most beautiful woman in this room," I say.

She swats me not so lightly on the arm.

"Ouch," I say, rubbing my arm.

"That's what you get for trying to distract me with silly, flirty compliments."

"Who said I was talking about you? Maybe I was talking about Nancy," I say, pointing to Nancy, who is trying to help Miles and Gillian, as they somehow managed to make their icing too thick, so much so that their spoon is stuck in it.

Gwen swats me on the arm again. "Not funny."

"Ouch, you're right, your hits are not funny. I think I may have a bruise now." I rub my arm even more dramatically.

She turns to face me, placing both hands on her waist and giving me one of her best glares.

Hands up in mock surrender, I say, "Okay, okay, I surrender. It's really you. You're the most beautiful woman in this room, Rose."

"Aww, now aren't you two the sweetest things," says Tammy as she walks by and picks up a bowl from the extra supplies Nancy had out.

"Err . . . thanks," says Gwen, her cheeks growing pink.

Rolling her eyes at me, Gwen turns back to face the color options, but I can see the small smile crinkling her eyes. She picks out a light blue, a yellow, and a sage green.

After we mix the colors, Nancy shows us all about the different decorating tips we can use, giving us examples of what each would look like. Then she instructs us on how to add the icing to the piping bags without making too much of a mess. Proud of myself for not getting icing all over the place, I glance over at Gwen, who has managed to get her icing in the bag with less mess than me.

"Show off," I mutter, bumping her with my hip.

"You better watch it, Niall. I have a piping bag full of icing, and I know how to use it."

"Oh, is that so, Rose?" I lean in close to her.

"Yes," she says matter-of-factly.

Before she has time to react, I take my piping bag and leave a dollop of the red icing on her nose. Scrunching her face, she doesn't even miss a beat as she places a dollop of blue icing on my nose.

Nancy clears her throat, having appeared right in front of our table. "Now, the icing is supposed to be for the cupcakes, not noses."

"Yeah, Gwen, didn't our mother teach you manners?" says Greg from a few tables over, smiling. He's one to talk. The icing is coming out of the top of his piping bag no matter what Holly does to try and help him.

Gwen looks alarmed at what she's done, but the whole thing has me cracking up, and before I know it, she is laughing right along with me.

"Here, let me get that." I reach over, holding her face in my hands. Her laughing immediately stops, shock at my touch causing her beautiful hazel eyes to grow wide.

"Don't worry, Rose, I'll be gentle with you," I say.

She makes a slight nod and lets out a breathy, "Okay."

Holding her so close, it would be so easy to just kiss her. Her full lips are lightly parted after her reply, her breath warm against me as I stand close to her. I take one finger, tracing her nose as I remove the icing from it. I plop the dollop of icing in my mouth. "Tastes delicious. We make a mean icing."

She nods, still frozen. Then, she reaches up and wipes the icing off my nose and licks the icing off her finger in what feels like slow motion. The pop of her mouth and finger sets off a gentle whirlwind of emotions within me. Oh feck, what she does to me.

I clear my throat. "Thanks."

"Now about these cupcakes," she says, "it looks like we are the ones behind now."

Gillian and Miles have already iced a handful of cupcakes, and Trent and Margot aren't far behind them. Holly is already on her eleventh perfectly iced cupcake.

"Right," I say, "let's get to icing."

After we finish, we each eat one of the cupcakes.

"We did good work," I say between mouthfuls.

"We sure did," says Gwen.

Next on the itinerary is laser tag, which sounds like something definitely added to the wedding activities by Greg. On the way there, Greg drops back to talk to me. "So, tomorrow Holly and I are going to the couple's yoga class. I was thinking you should take Gwen since she loves yoga so much."

"Exactly what I was thinking," I say.

"Great," says Greg, catching up with Holly.

When we walk into laser tag, the whole group is here except for Bradley and Tammy. Maybe they won't show up, which I know would be a nice break for Gwen.

The set up of the arena is truly amazing. Each group is a separate alien race, the Kriphits versus the Phevaihs, trying to take over the new world so their species can live on it.

We decide to do a boys-against-girls game. "We're going to be the Kriphits," says Holly. "It sounds like Griffins, which of course I love." The girls all nod in agreement.

"Sounds perfect to me," says Trent. "You won't stand a chance against the Phevaihs."

"Oh, there you are!" exclaims Vivian.

We all turn to see Tammy and Bradley.

"I wasn't sure if you two would be making it," says Vivian.

"Oh, girl," says Tammy, "we wouldn't miss it. Bradley was so happy when he found out the cruise would have laser tag. Right, Bradley Boo?"

"Right," says Bradley. Then looking at Gwen, he says, "I hope you don't mind that we've joined you."

"Of course not," says Gwen.

But one glance at Gwen doesn't have anyone convinced. Yep, she'd definitely gotten her hopes up that they wouldn't be here.

"Well," says Holly, quickly changing the subject, "we are playing guys against girls, but the guys are already one short. Would you mind being on the guy's team, Tammy?

"No worries," Tammy says cheerfully. "I'm horrible at this and can be on the guy's team. I'm just here for my Bradley Boo."

"Alright then, let's play," says Trent. He stars humming "Night Fever" by the Bee Gees. Greg, Miles, and I jump in to sing when he gets to the chorus.

Laughing, we all suit up.

Gwen makes eye contact with me, and I head over to her.

"How can I be this unlucky?" she says. "I thought they weren't going to make it. Why couldn't they have missed this event? It's like I can't avoid them at all."

I place my hands on her arms. "No worries, Rose, we can handle this." I turn and stand next to her as the instructor goes through the necessary safety talk. The space is dark with minimal lighting overhead in the labyrinth of the arena. The walls and fake rocks give off a slight glow, adding to the eeriness of the arena.

We're given a moment to run in and find a place to start the game. A beeping overhead counts down before the final buzzer sounds, letting us know the game has begun. Our vests and laser tag guns come to life.

Cutting around a path, I'm quick to get points for our team, finding Margot first, then Gillian. I keep inching around through the arena. A few minutes pass before I see her. Auburn hair zooming around a corner toward the back of the arena. I backtrack and cut through a path, hoping I'm heading to the same place as Gwen. She is sly though and is crouching behind a rock as I come around the corner. I'm open fire for her. She stands and shoots me square on the chest, and my vest lights up.

"Gotcha," she says then smirks at me.

Unable to fire until my hit wears off, I stalk toward her, backing her against the wall. "Oh, you do, do you?"

"Yes," she says, lifting her chin in stubbornness. My feisty Rose.

I drop my laser tag gun and let it dangle down next to me as I place both hands on either side of her, essentially trapping her in.

"Looks like I've got you now," I say, lowering my face slightly to line up with hers.

"Looks like it," she says, biting her lip, her chest still rising and falling rapidly from the adrenaline of the game. The sight of it makes me moan with want.

A sudden change in expression zips across her face, shock followed by frustration.

"Kiss me," she whispers.

Why would she ask me to kiss her? *Don't be an eejit. A beautiful beore asks you to kiss her, you kiss her.*

I lean down and place my lips against hers. Gwen presses into the kiss. I slide one hand from the wall to the back of her head pulling her in closer to me, kissing her deeply now. Our mouths dance in their own rhythm, exploring and enjoying the taste of each other. My desire for her overtaking all my brain cells, I don't know what to make of her suddenly asking me to kiss her, but I am going to enjoy this kiss, here and now.

The sound of my vest's sensor resetting breaks the bubble of our kiss. Pulling slightly back, I smile down at her, resting my forehead against hers.

"I like kissing you," I admit.

"Me too," she sighs, but then quickly adds, "I saw Bradley and Tammy coming around the corner, so . . ."

"Bradley and Tammy?" I ask.

"Yeah, it's one of our rules, kissing when necessary. I thought they were coming our way, but they must've gone a different direction."

Right, the rules, the agreement. Is that the only reason Gwen asked me to kiss her? For show in front of Bradley and Tammy?

"You're right," I say, giving her a soft kiss to her cheek and letting go of her. "That was one of our rules." Sounds of the arena bring me fully back to the moment. Laser tag arena, the game, right. "But I haven't forgotten we're in the middle of a game." I give her a playful smile and aim my laser gun right at her.

"You wouldn't," she says.

I only respond by pulling my trigger.

"Just you wait," Gwen says, crossing her arms. "I'm going to get you back for that."

I laugh as I turn the corner. "I hope you do."

CHAPTER 21
Gwen

The girls ended up beating the guys and Tammy barely, but a win is a win. So, of course, we have bragging rights. Tammy, Bradley, and Vivian head off on their own, thank goodness, and after an early dinner at the Duke's Diner, we all change into our swimsuits and head to the pool for a movie.

Many families are drawn to the pool deck for movie night. Everyone is laughing and having a good time either going down the slides, swimming, or just lounging and watching the movie.

After sitting on my lounge chair, I pull out my phone to check the itinerary for the rest of the day and tomorrow. Everything looks to be in order, so I message Becca.

GWEN

> Hey Becca, how'd the Paterson and Co. company retreat go?

She's quick to reply.

BECCA

> Everything went to plan and Larry Paterson has already booked us for next summer's retreat, he's thinking of having it over at the marina. I planned to chat with you and Trent about it once you are back from your cruise.

> Excellent news, I'll be sure to set that meeting up when I'm back in town.

"Auntie Gwen, Auntie Gwen," calls Maggie, skipping over to me dripping wet.

"Look at my swim vest!" Maggie exclaims, hopping up and down.

"It's so pretty Maggie," I say, trying to block my phone from the water she's throwing everywhere.

"I know, I picked it out *all* by myself." She twirls around like a little ballerina in her tutu swimsuit and bright pink swim vest.

"Did you see me jump in the pool?" she asks, giving me a big hug.

"No, sweetie, I missed it. I'm sorry. Can you show me again?" I say.

"Fine, but this time watch me swim to the other side once I jump in, okay?"

"Of course. I can't wait to see!" I exclaim. My phone beeps, and I glance down to see another text from Becca.

"Auntie Gwen, watch this," says Maggie on the side of the pool.

I give her a wave, while I respond to Becca. "I'm watching."

"Are you sure you're watching?" she asks again.

I give her a thumbs up, but my phone beeps again, and I can't help but read another of Becca's texts. I'm looking down too long, because when I look up, Maggie is marching back over to me with her little hands on her waist.

Uh oh.

"You missed it, Auntie Gwen," says Maggie, stopping right in front of me. "I showed you, and I was super fast, and you weren't looking like you promised."

"I'm sorry, honey. I was taking care of something for work. Maybe you can show me again?"

"No, I don't want to. You're always on your phone." Her lip trembles, and tears slip down her face as she stomps off to her chair to watch the movie. My heart aches that I was so wrapped up in my phone I missed spending time with my niece.

The moment I became an aunt was one of the best moments of my life. Holding little Maggie the day she was born, so small, so innocent, was the moment I knew that one day I'd want kids of my own.

The thought jolts me back to the loneliness I felt before the cruise. Is the path I've been on taking me toward that goal? Or have I been putting so much time into Whimsy and Wonder Events by Gwen that I'm distancing myself from the possibility of having a family of my own?

I know my current life has been all about growing my event-planning business. The business has been my own baby for the past however many years, but I know that I need to slow down a bit so I can spend time with the people I care about. I need to make them a priority. I turn my phone on silent and slip it into my bag. No more distractions.

I get up and head over to my niece. "Hey, Maggie, I'm so sorry I missed your jump." She wraps her arms around me and smiles, and I quickly embrace her, not even caring that I'm getting soaked. "How about we go swim together, and you can show me that jump?"

"Yay, let's go!" says Maggie excitedly.

After I'm in the water, Maggie jumps off the side right toward me.

"Wow, Maggie, you jumped in all by yourself! You're such a big girl. I'm so proud of you."

"Yeah, I know. I'm pretty amazing. Oh hey, let's race to the other side of the pool, okay?"

"Let's do it!" I say.

We laugh and do a few more laps before we sit on the side of the pool and kick our feet while we watch the movie on the screen.

"Look, Maggie," I say, pointing to a waiter near us, "he's dancing with a glass on his head." Not only is he balancing a full tray of drinks, but he has one atop his head as he shimmies and dances to the music.

Maggie giggles then runs up to her parents, making sure they don't miss out on the cool trick. They're giving her their full attention, and a wave of shame washes over me. I need to be better about balancing my work life and my personal life. Maybe I have been letting some relationships slide while trying to build my business.

After Maggie and I are both worn out from swimming, Maggie returns to her parents to get some food, and I settle back in my lounge chair.

I notice Niall looking at me from a few chairs down. My stomach flutters at the realization that he's been watching me, but also at the expression on his face. It's different, not flirty or smug, but soft and kind of sweet. So completely opposite of the heated look he gave me in the laser tag arena. Just the thought of that kiss causes my cheeks to warm.

What is happening to me? I'm never like this over a man. I don't have time for a real boyfriend, and this is all for show. But if it is all for show, why did it feel so right? And why did just looking at him make me want to kiss him again?

Shaking the thought from my mind, I turn and focus on the movie as Maggie comes back to sit with me. I wrap her in my arms as Niall approaches us. He looks amazing in his swim trunks, unfairly so.

"Mind if I join you for a moment?" he asks.

"Okay," says Maggie, answering for me.

"Thanks, Maggie," says Niall. "I just have a quick question for your Auntie Gwen."

"Okay," Maggie repeats, turning her attention back to the movie.

Niall turns to me. "I'd like to take you to an exercise class tomorrow morning," he says.

"That's not a question," I say.

Niall chuckles, his eyes crinkling at my response. "How about this? Can you be ready by ten o'clock?"

"That's better," I say. "And why should I go to an exercise class with you?"

"It's another one of the rules," Niall says. "Spending time together."

"What rules?" asks Maggie.

"Nothing," Niall and I say in unison, more loudly than we should have.

Gillian turns toward us. "Is everything okay?"

"Everything is fine," I say. Not wanting to draw any more attention to us by arguing about going or not going to the exercise class, I tell Niall, "I can make ten o'clock work."

"Grand," he says. "I'll pick you up then."

The next morning, a knock sounds on the shared door. I startle and drop the water bottle I'd been drinking from, spilling water all over my exercise shorts.

I open the door to a too-cheerful-in-the-morning McHottie. "You couldn't warn a girl first?" I say, gesturing to my soaked shorts.

Niall whistles at the sight of me, then he picks up my water bottle. "Drop this?" he asks, in a chipper tone.

"You think?" I reply stoically. "You made me spill it all over myself at your unannounced knock." Grabbing a towel, I pat my legs dry.

"So, what you're saying is I make you all wet?"

My head snaps up at him, and I give him my best unamused scowl, eyebrow raised at his implication. Though, my scowls are becoming less serious the more time I spend with him. I still try to portray how maddening he can be.

"Plus," he continues as he fills up my water bottle, "I wouldn't say it was unannounced. Technically, a knock is an announcement in and of itself, right?" Tilting his head to the side, he watches me dry off, grinning the whole time.

"Knock it off," I say, flushed.

"At least you didn't answer the door completely naked save for a towel," he grins.

True.

My face heats at the memory.

I close my eyes and take a few deep breaths before standing to look at him and setting the towel down on the counter.

"So," I ask, wanting desperately to change the subject, "what exercise are we doing? Running track again?"

"It's a surprise," he says, opening the door to the hallway. "C'mon, Rose, we've got to go."

I down the last few sips of my coffee, grab my now-filled water bottle, and head out after him.

As we walk into the fitness center, I notice they are holding a group class.

Niall gestures grandly. "You mentioned you couldn't do it the other day because you didn't have a partner, so I thought I'd come with you so you could do couples yoga today."

I freeze mid-step.

Did he just say couples yoga?

Niall is beaming. How can he possibly think this is a great idea?

Couples yoga is all about trust, and some poses can be very . . . err, intimate. I barely know him. Okay, that's a lie, I know him at least a little now. But is Niall even any good at yoga? Ugh, he's going to make me hate my favorite form of exercise with this awful idea.

"Rose? Gwendolyn!"

The use of my full first name snaps me out of my head, and I blink at him.

"You said you love yoga, so I thought this would be fun," he says. His sincerity and enthusiasm make my fears ebb just a bit.

"Do you even know how to do yoga?" I ask, skeptically.

"A bit," he says, shrugging his shoulders.

"Well, then this should be interesting," I grumble.

"That's the spirit!" he says, leading me to a spot on the floor.

I freeze again, and Niall almost bumps into my back at my sudden stop. There, waving to us from a spot on the floor is Greg and Holly.

OMG, what a disaster. Couples yoga with Niall, plus Holly and Greg are here. What will they think of us spending this intimate time together? This can't end well.

Niall leans in to whisper in my ear. "Look, I can tell you're not so sure about this, but you need to take some time for yourself. Greg mentioned he and Holly were going to be doing the class, and I thought it would be something you would enjoy, something to help you take time for yourself and relax. And you love yoga, so I thought, 'Win-win.'"

I look over at him and his expression conveys such earnestness that I have no fight left in me.

"Alright," I say, walking a few places past Greg to an empty space.

"Hi, Gwennie," says Greg. "I'm glad you could join us. It's not too early in the morning for you, is it?"

"Hush up, you," Holly smacks him in the arm lightly. "You know perfectly well that Gwen regularly gets up around ten."

"Gee thanks, Hols, that makes it sound better." I huff out a laugh.

As Niall and I find a spot a little to the side of Greg and Holly, I groan as Bradley and Tammy walk in. *This just got even better.*

Tammy looks like she could teach the class in her yoga attire, but similar to karaoke, Bradley looks completely out of place. It dawns on me how much Bradley cares for Tammy if he is willing to put himself in these types of situations—ones he's not comfortable with but does anyway because she likes to do them. It's actually really sweet of him.

I think back on our relationship. When did I go out of my way to do something for him? How often did we really spend time together? True one-on-one time when I wasn't checking in with Becca or answering emails?

The instructor starts with some basic breathing techniques, moving into a sun salutation. We repeat the sequence for a few minutes, all the while focusing on our breathing.

I try to focus on the warmup but my mind keeps returning to my relationship with Bradley. I've done yoga for years, and would consider myself advanced, but I've never done couples yoga before. I need to focus. Couples yoga is a whole different world. Couples yoga poses not only test your balance and flexibility, but also your strength and communication as a partnership. There's a lot of trust, not to mention the amount of physical contact involved. I try to steady my breathing. *You can do this, Gwen.*

Once we're warmed up, we start with some simple moves. A couple's chair pose has us back-to-back. Niall is warm and strong against my back. We are the picture-perfect pose, holding longer than any other couple in the class. I'm surprised by his flexibility and how in sync we've been with our poses. I think he's done more than "a bit" of yoga.

The next pose, temple pose, has us face-to-face and forearms-to-forearms. Niall stares into my eyes.

"Stop that," I whisper to him.

"What?" he asks in feigned innocence.

"You know what. Your face, you're being distracting."

"My face distracts you?" he asks, lifting a brow.

"No," I huff, "The faces you are making. It's distracting. We need to concentrate and focus on our breathing, and I can't do that with you doing . . . well, that."

"Got it, no faces because I make you breathless," he says, eyes twinkling.

I roll my eyes as the instructor calls for us to raise back up. I'm glad that we are a couple people away from Greg and Holly. This is already too close to Niall for my liking, and even though it's a class, I don't want Greg or Holly getting any funny ideas about us.

These poses have caused me to be extremely aware of Niall's body, and I already know he deserves the nickname McHottie, with his perfect abs and perfect arms. The constant touching has me so turned on that I'm ready to bolt from this class. Especially when the instructor calls for one final pose before we start our cooldown poses.

Not a difficult pose by any means, but the couples camel pose has Niall and I facing each other while kneeling on the ground, knees touching and lower body touching up to our hips. Being fairly tall myself, Niall and I are close in height, and this pose has us leaning into each other in some intimate places. Our pelvises push into each other as we both lean backward, letting our heads fall as we hold onto each other's arms to steady ourselves.

I feel every breath, every movement of him against me. A sensation of being flooded with warmth passes through me, and I have a strong awareness of my heartbeat. It thumps erratically, and even though I'm supposed to be controlling my breath, it comes out in a quick rising and falling of my chest.

I'm not the only one feeling something. I can tell in the way Niall is breathing that this pose is affecting him as well.

When we are called to release the pose and ease back up, our eyes meet, and there is a fire burning in his. The blue eyes which normally hold so much humor and light are now like ocean waves during a storm. Wild and untamable.

Without a thought, we are once again close to each other, our faces mere breaths apart.

"Niall?" Greg asks. And our spell is broken. We quickly jump back from each other. Greg is looking at us with concern, but Holly seems pleasantly surprised.

"I, um . . ." says, Niall.

"We were . . ." I start, but we're saved from answering by a sudden commotion.

Bradley and Tammy have managed to fall over into a tangle of limbs on their mat. I breathe a sigh of relief, glad for the distraction. I'd forgotten they were even in the class. Niall seems to keep having that effect on me.

If I can have this much fun and feel this good with someone I practically just met, even if he's just pretending to date me, was I ever truly happy with Bradley? It's something I'm starting to question.

The shock of that hits me, causing me to sway slightly.

"Whoa, you okay?" Niall asks, worry creasing his forehead, as he holds my arm.

"Yeah, no, I mean, yes, I'm alright," I say, shaking my head a bit. The warmth of his touch brings back a desire to be physically close to him again. I shouldn't be wanting that. *We're just fake dating, Gwen, get ahold of yourself.*

"How about we go get a bite to eat?" Niall suggests, glancing at his watch.

"I could eat," I say. "This session wore me out."

"What are you two up to?" asks Greg, with some concern in his voice, as he and Holly approach us.

Did we go too far? Does Greg think there is something going on between Niall and me? I hope not. I can't even wrap my head around how I feel about Niall. How am I going to discuss this with my brother?

"I was going to get something to eat," I say.

At the same time, Niall says, "We were going to get lunch." Niall and I exchange looks.

"Maybe we'll join you," says Greg, eyeing us both.

"No, we won't," says Holly, giving me and Niall a hopeful look. "We're going to go get cleaned up and rest before we head out on our excursion for the day."

"Don't you want to grab some food?" Greg asks Holly.

"I think we should do room service," says Holly.

"But, what about—" Greg starts.

"Room service," Holly repeats, giving Greg a flirtatious look.

"Room service it is," says Greg. "See you two soon." He grabs Holly's hand, and they head out of the fitness center. Holly throws me a wink before they're out the door.

"Did she just wink at us?" asks Niall.

"Nope," I say. "Definitely not."

Niall and I snag a table at Imperial Café that looks out over the ocean. The sight is beautiful. Blue skies and blue ocean as far as the eye can see.

After ordering and getting our food, Niall asks, "So, all of you grew up in Chessie Valley?"

"Yeah, except Holly, Margot, and their family. They moved in when Holly and I were in the sixth grade, but we've been inseparable ever since. Well, except during the time Holly lived away with her ex. Thank goodness that's all over!"

"You didn't like the guy?"

"No, I hated him. Holly was too good for him." I take a bite of my frilled pineapple. "She's too good for my brother too, but sometimes love works in mysterious ways."

"I'd always thought it peculiar that Greg never found someone, with how many lassies were interested in him over the years. It was nice to finally find out the reason why," Niall says, biting into his sandwich.

"He kept that secret for so long," I say. "Even from me. I was floored at first, but seeing them together . . . it all made sense."

Niall nods, then sips his orange juice.

"I bet you were the same way growing up," I say, taking a sip of my coffee. "Lots of girls showing interest in you."

"Oh you do, do you?" he asks, eyebrows raised at my statement.

I nod, keeping my face blank.

"Well, you'd lose that bet. You're looking at a kid who was gangly and dorky growing up," he says.

"I have a hard time believing that."

"It's true. Mix that with being an only child, and that spelled a recipe for disaster. You know, I used to envy those kids with big families, as it was just my mam and me, but thankfully, my mam was like a second mam to all the kids in the neighborhood, so we always had someone over at the house."

"Do you like living in Boston?"

"Love it. I mean, my mam was there, and I still have a handful of friends that live around there. But we're not too close like you guys are. You know, it wasn't until I met Greg and Trent that I felt like I'd found true friends. We were inseparable in college, like brothers," he says. "But after my mam's passing," his eyes glaze over with a sadness, "I mainly spend time with my brothers and sisters from the firehouse."

The grief on Niall's face doesn't sit right with me. I want to reach over and pull him into a hug.

"Mind if we join you?" asks a familiar voice.

CHAPTER 22
Niall

"Of course we don't, do we, *mo ghrá*?" I say, shifting so Gwen and I are closer to each other, allowing Tammy and Bradley to sit on the other side of the table from us.

"No, don't mind at all," agrees Gwen.

"Great," says Tammy, "that is so kind of ya'll. We've been walking all over and haven't been able to find a place to sit, then we spotted you and thought, 'How perfect!'"

"Right," agrees Bradley.

"Wasn't yoga so much fun this morning?" asks Tammy, clearly not at all feeling the absurdity of this whole thing.

"Yes, actually," says Gwen, placing her hand on my arm. "It was the first time Niall and I have tried a couples yoga class."

"You did always like your yoga classes," adds Bradley.

Tammy turns to me before asking, "What about you, Niall, do you like yoga? You seemed to be pretty good at it from what I could tell."

"I do actually," I say. "We do a bit of yoga at the firehouse to help keep us nimble."

"You're a fireman?" asks Bradley, his eyebrow raised.

"I am. I've been with a firehouse in Boston for the past six years."

Gwen smiles up at me as Bradley says, "That's impressive."

"Oh, you live in Boston," says Tammy. "That must be dreadfully hard to have a long-distance relationship and all."

"We find a way to make it work," says Gwen, giving my arm a light squeeze.

I lean over and give Gwen a light kiss on the cheek. "That we do."

"So then how did ya'll meet?" asks Tammy. "Bradley and I met at an after-hours work function. Started talking and hit it off right from the beginning."

Bradley smiles at Tammy and takes her hand.

"We actually met through her brother, Greg," I answer. "I went to college with Greg and Trent in Boston."

"Greg and Trent are good guys," says Bradley.

"They are," I agree.

Gwen motions to our plates. "Well, looks like we are all done. We should hurry up and get ready so we can meet up with the others for our excursion."

"See you around," says Bradley before taking a bite of his biscuit.

As Gwen and I leave, I think about how amazingly Gwen handled that late breakfast with Tammy and Bradley. I can't be sure, but maybe she's finally getting over him. Or starting to feel more like herself, like Greg wanted for her. She does seem lighter, happier since the first day on the cruise ship.

After a quick shower, I pull on my swim trunks and shirt, brush my fingers through my hair, then slide on sandals. Glancing around the room, I go to pick up my sunglasses, bandana, and frozen water bottle before heading over to Gwen's room.

Seeing me coming around the balcony, she waves me in.

"Give me just a moment. I can't find my sunglasses," she says, as I close the balcony door behind me.

"I'll help you look," I say.

"Thank you. I feel so scattered. Normally, I'm on top of everything, but somehow everything I laid out last night has got up and walked away."

I survey the room, and when my eyes land on Gwen, a smile breaks out across my face. "Ah, here they are," I say, stepping over to her and plucking the sunglasses off the top of her head.

"What? How did I not notice? I've seriously been looking all over for them!"

I hand them over to her, and she clips them to the front of her dress.

Taking her arms in my hands, I gently turn her toward me. "Hey, what's wrong?"

Deflating a little, she sighs. "I've been a little off-kilter since we got back from yoga and breakfast."

"Want to talk about it?" I ask, pulling her into a hug. She doesn't stiffen this time, and I continue, "I'm always here for you."

She nods, then shakes her head. "Yes and no. I guess I'm having a difficult time processing, well . . . everything. And I don't want to burden you with my emotions. That wasn't part of our dating agreement."

"Gwen, I hope that through all of this, you consider me a friend. I mean, we are fake dating and everything," I tease. "But as your fake boyfriend, I want you to know that I'm here for you. Whether it's fake-dating charades or heart-to-heart conversations. If you need someone to unburden yourself to, I'm your man."

"Thank you," she whispers into my embrace. "It's just that I'm realizing that Bradley might not be entirely at fault for our breakup. It's hard to admit, because since the breakup I've blamed him, and I haven't let myself see the part I played in our relationship ending. I've thrown myself into my work, trying to prove to Bradley that I had to spend so much time on my business so that it could be successful. But now that it is doing really well, I'm realizing that there was some truth to him saying I make work too much of a priority."

"That's good that you're recognizing it, right?"

Gwen shrugs and continues, "And being on this cruise with everyone, it's become obvious that I need to pull back from work, dedicate more time to my friends and family, to my personal life. I need to focus on what is most important: the people I care about. Work will always be there, but I don't want to wake up one day and not have my friends and family. I don't want to be that person who just goes to work, comes home to sleep, and then rinse and repeat over and over."

I hold her tight, her words like a punch to the gut. It's exactly what I've been doing the past twelve months since my mam's passing. The realization is shocking. We've both gone through two major life changes, and each of us has handled it in similar but different ways.

"Are you okay?" Gwen asks.

"Of course I am," I say.

"It's just," Gwen says softly, "I can see the look on your face when you go off into your memories. It can't be easy being around our families when you've lost yours."

That realization stings. I step back from her to give myself some space. "I'm fine," I say and turn and look out to the balcony away from her. I need to just keep it in. No need to burden her with my struggles.

"Niall." She places a hand on my cheek and turns me to face her. The sincerity and care in her eyes have me melting.

No one has looked at me with such genuine concern since my mam's passing, and it breaks something within me.

I sigh before letting the words pour forth, like a dam breaking from the weight of all my emotions. "It is hard. My mam was my best friend. We were all each other had in the world, but then she was taken away from me too soon. I've been struggling with that and trying to make myself be happy again. I almost didn't come on this cruise, but I knew I didn't want to let Greg down, and I knew my mam wouldn't want me to miss this either. I needed a chance to get away from Boston, from the constant reminder that she is gone."

Gwen nods, encouraging me to continue.

"I know everyone feels sad about it, and they've tried to reach out, but I haven't wanted to let them help. I haven't wanted to burden them with my emotions. I was so strong for my mam while she was sick, but there are times when I feel so lost without her. She was my one constant for my whole life, and without her I feel . . . alone. It's just me now."

"Oh, Niall," Gwen says.

I brush a tear from her face as I say, "See this is what I mean. I'm causing you sadness."

"Yes, but it's only because I hate that you feel so alone. You're not alone, you know? You've got Greg and Trent. My mom and dad talk as if you're their son too. And not that it's much, but you've got me. Just as you said to me, I'm here for you. Anytime you feel like you want or need to talk, I'll be an ear for you."

I pull her in for a hug, my chest pounding rapidly at her kind words. It's time I let my friends in, because she's right—I'm not alone. I have a great group of friends who feel like *mo thaeghlach*, just like I've got a great crew at work who are also like family. I've been looking at this all wrong for too long, and it's time to change that, to lean on the people that care about me.

"Thank you," I tell her. We stand embracing each other, looking out over the ocean for several moments.

My phone vibrates, and I pull it out of my pocket.

GREG

> Where are you? We're about to head out.

"We better go," I say. "The others are going to wonder where we are."

NIALL

> Heading your way now.

We hurry out of the room and off the boat, meeting up with the rest of the party just after the pier.

"Finally!" says Margot. "We were worried you weren't going to make it. Wait, were you two together?"

"Yep." Gwen shrugs. "Just grabbing some food."

After a round of hugs, the grandparents leave with Maggie to go to the beach. The rest of our group heads to the off-roading four-by-four adventure through Aruba Arikok National Park.

A very bumpy, very dusty ride takes us through the national park. We see burrowing owls and other local wildlife as well as all sorts of flowers and plants. The view is amazing. But by the time we get there, we're all ready for the refreshing waters of Conchi, a natural pool.

The tour guide gives us a brief history of the area. The Conchi, which means bowl, has unique natural pools created by the ocean's relentless crashing waves. He explains that the Conchi has two natural pools: a larger bottom one and a much smaller upper pool. The upper pool is only deep enough for a small handful of people to swim in it at once.

We gather our belongings from the four-by-four and find an area on the small beach to lay our towels and packs. The view is breathtaking with dramatic shows of water spraying over the rocks as the ocean ebbs and flows against them. Within the pool, the water is calm and crystal clear.

Some of the group from the excursion has already rid themselves of their shoes and extra clothes and are swimming in the water. The more adventurous are heading over to the rocks and cliff jumping into the pool.

Gwen and Holly quickly wade into the water and wait for the others to join them.

"The water feels amazing," shouts Holly.

"Definitely refreshing after that ride," agrees Gwen.

"Come on, slow pokes," they yell out to us, heading over with their snorkeling gear toward the rocks closer to the ocean.

After snorkeling for only a few minutes, Trent says, "I'm going to try cliff diving."

"*Cúla búla*," I say. "I'll join you. Greg, you game?"

"I'm in," he says. Then looking back to Holly, he adds, "Be back in a minute."

We climb up the path to the spot in the rocks that's just right for the jump.

Trent doesn't even wait. As soon as he's at the edge, he jumps. "Woohoo!" he yells before splashing into the cool water below.

As soon as Trent surfaces, I tell Greg, "See you below," before jumping in. The jump is freeing as the air rushes by me before I hit the water. I pop back up just in time to see Greg as he hits the water.

"That looks crazy," says Margot as we swim back to the girls.

"It's a blast," says Trent, splashing them.

"I prefer the calm, less deadly swimming," says Holly.

"Ah, you know you love the thrill," says Greg. "I couldn't keep you off the black diamond runs at the cabin last winter."

Nodding, she splashes him with water, managing to get me in the crosswind.

"Hey, what'd I do?" I ask in mock horror.

"You encourage them both," Gwen says and laughs.

"You going to jump?" I ask.

"Ooo that sounds fun," says Margot, looking between us both excitedly.

Gwen bites her lip as she looks from me to the cliff.

"I mean, this can't be any worse than a black diamond run," Gwen says.

"Grand!" I say.

"Yeah, let's do it," says Trent, already swimming back over to the path.

"You all have fun," says Greg. "I'm going to hang back here with Holly."

Trent leads the way as Margot, Gwen, and I all follow.

Margot catches up with Trent and doesn't hesitate before jumping off the cliff and into the clear water below.

"She's fearless," says Trent. "See you all down there!" He jumps into the water below, then comes up laughing as his head breaks the surface.

Looking at Gwen, I notice she's watching the water spraying up and over the rocks.

"It's so dramatic," she says. "If I didn't see the calm pools of water with my own eyes, I'd never believe it could be hidden behind those rocks."

"True, so many things can be easily hidden when people don't take the opportunity to look," I agree, then I motion to the edge. "You ready to jump?"

Her starburst eyes pierce mine. "It's a long way down."

"You're not wrong. The five-foot jump is down a bit further on the trail. This one is just about a fifteen-foot drop."

"'Just,' ha, right," she says, fidgeting as she looks over the edge.

"What did you say about black diamonds? This can't be worse than that, right?"

"Psh, well, now that I'm up here, of course it's worse. A black diamond is easy. I have total control the whole way down the mountain. With this, it's a free fall. I have zero control over anything."

"What if we jump together? We can even hold hands?"

"You'd do that?" she asks.

"Of course, Rose, I'd do anything for you." I reach out my hand to her. "Do you trust me?"

Nodding, she takes my hand and says, "Let's do this."

"That's my girl," I say.

Grinning, we link our fingers. "Three, two, one . . ." I say, and we take off running, jumping just as the edge nears.

When we break the surface of the water, the laughter and pure joy emanating from Gwen causes my breath to hitch. She's gorgeous. More than that, she's a stunning woman inside and out.

We swim back over to the group. Margot and Trent convince some of the others to jump with them again. But Gwen and Holly head to the beach to lie out, leaving just me and Greg.

Greg swims closer and, in a hushed tone, says, "I knew you'd be good for Gwen. It's almost like she's her old self again, before that jerk dumped her."

"That's good to hear."

"If you want some advice, she loves Mexican food and Putt-Putt golf."

"I'll keep that in mind."

"Thanks for doing this, man."

"Don't feel like you need to thank me. She's the *craic* to hang out with."

"I love to hear it," he says. "It hasn't been too hard getting Gwen to hang out with you, has it?"

"Not really," I admit.

"Well, that's good," says Greg. "And, um, things are still friendly between you two, right?"

My stomach churns slightly at the guilt I feel in deceiving Greg. Not only about the deal I made with Gwen, but also about my feelings that are growing stronger for her the more I'm around her.

I have the urge to confess everything to Greg, but one look at the beach, seeing Gwen so peaceful, has me biting my tongue.

I cannot betray her trust. If I can't have more with her right now, at least I have her trust. And her trust is worth more to me than anything else.

"Yes, just friendly."

CHAPTER 23
Gwen

By the time we get back to the port, my stomach is grumbling. I'm ready to eat when we meet up with our parents and Maggie for a late lunch in the city, Oranjestad.

"Did you know the style of these houses is Dutch Colonial?" asks Dad. "We stopped by a little museum and found out all about the history, didn't we, Maggie?"

She scrunches her nose at the mention of the museum. I guess it wasn't one of her favorite things to do.

"What do you think of the houses?" I ask her encouragingly.

"I think they look like bright gingerbread houses," she says, then giggles, "like Easter and Christmas collided."

"Hmm, isn't that a fun idea," says Holly. "Maybe we can make one this Christmas to put in my storefront window."

Maggie nods excitedly, "Niall, could you make one with us?"

"Oh, umm, I don't know, Maggie," Niall says. "I live pretty far from Chessie Valley, you know?"

Why does that make me sad all of a sudden? I know he's only here for the wedding, and then of course he'd be going back home. I catch Niall watching me, so I plaster a smile on my face.

"Who's hungry?" I ask with feigned enthusiasm.

Trent claps his hands together. "Now that's what I'm talking about. I'm famished."

We make our way to a little restaurant and order some of the local cuisine: nutty Dutch cheeses, pan bati (which I find out is really just a pancake made from wheat and corn flour), empanadas, and arepas. The flavors overwhelm me. Everything is delicious, and we stuff ourselves like it's Thanksgiving.

After lunch, we go to a beach that's walking distance from the pier. It's a relaxing afternoon, and with full bellies, we take our places on lounge chairs. Maggie drags her parents into the ocean and uses our snorkeling gear to see if she can find any fish or shells.

Smiling, I watch them. I'd love to bring my kids on a cruise someday, to visit new places with them and watch them as they explore the world outside of Chessie Valley.

"You're quiet," says Margot. "What's on your mind?"

"Hmm, oh nothing, really, just thinking how nice the cruise has been. Are you liking it?"

"It's been great, and perfect timing too. Early to mid-July is when I have a bit of a break at work."

"That's right, I forget how busy you can get. Are you excited for this year?"

"Yeah, I've been done with the internship portion for a while and am a full-time athletics trainer. It's been everything I could have hoped for. I love football, and working with an NFL team is a dream come true. Especially one close to home."

"I'm so happy for you, Margot! I'll have to come to one of the games."

"You better!" she says.

At the sounds of Maggie giggling, I glance to my left. It seems she, Holly, and Greg somehow convinced Niall to let them bury him in the sand. He's covered from the waist down in what appears to be a mermaid tale over his legs.

I laugh, and Niall's head whips in my direction. He gives me one of his sexy half smiles.

"You don't think I make a grand mermaid, Rose?"

"I think you make a fantastic mermaid, very manly," I say, trying to stifle another laugh.

He tilts his head back and laughs, "You're not wrong."

The group works together, and before long, Niall has beautiful scales and shells lining his tail.

"Alright, kiddo," I tell Maggie, "we've got to let Niall up or else he might miss getting back on the boat." My phone pings, and I pick it up to a notification from Becca about the birthday party. Something is wrong with the entertainment.

"Everything okay?" Niall raises his eyebrows in question, as if really asking, *Are you going to work or are you going to spend time with us?*

Glancing at him, I tilt my head to the side, thinking before answering, "You know, I think it will be." I send Becca a quick response telling her that I trust her to handle the situation and then silence the phone and place it back in my pocket. It's nothing that Becca can't handle.

A slow smile builds on Niall's face. It makes me feel warm inside. I'm snapped back to the moment at hand when Maggie says, "But he's a mermaid. He can swim to the boat."

"Afraid not," I say. "This sand tail will wash away in the water."

"Sadly, I'm only a beach mermaid," adds Niall, looking more distraught than Maggie.

Giggling at his expression, she turns to me for help. "Auntie Gwen, can you help me get him out?"

"Sure thing, kiddo."

I kneel down next to Maggie, and we start brushing away the sand from Niall's legs.

"Thanks for rescuing me," says Niall.

"No problem. Can't have a groomsman miss the wedding because he is stuck in the sand," I say, lightly bumping Maggie's shoulder.

Smiling, I glance up at him to see one of his half smiles. He's got such a gorgeous face, and the way his eyes shine . . . it's just not fair.

I keep working to move away the sand, with Maggie helping. As my hands brush against Niall's warm skin, a tingle runs through me. My cheeks turn hot at the touch.

Maggie and I finish getting most of the sand off Niall, and he pushes himself fully upright.

Niall brushes off the remaining sand. "I'll definitely be needing a shower after this. I have sand in all the wrong places," he says.

Maggie giggles, and I can feel my face growing brighter. *Do not think about him in the shower. Nope, don't do it.*

An image of Niall in nothing but a towel fills my mind as I lock eyes with him.

"I'm just going to . . . Maggie, let's go help pack up." I quickly reach for Maggie's hand before turning to find anyone who needs help packing up. I can feel him watching me walk away, and I swear I hear a slight chuckle from behind me.

Shaking the memory of Niall and his too little towel from my mind, I tune into what everyone else needs and keep busy until we head back to the ship. We break off in groups, and Maggie falls asleep on her dad's shoulder during the walk back.

With the distraction from the others in the group, I manage to make it all the way back to the ship without thinking about Niall. But the moment I'm back in the quiet of my room with the shared door as the only thing separating our rooms, my mind is once again back to Niall in that towel, droplets of water falling from his wet hair to his bare chest.

CHAPTER 24
Niall

Growing up near Revere Beach, I'm no stranger to sand. But it's been a very long time since I've been buried in it, and I completely forgot how uncomfortable sand is when it gets under the clothes. After taking a long shower, making sure I removed all the sand, I dry myself off and throw on a pair of shorts. We haven't left port yet, but it won't be long now.

The view from the balcony room looks out toward the ocean. Sliding the door open I step out to enjoy the breeze. Out of the corner of my eye, I see Gwen on the balcony with a book.

"What are you reading?" I ask Gwen.

She shrieks and drops her book. "Now look what you've done. You've gone and made me lose my place," she says as she picks her book up.

Chuckling, I try to see what it is she's reading.

"Don't you know that snooping isn't nice and—" she says, looking over at me before freezing mid-sentence.

Her eyes slowly roam over me, and it causes my pulse to race. Being a fireman, I'm used to the occasional ogling from women when my house brothers and I go for our runs and when we're cleaning the fire engine. I know I look good, but I've never felt like this before from just a look.

Or ever, really.

I've always been dedicated to the job and taking care of Mam that I'd never really gotten serious about dating someone. My firehouse brothers tease me constantly, saying I'm a player, but nothing could be further from the truth.

Do I take the occasional *beore* out on a date? Sure, I'm not dead inside.

But I always let them down easy and typically stay on good terms as friends, or I set them up with someone I think would be good for them. A couple of the pairings started to turn serious. But it wasn't something I'd been looking for.

Not, that is, until Gwen. She makes me want to throw my reservations overboard and jump headfirst into a real relationship with her. That thought scared me at first, but the more time I spend with her, the less scary it seems, and the less alone I feel. *Is this what Mam meant when she said I'd find the right person if I just open myself up to it? Because Gwen is definitely someone I am starting to think could be the right person. . . . And Mam would have loved her.*

Gwen finally glances up and meets my eyes, her cheeks going that delicious flushed color. A darker shade of pink that tells me she's not upset by my lack of shirt.

"Like what you see?"

"No," she narrows her eyes at me. "Just wondering why you don't have a shirt on. You'll get a sunburn."

"Oh, I'm feeling the heat alright, but it's not from the sun." I step closer to her, and she sighs.

"Can't a girl read her book in peace?"

"Didn't mean to stop you. I honestly had no clue you were out here. Lucky coincidence." I shrug. "But now that I do have your attention, I'm cashing in on one of our dates."

She stares at me blankly, just blinking.

"Rose." I wave my hands in front of her. "Did you hear me?"

"Uh, yeah, I . . ." She clears her throat, shaking her head before adding, "I mean, yes, I heard you. I just didn't think you were serious about that rule."

"I was definitely serious about it. Deal-breaker, remember?"

"Right."

"I was thinking mini golf."

"I'm good with that."

"Grand! Leave in five minutes?" I ask.

"Five minutes?" she says, her eyes wide.

I nod.

"Okay," she says, and she grabs her things and heads into her room.

Walking back into mine, I put on some sandals and throw on a shirt. Slipping my glasses on my collar, I head out to the hallway. When Gwen walks out, I freeze.

She's sexy in short jean shorts, a tight, white tank top, and a flowy top over it.

I resist the urge to pick her up and carry her back into her room. *That's not part of our agreed-upon rules*, I scold myself.

"You look amazing," I say hoarsely.

"Oh, thanks," she says.

When I make no motion to leave, she asks, "You ready?"

I clear my throat and say, "Erm, I am. Let's go."

The mini golf is at the back of the boat on the top floor. By the time we get up there, the boat has started moving out of port, and, thankfully, there are only a few people on the course.

"Not too crowded," I say.

"Well, that's good for you," says Gwen.

"Oh, yeah? Why's that?"

"Less people to see you lose horribly," she says, laughing.

"We'll see about that!"

I've played mini golf before many times, but playing against Gwen makes me feel like an amateur.

She's a sexy, competitive bombshell, and I love watching as she lines up the swing, swaying her hips slightly from side to side. Needless to say, I'm a bit distracted, and my game is off.

The course is fairly simple. There are only nine holes, but with Gwen's competitiveness, we treat it like we are on a professional golf tour. She's currently a couple swings ahead of me.

We're at the seventh hole, and she aims. The ball bounces slightly off one of the walls, curves around the side of the hill, and drops into the hole with a soft plunk. Gwen jumps up and down, doing a little victory dance. "Oh, that feels amazing. I needed a win lately," she admits.

I lean down and pick up her ball. "Fair play, Gwen! That was a terrific shot."

Reaching my hand out to give her the ball, I'm taken by surprise as she jumps into my arms, wrapping hers around my neck.

Feeling like the luckiest man in the world, I wrap my arms around her, pulling her in to me. I pick her up for a little celebratory spin. As I set her down, she doesn't let go. Instead, she pulls my face toward hers and kisses me. It's just a little peck, but time freezes. Hope races through me like a dam bursting.

A look of shock appears on her face as she realizes she's kissed me. "I . . . I know that was against the rules."

Not giving her another second, I lean back in and kiss her back.

But not just a peck. No, I let that all-consuming hope continue to weave its way through my soul and act on instinct.

Sliding one hand into her hair and the other around her waist, I pull her even closer to me. She doesn't resist but kisses me back eagerly. Dropping her club, she puts her hands on my neck. I groan against her mouth as her hands play in my hair at the base of my neck.

Her strawberries-and-cream scent envelopes me as the wind rustles lightly. She tastes like a dream, and I never want to wake up. I've never been so attracted to someone in my life, and this firecracker is going to ruin me for anyone else.

Our tongues dance as our mouths meld together, and everything else fades away. I feel her chest rising and falling in quick breaths in rhythm to mine. The feel of her soft skin at her waist as her shirt raises slightly up drives me insane. She shivers at my touch, and I can feel myself growing more needy.

A voice clears behind us, and we slowly pull apart. I remember that we are standing in the middle of the Putt-Putt course. Looking over, I see Bradley looking at the ground embarrassed and Tammy with her hand covering her mouth, trying to suppress a giggle.

CHAPTER 25
Gwen

"Fancy meeting you here," Niall chimes cheerfully, drawing me in by his side. His arm wraps around me, making lazy circles with his thumb on my skin. His touch ignites a spark that surges outward, electrifying my senses.

"Apologies for holding things up," Niall continues, gesturing toward me. "Gwen just aced a hole-in-one, and I guess we got a little carried away celebrating."

Tammy, her eyes sparkling with giddiness, says, "Oh, no worries at all. I'd be just as happy if I were in her shoes."

With a gentle turn, Niall guides me back toward our abandoned clubs as he says, "Well, we won't hold you up any longer." We gather our belongings and move onto the next hole. Niall quickly finishes hole eight in just two strokes.

I marvel at his focus, considering the playful escapade we'd just shared. What amazes me even more is how I yearn to continue what we started with that kiss. My feelings are a swirl of confusion. "This date wasn't so bad," I tell Niall.

Niall chuckles, a warm sound that eases my embarrassment. "Well, this not-so-bad date isn't quite over yet."

"No?"

"Nope. Ready for some Mexican food?"

"I love Mexican food!" *How did he know?*

"*Cúla búla*," Niall grins. "There's a little restaurant just on the other side of the ship. I've heard their nachos are amazing."

After reaching the restaurant, we place our orders and find seats by the windows overlooking the mesmerizing expanse of water. The ocean's beauty never ceases to amaze me. From the corner of my eye, I catch Niall's gaze fixed on me.

His curiosity can't be ignored. "Something troubling you?" he asks, his eyes probing.

"No, everything's fine," I reply, though thoughts of that unforgettable kiss swirl in my mind. *Why did I have to get caught up in that moment?* But it's a kiss I can't, no, won't regret—it was electric, unlike any other.

"Right," he says, a hint of amusement in his tone.

"Don't 'right' me. You don't know what I'm thinking," I say, trying to conceal my thoughts, as if he really could read my mind. Sometimes I wonder about the way he's so in tune to my emotions, to my expressions, to me.

Our plates arrive, laden with nachos and tacos, and we devour them eagerly.

"Feck," says Niall, "the nachos and tacos vanished faster than I anticipated. Should we order more?"

"No," I respond. "I think I'm sufficiently stuffed. I wouldn't want to doze off during trivia tonight."

"Good call. Shall we?" he asks, extending his hand to help me up.

I glance at his hand; my brief hesitation melts away. "We shall," I respond, amused by our formality. After all, we just devoured some of the messiest food.

An exhilarating thrill courses through me as I take his hand in mine. He's momentarily stunned before he breaks out into a smile.

"We have time for a game of ping pong before trivia if you're interested," he offers.

"I'm game. Though, as you know, I can be a bit competitive."

"Seems so. I'm not complaining though. It worked out quite nicely for me last time." He grins at me and squeezes my hand lightly.

"You're incorrigible," I laugh, bumping him with my hip, as we walk around to our spots at the ping pong table.

Niall takes one side, grasping the paddle with a confident grip. His eyes lock on me, an inviting smile playing on his lips. I stand opposite him equally poised, excitement and determination coursing through me. *See, I can have some fun; I'm not always all work and no play.*

The table seems to stretch between us like a stage for our duel. I lightly drop the ball, the soft thud echoing in my ear, marking the beginning of our match.

The ball sails easily through the air, a white streak of anticipation. My serve is crisp and well-calculated, bouncing near the edge of the table, a challenge Niall is more than willing to accept.

He responds with a swift return, his focus unwavering and his grin never leaving his face. His eyes dance with his excitement from the game.

Frick, why is that so sexy?

I may not have as much confidence in my swings, since it's been years since I've played, but I'm able to meet his shots with grace, my eyes staying locked onto the ball as if my life depends on it. The occasional times I glance up at him cause chills to run through me, excitement and a promise of a good time filling me with both exhilaration and nerves.

Gone is our light banter. We are both focused on the task at hand, neither of us willing to back down. I send a particularly tricky shot to Niall, sending the ball skimming just above the net.

His response is swift and unexpected, the ball ricocheting off his paddle with finesse and leaving me momentarily stunned. Applause from nearby observers adds to the electric atmosphere, turning our private game into a small show.

I'm happy. It's nice to take a break from stressing about everything all the time.

Niall wins, and while the competitive part of me is upset, he is just so happy that I can't help but be happy too.

"I guess you do have a bit of the luck of the Irish," I say. "You were bound to win at something eventually."

"You didn't just say that," Niall laughs throwing his head back, his whole body shaking from laughter. Pure joy radiates from him, his laughter infectious as I join in.

Glancing at his watch, he turns it to me, "Looks like it's about time we head over to the Knight's Tavern."

Nodding, I set down my paddle and follow him. I'm beginning to think Niall could make anything fun. Usually, I get so competitive that I lose sight of the fun, but with him, he makes just eating nachos or sitting on the beach exciting.

The Knight's Tavern is a haven of twinkling lights and cozy corners. Decorations of fishing nets, crab boxes, and images of krakens and shipping vessels line the walls. By the time we get there, the others are already sitting near the piano where the trivia host is setting up his station.

We sit down just in time as the trivia host picks up his microphone. "Welcome, everyone, to the Way Late Trivia Challenge!" The host's voice booms, sending a ripple of excitement through the large crowd.

I'm honestly surprised by the amount of people here with it being so late, but I guess on a cruise people are awake at all hours.

"We're about to embark on a journey through the realm of random facts and knowledge," the host continues enthusiastically. "I hope you all are ready! If you haven't picked up your paper and pencil, we have plenty up here for everyone."

A few people move to pick up their pencils and papers then head back to their groups.

Glancing around at our group of six, I see that Margot is leaning forward in her seat, determined and ready for the questions to start. Niall, sitting comfortably next to me, oozes confidence and a laid-back charm. Catching my gaze, he gives me a flirty smile. Holly holds the pencil and paper poised and ready to go.

Next to her, my brother sits giving Holly an endearing smile. They really are so perfect for each other; I don't know why I didn't see it sooner. And then there is Trent. His face is already adorned with a mischievous grin. Smacking his hands together in excitement, Trent says, "Let's get this party started!"

The host chuckles at his exuberance, picks up the microphone, and announces, "Without further ado, let's dive into your first question!"

The question is called out, and Margot whispers the answer to Holly, then says, "I've got this one, guys. Prepare to be amazed at my medical knowledge!"

The questions continue, each one a unique challenge that showcases our group's strengths and quirky hobbies.

"I'd be surprised if we don't win this thing outright," says Niall.

"Shh," I slap him on the arm, "You can't say things like that in the middle of a game. You'll jinx us!"

"Ouch, okay, okay, I get the point," he rubs his arm in mock pain.

Rolling my eyes, I say, "Oh don't be a big baby. I didn't hurt you."

"You're right, but maybe you could kiss it and make it better," he whispers in my ear.

A shiver runs through me at the mention of a kiss. My mind jumps back to the multiple kisses we've shared now, the sounds of the room disappearing, and my cheeks heat.

"G, what's the answer?" Holly asks me.

Looking around, I blank. "I . . . what was the question?"

Holly looks at me curiously as Niall tries to hide his amusement behind his hand, and I catch Margot giving me a smile.

After they repeat the question, I give them a quick answer.

The last question gets asked, then the host goes over the rules for scoring. Cheers and groans fill the air as correct and incorrect answers are revealed. The room echoes with the sounds of laughter and a good time.

Three teams tie for first place, including our group.

"Alrighty, we will ask one final showdown question," says the host. "Our three teams that tied for first will give an answer and the one who is closest to the correct answer wins. Ready?"

We all cheer then huddle closer together so no one overhears us when we discuss the final question.

Grinning, the host does a drumroll on the top of the piano before saying, "For the grand finale and the chance to win these logo cozies: How many countries does the equator pass through?"

"There's Ecuador," I start us off, "Colombia, and Brazil."

"And Gabon and Republic of the Congo," adds Greg.

"Don't forget about the Democratic Republic of the Congo too," says Margot.

"I'm pretty sure Uganda and Kenya are both in that general area," adds Trent

"Somalia, Maldives, and Indonesia," Holly continues, adding tallies on her paper. "That's eleven. Is that correct? Are there any others we missed?"

"Two more, I believe," says Niall. "You left out Kiribati and São Tomé and Príncipe."

"I don't think I've heard of those before," says Margot.

"Alright teams, ten seconds," announces the trivia host.

"Eek, hurry," I say, my competitiveness coming out again. "Let's add them all together, what does that give us?"

Holly quickly double checks her notes. "Thirteen. Okay, that's our final answer."

We put down our pencil right as the host calls time.

"Alright, will one member of the winning team bring up their paper to show me their answers?"

Holly practically runs over to the host. The other two teams' representatives head over as well.

Once all three teams have given their answers, the announcer reviews them.

Holly sits down as the announcer says, "Everyone was very close but only one team got it right. The question was: How many countries does the equator pass through? The correct answer is the equator passes through . . . thirteen countries. Holly, congratulations, your team is tonight's winner."

Laughing that we got it right, we share triumphant high-fives and fist bumps.

"See, Rose. I told you we had this!" says Niall.

"Alright, alright, you were correct," I concede.

CHAPTER 26
Niall

Our group stays in the Knight's Tavern as many of the other groups disperse to other areas of the ship. Given the time, many are probably heading off to bed.

Music is playing, and we take our drinks and move closer to the balcony that overlooks the Grand Promenade below to watch the singers and listen to the music. A group of people start to dance.

"Let's go dance," says Margot, pulling Gwen and Holly along with her. Neither are reluctant. The joy in Gwen's eyes is evident. The girl's wave to us as they leave, telling us they'll be back soon.

Trent, Greg, and I stay up in the lounge, sipping our drinks, while relaxing and chatting.

"Thanks for inviting me," I say to Greg.

"Of course, man, couldn't get married without you and Trent here with me," he says.

"I love my boats back at the marina, but I have to say, this boat tops those," Trent laughs.

"I bet," says Greg, "though I wouldn't say this is just a boat."

"What's it like managing the marina now?" I ask Trent.

"Oh, you know, every day is something new. Some days I'm captain, other days a janitor. The elderly come to fish off the docks, and on those occasions, I multitask as a therapist and occasional fish whisperer all rolled into one. There's this one elderly man who comes every morning at sunrise, like clockwork. He's a sweet old man. His wife recently died, and I think he's a bit lonely, but we have some of the best conversations," Trent answers genuinely.

"Sounds nice," I say with sincere honesty. The memory of my mam hits me in the gut. I feel for the old man having no one around anymore. No one should be lonely.

After taking a sip of his drink, Trent adds, "Some days, I swear I've got more sunscreen on me than a lifeguard at spring break! But seriously, it's a labor of love. I wouldn't trade it for the world. I mean, where else can you fix a boat engine while belting out sea shanties and debating the horror that is pineapple on pizza?"

"Hey," says Greg, "I happen to love pineapple on pizza."

"Yeah, and dude, you're weird," Trent says. Then turning back to me, he adds, "But it has been nice having Greg here rehabilitate our website and social media presence. Nowadays, we have a party or event going on almost every weekend. It's definitely revamped the sense of community that the town has in the marina, for which I will be eternally grateful."

"Even if I like pineapple on pizza?" Greg asks.

"Well . . ." Trent says, "to be determined." The two laugh with each other before Trent continues, "With all Greg's done for the business, my parents finally feel like they can see retirement in their future because Greg and I have everything handled."

"Sounds like you have a *craic* of a time," I say. "I'm definitely going to have to come down for a visit soon. I hate that I feel like I've shut you all out recently with everything going on. I'm sorry about that."

"Don't worry about it, man," says Greg.

"I'm going to be different moving forward," I say. "More open. Being on this cruise has been good for me. It's showed me that I've just been living each day on repeat. But I realize it's time to move forward and process my mam's death. I need to figure out what I'm going to do with her stuff; I can't keep living like she's going to walk back through the door any day."

I haven't thought about the house or about going through my mam's things since I've been on the cruise. A certain spitfire of a woman has kept me occupied, and I've felt more like my old self these past few days.

Glancing down to the Grand Promenade, I see that beautiful auburn hair. Gwen and the girls are dancing. Gwen looks happy and carefree.

"We'll always be here for you," says Trent. "You shouldn't ever feel like you can't reach out. We've got your back. As for your mam's house, you could sell it."

"Or keep it and rent it out," Greg adds. "You can move anywhere, do anything."

"Oh yeah, dude," says Trent, enthusiastically. "You could come to Chessie Valley. You're a firefighter. Everywhere needs a firefighter! You don't need to stay in Boston all by yourself. You can come be with us."

"Trent," laughs Greg, "you are always trying to get people to move back to Chessie Valley."

"Maybe I just know what's best for everyone," says Trent as he sits up a little straighter.

It would be nice to be around Greg and Trent more. They're like family to me, and they're right too. What is holding me in Boston? A sense of duty to my brothers and sisters at the firehouse? But they're the ones that encouraged me to move forward. Right now, Boston is full of reminders of the past, and Mam didn't want me moping around by myself forever.

Mam would want me to continue to live my life. And I wasn't truly living my life while I was taking care of her. I put everything on pause: friendships, dating, all of it. I was so focused on Mam and what she needed. Maybe it is time to start thinking about what's best for me.

The sound of laughter hits my ears, and I turn to see Gwen, Holly, and Margot making their way up the stairs to where we are sitting. Gwen . . . now she is someone worth living my life for. She's funny, smart, full of life, and feck is she beautiful.

I smile as she glances up. I can see the pink in her cheeks grow once she realizes I'm looking at her.

"You all have fun?" asks Greg, as Holly sits down on his lap and gives him a kiss on the cheek.

"We did," Holly says. "I love dancing. It's so much fun, but now I am beat. It's been such a long day, and we have another port day tomorrow. I'm ready to head off to bed."

We all agree with a chorus of "same" and "me too," then head off to our respective rooms.

A wave of energy hits me once I'm back in my room. I tidy up, picking up my brush off the dresser and picking up clothes that I've strewn around the room as I walk back out toward the sitting area. Afterward, I take a shower, hoping it will help relieve some of this energy, but nothing helps. After throwing on some pajama pants, I head out to the balcony and pace back and forth.

The vastness of the ocean before me seems to mirror the endless possibilities of my future. The gentle breeze carries a salty scent of the sea, and the moon casts a silvery path on the water as if inviting me to follow it into the unknown.

What is my problem?

Is it that I might be considering moving away from Boston? Selling my mam's house and moving to Chessie Valley? There's nothing bad about that. Nothing that would cause me to feel this pent up. I feel like I could run a marathon right now and still have energy left over. It's the unknown, like I'm at a crossroads for my life, and that feeling is unsettling to me.

I've never wanted to settle down, but now . . . now that's changed. The thought of a relationship, a real relationship with Gwen excites me. Something I never thought would happen. *But Mam knew.* It wasn't any one thing with Gwen, but a bunch of little things. I'm happy around her, truly happy, not just hiding behind a fake wall of happiness.

Her spunk and caring nature draw me in. She's so easy to be around. And unlike anyone I've ever dated before, I want to be with her. I want to try new experiences and see her face when it lights up with happiness. To fix her problems when she's upset, just to see her smile again.

The sound of singing causes me to stop my pacing. It's a melody so pure it's captivating, seeming to both wrap around my heart and hold me still.

My breath hitches when I realize it's Gwen. Her balcony door's ajar, letting in the ocean breeze. A gentle light from inside her room casts a soft glow on the balcony. I feel drawn to her. Each word is like a thread pulling me closer.

Moving over to her side of our shared balcony, I listen to her as my heart beats in rhythm to her song. Her rendition of "Conversations in the Dark" by John Legend is stunning. I'm frozen listening to the words coming from her cabin and watching her dance. She's captivating.

I'm hit with a realization so strong it takes the breath from my lungs—a realization as clear as the moonlight reflecting on the water. The depth of my emotions surges forth like a tidal wave, knocking into me with such a force I can do nothing but stand here and catch my breath.

In the midst of this tidal wave crashing over me, truth dawns on me. The way my heart quickens at the sound of Gwen's voice, the way her presence feels like the missing piece of a puzzle I didn't even know I was trying to solve. I want to be more than her fake boyfriend, more than just a friend. I want to hold her hand as we navigate the seas of life together.

With every note, a downpour of thoughts and images flash through my mind: shared laughter, stolen glances and kisses, moments of a life with Gwen, a future with her.

With this realization, the final piece of the puzzle clicks within me. I've fallen hard for her, slowly and deeply. I have never felt this way about someone before. I may have taken off the whole allotted year my mam gave me, but I think I have finally found someone worth trying with.

As her song reaches its end, I'm full of hope for a new beginning for us. I want to be the one to make her laugh, to hold her close when she's sad, to support her in her hopes and dreams. As the waves lap against the hull of the ship, I feel as if it's encouraging me and pushing me toward a new future, one I never saw coming. One that is beginning to mean the world to me.

Though her door is ajar, I softly knock on the glass of the balcony door, not wanting to disturb the sereneness of the night. Gwen answers in just her pajama shorts and tank top, causing me to swallow hard at the sight of her. She's breathtaking.

Cheeks still a little flushed from dancing around her room, she slides open the door a bit wider.

"Hi," she says. "Is everything okay?"

I'm quiet for a beat, so many thoughts running through my head. What if I'm misinterpreting everything? *Sometimes you just have to take that first leap and hope you'll land safely on the other side,* I think to myself.

Shaking my head to quiet the thoughts, I finally say, "Gwendolyn, I don't want to be fake dating anymore. . . . I, I don't think I can."

Gwen gives a sharp intake of breath, her cheeks heating up, before saying, "But . . . the plan. We had a plan. You promised."

Placing my finger to her lips to stop her spiraling, I say, "You misunderstand, *mo ghrá,*" the breath from her mouth on my finger stirring even more emotions in me.

"You misunderstand," I say, brushing a strand of hair out of her face and behind her ear. "I don't want to be your fake boyfriend; I don't even want to be your friend. I want to be more than friends. And I don't know what that means for the future, but for now, for the rest of the time I have with you on this cruise, I don't want to pretend anymore. If I'm being honest, I haven't been pretending at all. My feelings for you are true. I want to be yours, for real, for as long as you'll have me."

CHAPTER 27
Gwen

"I know this is unexpected," Niall says, his eyes holding mine with an unwavering sincerity.

His vulnerability in this moment touches my heart. Even though said heart is beating around a million beats per second. His confession changes everything between us. He hasn't been pretending, but that's what our agreement was. It was a fake pact to be boyfriend and girlfriend for the duration of the cruise. It wasn't supposed to turn into something real, something tangible and whole.

Breathe, Gwen, and answer the man. He's standing there so patiently while you are having an internal freak-out session.

"Gwen, you okay?" he says timidly. He reaches out to touch me but pulls back. Maybe he's afraid that if he touches me, I'll make a run for it. But really, I need one of his hugs to help hold me together while I sort through the thousands of emotions ping-ponging their away through me.

"I . . . yes, I'm . . ." I manage to say. Taking a settling breath, I try again. "I'm okay. I just, I wasn't expecting this. I need time to process everything, time to think about what you just told me."

"I'll give you all the time you need, and don't worry, I'll still be your fake boyfriend while you are thinking things over. If you need to talk things through, well, you know where to find me. Goodnight, Gwendolyn." He backs away then enters his room.

The fresh morning breeze sweeps across my skin like a whispered promise of a new day. Last night after Niall went to his room, his declaration hung in the air, leaving me to navigate the rush of emotions he stirred within me. The weight of his words lingered in his absence as the stars continued to blink in the night sky.

After tossing and turning all night, I get up before the sun, needing a run to clear my head. With each stride, the rhythmic sound of my footsteps harmonizes with the soft hum of the ship's engines. The track stretches ahead of me, calling to me, inviting me to embrace the solitude of the morning quiet.

As the sun begins to cast its shimmering golden rays over the horizon, I dive into my own feelings and grapple with the echoes of Niall's declaration. Our shared plan is still an option, but now a second path has emerged, one that gives the hope of possibility. His wish for more floats in the air, inviting me to acknowledge my own heart's desires.

The image of our shared moments together is vivid with laughter and friendship. Yet beneath it, a whisper of doubt unfurls within me—were those moments truly the unearthing of genuine emotion? Is there more to them than the rules of our deal allow?

Niall's presence has been a comfort, a constant companionship. His easy charm and friendship are a reflection of the deal we'd made. Can there be more than just friendship? Do the ripples of laughter and the care in his eyes hold a deeper meaning?

According to him, they do.

My stomach flutters as I consider the possibility of us.

What if the rules we'd set for our fake relationship were to blur? Hadn't they already? In the quiet corners of my heart, the image of Niall takes on a different perspective—not just the fake boyfriend per our deal, but someone who really does make my heart skip a beat. I realize that over the past few days, I've been more myself, and because of that, I may be more on board with the idea of us.

Memories surge forward, each the undercurrent of something more. The touch of his hand as he's steadied me countless times—it carries a weight beyond friendship. Those fleeting glances exchanged during conversations we'd shared—were they glimpses into the unspoken connection we share?

And then the tender forehead touches, the stolen caresses, the confidence I'd gained back just from holding his hand, and that breathtaking kiss. Were these more than just an orchestrated performance for our fake relationship? Do they carry within them the essence of something more? Something genuine?

My breath catches in my throat when I realize that almost every time he's kissed me, it was just the two of us. No one to put on a show for.

My thoughts dive into the amazing man that Niall is. He came to my rescue before he even really knew who I was. I hadn't realized how much his genuine care meant to me. How it helped me come back to myself and move past the hurt from Bradley.

I'd tried to push away all those negative emotions that came from Bradley and my breakup. But seeing Bradley on this cruise and realizing he had a fiancée made me have to face our breakup and the role I played in it. I've even learned to be happy for Bradley. I'm shocked that I have no resentment toward him and Tammy anymore. They are clearly enamored with each other. Otherwise, why would Bradley have faced his stage fright and done karaoke? Why would Tammy be willing to take on rock climbing when she clearly wasn't the outdoor adventure type? They clearly love each other. And I'm happy for them, truly happy for them.

Bradley and I, we never had a love like that, did we? Thinking back on it now after seeing them together, I feel like he and I were just placeholders for each other. We were never truly happy together. He was someone I enjoyed talking to and doing things with, but not someone I was meant to be with long term. Maybe deep down I'd known that about us. And he was right, there were times that I put work before him. Work was something I truly cared about, something I wanted. Bradley wasn't.

As for Niall, did he embrace every touch, share each stolen glance and cherish our breathtaking kisses as something more? Based on his declaration last night, I'd have to say yes.

But the question is, do I?

The time has come to unveil the truth within me. Is what is happening between us something more? It's clear to me that somewhere along the way, Niall worked his way into my closed-off heart, and among the laughter and friendship, real feelings bloomed.

Am I ready to open myself up to another person?

As I finish another lap around the ship, the question is no longer "do I have feelings for Niall," but rather "am I ready to open my heart to the possibility of heartbreak?"

Can I take that again?

I've always been the type to go headfirst into something and figure things out later. Over the past year, that same spunky, go get 'em attitude has morphed into someone more reserved. Less risk-taking.

Am I ready to be that version of myself again? A risk-taker?

Is that version of Gwen gone forever or is she still here, hidden beneath the hurt and ready to break through? In the few days I've been on the cruise, it seems like that part of me is coming to light again.

My phone pings with a text from Holly.

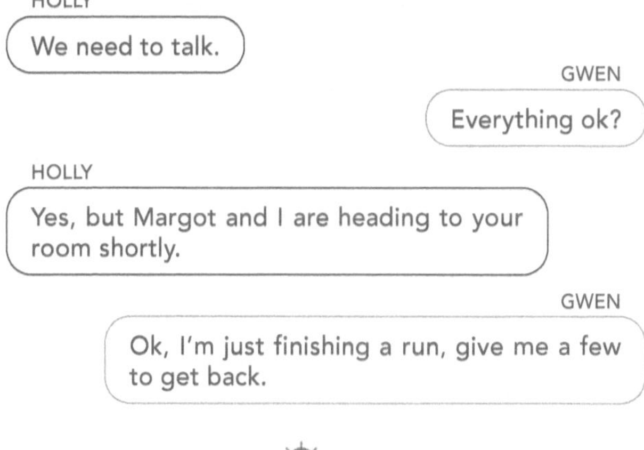

After changing my clothes, I answer the knock at my door. Like promised, Margot and Holly are waiting for me.

"Walk with us," says Holly. I exit my room, and Margot links her arms with mine. "So, spill the beans, Gwen," she says. "What's happening with you and Niall?"

"What are you talking about?" I say.

"Don't play coy," Holly says. "We know something is going on."

"Okay, okay," I say, "but it's really nothing. We're just having fun and enjoying the cruise." I'm trying to come off as nonchalant as I can manage because, after Niall's confession last night, it might be a lot more than a little fun.

"Well," says Margot, "you seem to definitely be enjoying the cruise more than I am."

"Hey," says Holly in mock outrage, "we've been having a lot of fun."

"I know," agrees Margot. "Just not *that* kind of fun."

"Margot does have a point," Holly says conspiratorially. "It does look like you're having a bit more 'fun' than what was outlined in the wedding activities, G."

I only shrug.

"Don't make me bring it out," says Holly.

"Bring what out?" I ask.

Margot pulls a folded piece of paper out of her pocket.

My stomach drops through my body, through the floors beneath me, through the hull of the cruise ship, then deep into the ocean below.

"Where did you get that?" I ask, reaching for the paper, but Holly pulls her hand back. Opening it up, she confirms what I'd dreaded most.

"Rule one," she reads, "Our friends can't know we're fake dating."

I try grabbing for the paper again, but Holly is too quick.

"Rule two," she continues, "Go on dates, just the two of us, as a fake couple."

This time I snag the paper with the tips of my fingers, but Margot comes to Holly's rescue and easily steals it back from me.

"Rule three," reads Margot, "and my personal favorite, when fake dating, PDA is acceptable, but kissing is only allowed if necessary."

"Alright, alright, alright," I say in defeat. I shush them both and glance back behind us in the hallway. I'd be mortified if one of the guys overheard this conversation.

"So," says Holly, "Margot and I have both looked over this list and have been waiting for you to tell us about it."

"Well, about the pretend dating," says Margot.

"But you haven't said anything," says Holly, "so, now we're asking you."

"How did you know the paper belonged to me?" I ask.

"That's easy," says Holly. "I found it on the floor outside your room. I wasn't sure it was yours, but then I saw you and Niall in the laser tag arena. . . ."

I freeze, growing red at the announcement. *Oh no, Holly saw the kiss.*

Margot looks back and forth between me to Holly. "What happened during laser tag? I miss all the juicy gossip!"

"It sure did look juicy," says Holly before giggling.

"Truth is," I say, "I don't even know where to start."

"The beginning is always a good place," says Margot.

"You're hilarious," I say.

"Really, G," says Holly, "what's going on? You know we're here to help you through anything, so how did this fake-dating thing happen?"

The looks on Holly's and Margot's face are so earnest and trustworthy that I end up spilling everything to them. From the first run-in with the non-rideshare to seeing Bradley and Tammy to Niall playing along as my fake boyfriend to deciding to be in a fake relationship for the rest of the cruise. And finally, to Niall's confession last night and the decision I have to make.

"Wow, that's huge," says Margot.

"I know," I say, "it was just supposed to be him pretending to date me around Bradley and Tammy, but obviously, a lot has happened with us since then. And now, with Niall's confession, everything's changed."

"It makes so much sense now," says Margot, "why Bradley's seemed so annoyed around Niall and why Niall has been sticking so close to you."

"But please don't tell the guys," I say. "I don't know how Greg and Trent will take the fake dating, let alone Niall having feelings for me. Unless you've already told them?" Panic courses through me at the thought of it.

Margot shakes her head.

"No," says Holly, "I haven't talked to Greg yet. I wanted to see what you had to say first."

"Okay, good," I say. "I don't want to deal with what Greg and Trent might think on top of trying to figure out what to do with Niall."

"So," asks Holly, "what are you going to do about Niall?"

"I honestly have no idea yet," I say.

CHAPTER 28
Niall

I haven't talked to Gwen since last night, which has been keeping me on edge. The unknown is a heavy weight sitting on my chest.

I hope I didn't unsettle her when I told her how I felt last night. But when the realization that I was falling for her hit me, I had to say something. I've learned the hard way that life is too short to let moments slip by. Waiting might mean missing out on something extraordinary.

Today, we are at Mambo Beach. The waters are calm and tranquil with the rocks stopping the current from coming through to a little lagoon. The sun hangs high in the sky, casting a golden glow over the sandy shore. A gentle breeze carries the calming scent of the saltwater as the sounds of laughter scatter around us. Umbrellas and colorful towels dot the beach, forming a cozy haven of relaxation and family fun.

Maggie doesn't waste a second in building a sandcastle, Miles and Gillian setting down their beach gear before joining her. Waves crash to the shore in an unpredictable ebb and flow, leaving a trail of shells in their wake. Vivian settles herself in a lounge chair next to her parents, who've already claimed their spots, and immediately plugs in some earbuds and lays back.

Greg, Trent, Margot, and Holly start a game of frisbee. I lay out my towel on the lounge chair next to Gwen. Taking a deep breath to ease my racing heart, I lean down next to her and whisper, "Would you like to go out to dinner tonight?"

She pulls down her sunglasses a bit, staring at me, her eyes a fusion of warm earthy tones with hints of green and gold. She radiates a quiet intensity in her gaze. A few heartbeats pass before she answers, "Yes, that would be nice."

My heart, having frozen in time while waiting for her answer, skips a few beats at her affirmation. This has to be a good sign, right?

I sit next to her and watch the others from the cruise along the beach. My natural instinct is to be on alert and consistently assess my surroundings. However, today is a perfect day with calm waters, barely a cloud in the sky.

The world seems to slow down, giving a leisurely feel to the day. Gwen cracks open a book, the rustling of pages mingling with the gentle hum of the ocean and creating a harmonious duet of tranquility. It's not long before the melody of sounds lulls me to sleep.

A frisbee to the stomach wakes me. "Hey, man, you wanna play?" calls Greg.

Sitting up, I sling the frisbee back to him. "I'm in." I jog over to him and the others as they spread out to allow more room for me to join in.

Trent launches the frisbee with a grin, calling out, "Alright, now that the whole gang is in, who's ready for some serious frisbee action?"

Holly, running forward with arms outstretched, goads, "Bring it on, Trent. You're looking at the reigning frisbee champion right here."

Laughing, Margot catches the frisbee before Holly can grab it. "Oh please, I've seen you trip over your own feet, Holly," Margot teases.

Sticking her tongue out at her sister, Holly says, "That was all Murphy's Law, not my doing. Plus, I've been practicing my frisbee skills."

Joining in on the fun, I say with a wink, "Watch out, I've got some frisbee magic up my sleeve."

Margot tosses the frisbee and Gwen catches it, "Alright," she says, "let's see if you've all got what it takes. Ready, set, go!" She throws the frisbee.

Holly dives dramatically. "I've got it, I've got it!" Holly hits the ground followed by the frisbee.

Margot laughs. "Wow, Holly! That almost made it look like you knew what you were doing."

"Hush, you," says Holly. She stands before picking up the frisbee.

Trent teases, "Where were those secret frisbee techniques you'd been boasting about?"

Holly's only response is sticking her tongue out at Trent and tossing the frisbee.

"Don't mess with my bestie," says Gwen playfully in Holly's defense.

The frisbee, flying through the air, looks like it's flying right to Trent, but Greg intercepts it with ease. "Nice try, Trent, but this one's mine. Can't have you teasing my bride-to-be and getting away with it."

"Dude, not cool, that was so mine," says Trent, jogging back to his place.

"My man's got moves," says Holly, going up on her tip-toes to kiss Greg on the cheek.

Right as I catch the next toss of the frisbee, Margot walks toward me and whispers out of the side of her mouth, "So, what's happening with you and Gwen?"

The question catches me so off guard that I end up throwing it past Trent and Greg, causing them to run farther away from the group. Glancing around, I notice Holly eyeing me and Gwen sending me an "I'm sorry" glance.

Ah, so they know.

I turn to Margot. "It really depends on Gwen."

Margot nods, Holly smiles, and Gwen's cheeks turn a captivating shade of pink.

I'm grinning like a eejit by the time Trent and Greg are back with the frisbee. The girls know about us. I don't know how much, but it seems like they might be sound with the idea of Gwen and me together. Now, hopefully the guys will think that too when they realize I have real feelings for Gwen.

"What was that long toss about, Sully?" asks Greg, as they finally get back to the group.

"Yeah, dude," says Trent, feigning exhaustion, "I didn't sign up for marathon running on the beach. That frisbee went far out."

"What can I say?" I shrug. "At least it didn't go into the ocean."

"If that was the case," says Greg, "I'd have made you swim out to get it."

"Fair," I say.

"Enough jabbering," says Gwen. "Let's get on with the game."

"Yeah," says Margot, "let's finish this game, and then someone owes us a round of tropical drinks!"

"And the winner gets bragging rights," I say, "until the next game, of course."

Laughing, Trent adds, "Let the frisbee final show-down begin!"

The winner ends up being Greg, and he buys us all a round of drinks as the afternoon sun begins to descend. Shortly after, we pack up our things, heading back to the cruise ship.

After dropping off our beach gear in our rooms and changing into something a little less sandy, we meet up two hours later and head to the theater to watch the *Mamma Mia!* musical. The energy in the theater is high, especially from our group. As the show gets to the "Super Trouper" song, Holly, Gwen, and Margot sing and dance in their seats in sync with the actresses on the stage.

When the show ends, we take the stairs up to head out the back of the theater. The ship is sailing through some rocky water, and a few of us begin to feel its effects, sway-ing as we walk. The Kentons and Palmers walk out with Vivian, Miles, Maggie, and Gillian. Miles holds tight to his daughter's arm, steadying her with each step.

Holly and Gwen are in a fit of giggles. Margot stands off to the side, hands on hips like she's an exasperated parent waiting on her toddlers.

"Come on, lightweights," teases Margot.

"I don't know why it's hitting me so hard," says Holly, giggling as she tries to climb the stairs next to Gwen. "I have my Dramamine patch on."

"Me either," says Gwen. Tears sparkle in her starburst eyes from her laughter. Taking a step forward, she starts to tumble. Her hands reach out for the railing but miss. I quickly grasp her around the waist, gulping as my hands land on the soft skin.

"Don't worry," I say softly into her ear as I set her upright. "I've got you."

Her big eyes lock with mine. "Thank you."

Clearing my throat, I glance over at Holly and Greg. Holly isn't fairing much better than Gwen. Greg has her elbow in one hand and is using his other hand to guide her up the stairs. Watching as Gwen takes another shaky step, I steady her again.

Once we exit the theater, the rocking subsides and everyone feels a bit calmer. "Alright, everyone," says Gwen, checking the wedding itinerary on her phone, "you are on your own for dinner tonight, except for Holly and Greg. I've planned a special dinner at the hibachi restaurant for you two. You're going to get a cooking demonstration from the head chef. They'll lead you in a little mini class about hibachi, and you get to enjoy a romantic dinner and dessert at a table overlooking the ocean."

"Gwen, that's too much," says Holly, tears brimming in her eyes.

"Thanks, Gwennie," says Greg, giving Gwen a big hug. "That was thoughtful."

"Oh, well, it was nothing," says Gwen, "I just thought you two would like . . ." she trails off.

"It wasn't nothing," says Holly. "You are the best friend a girl could ask for."

Greg and Holly leave for the hibachi restaurant. Gillian and Miles break off from the group to take Maggie to kid's club so they can have a night out together. Vivian leaves the group, saying she's going to meet up with Tammy and Bradley. The Kentons and Palmers head off to the Duke's Diner.

"I think," says Margot, "I'm going to catch one of the World Cup games at the sports bar."

"I'll join you," says Trent. "We can catch dinner there too. You guys coming?" Trent asks Niall and me.

"They probably have other plans," says Margot, giving me and Gwen a large smile.

"Other plans?" asks Trent.

"Actually, Margot's right," I say. "I've already got reservations for dinner tonight . . . with Gwen."

Trent raises his eyebrows and nods, "Gotcha. Well, you two have fun."

Trent and Margot turn and head off together toward the sports bar.

"When did you make a reservation?" Gwen asks, once they're out of earshot.

"This morning before we all headed off to the beach."

"But you didn't know if I'd agree to dinner."

"I had hope. Shall we?" I hold out my arm to her.

She looks at me for a heartbeat, then nods and puts her arm through mine. "Lead the way."

The dinner at the steakhouse is delicious. Our meal passes with the two of us immersed in conversation that ebbs and flows easily, as if we've been going to dinner together for years.

It all seems so easy with Gwen, so right. I've been hesitant to bring up last night and what I confessed because I want to give her time to think everything over, but after enjoying the day and this dinner together, my nerves are all but shot.

"So," I start, then take a sip of water. "Have you given any thought to what I told you last night?"

She eyes me silently for a bit, causing my already quickening heart to beat rapidly. "You don't have to have an answer," I say quickly. "I just wanted to know if you've thought about it."

"I've been thinking about it," she says, "but I don't have an answer quite yet."

I nod, and surprisingly, we return to normal conversation, no awkwardness lingering between us.

After we're sufficiently stuffed from the delicious food and dessert, I guide Gwen out of the restaurant. "Would you like to take a walk through the gardens?" I ask.

"That sounds nice," she says.

We stroll the Royal Gardens, enjoying the cool breeze and the beauty of the inky sky dotted with stars.

Pulling Gwen to a stop, I turn to face her and brush my thumb against her cheek. "My mam always said if you wish on a star, your wish would come true. Close your eyes and make your wish, whatever your heart desires."

CHAPTER 29
Gwen

I close my eyes. When was the last time I wished on a star?

Taking a deep breath, I let myself take in the moment. The chill of the air around us, a slight breeze as the ship moves across the ocean. The smell of the restaurants we passed, delicious scents of savory and sweet. The sound of people in the distance chattering, music coming from the pool areas of the ship. The touch of Niall's hand on my cheek, warm and soft. Comforting.

When was the last time I'd been comforted by someone? When was the last time I let someone take care of me instead of me trying to take care of everyone else?

It's nice. This, this is what I want. I want someone to take care of me for once who I can be my true self around. I want to be with someone who doesn't slink away from me but rather digs deeper to get to know me. Someone who, regardless of my to-do lists, my obsession with my business, and my snarky quips, still sees the real me.

I wish for this feeling with Niall to never end. I wish for the courage to try and make something work between us.

Taking a deep breath, I open my eyes to see Niall's blue eyes staring back at me.

"You make a wish?" asks Niall.

"Yes," I say softly, not moving back from his touch. Instead I lean into it as Niall puts his other hand on my waist. I can feel the heat of his hand through the fabric of my shirt. Reminded of earlier when his hand briefly brushed my bare skin, I feel a shiver of anticipation jolt through me.

"Good," he says gruffly.

I'm unable to resist the pull that draws me toward him. I lean forward, wrapping my arms around his neck. I pause just before our lips touch.

Brushing against his lips, I quietly say, "I don't know when it happened, but I realized I haven't been pretending either. I want to try . . . us."

Niall pulls back slightly but only enough that he can look me in the eyes. "Are you sure?"

"Yes. I'm open to trying. I'd be lying to myself if I didn't admit that I have feelings for you too."

Niall sweeps me up in a hug and kisses me deeply. "That makes me so happy, *mo ghrá*," he says. "Those are the best words I've ever heard."

I laugh and kiss him back.

"Because of you," says Niall, "I've been able to keep the promise I made to my mam before she passed away."

"What promise?" I ask.

"My mam made me promise her that I wouldn't stay alone when she was gone. She told me I had one year to mourn her and then to get on with my life," he chuckles at the memory.

I smile, encouraging him to continue.

"She said to try and find someone who makes me happy, someone I can laugh with and makes it so I no longer feel alone. To really try and connect with someone. I wanted to keep my promise to my mam, but it wasn't until I met you that I felt like I could. So now, not only have you allowed me to keep my promise to my mam but you've made my wish come true too," he says before pressing his mouth gently against mine.

His hand holds me around the waist, pulling me closer to him as his other hand moves behind my head, cradling it. Our lips touch, and our tongues taste as we explore one another.

I have no idea how long we stay like that, making out in the garden like a pair of teenagers under the canopy of the night sky. The vast expanse is adorned with a breath-taking display of constellations, and the stars twinkle like diamonds against a velvety black backdrop. The world disappears, and there is nothing but the feel of Niall, the sound of my heart beating wildly in my chest, the taste of his lips on mine.

Breaking apart, Niall leans his forehead to mine.

"I don't want to say anything to the rest of the group," I say. "Not just yet, not with the wedding a few days away. I don't want to take anything away from Holly and Greg."

Nodding, Niall says, "I understand."

"But," I say, kissing him softly, "I'm not ready for tonight to be over. Can we . . . can we head back to our balcony?"

He looks deeply at me. "*Mo ghrá*, I want nothing more than this night to last forever."

We walk hand in hand back to our rooms. Before we step into our separate rooms, he takes my hand and bends down to place a kiss on it. "See you soon."

I nod mutely. *How is a kiss on the hand so hot?*

Flushed, I hurry to freshen up.

A moment later, there is a soft knock at my balcony door. Niall has taken off his shoes and cruise card lanyard, but everything else is just as he was a moment ago. Anticipation builds within me as I unlock the balcony door and slide it open.

Niall holds out his hand, and I take it, letting him guide me onto our balcony.

"Hi," he says.

"Hi," I echo.

He tucks a stray strand of hair behind my ear. Then, tilting my head up, he lowers his lips to mine. Still gentle, but harder than in the gardens. Almost . . . needy.

He needs me just as much as I need him.

A beat of a breath passes before we are in each other's arms. Hands wandering, needing to be close to each other. His lips leave mine and trail behind my ear and down my neck, causing me to shiver. His hands push my shirt up slightly, stroking over my skin just above my hips. The cool ocean breeze is a stark contrast to the warmth of his hands.

Running my hands through his hair then down his arms, I explore his body. My gentle tugging registers to Niall, and he pulls away momentarily to take off his shirt in one swift movement and throw it over the chair next to us.

I swallow as I touch his bare skin. Damn is he fine. A shiver runs through him as my fingers trace his abs down to the top of his shorts.

"May I?" he asks, hands on my shirt.

I nod, trying to remember how to breathe. Bolts of electricity surge through me as he slowly lifts my shirt up and over my head and tosses it on top of his.

He traces the straps of my bra, following it down to the curve over my breast. The touch sends an urgency through me. I want this man more than I've ever wanted anyone. How is that possible when just days ago, he was infuriating me?

"You're so sexy, *mo ghrá*," he says in between kisses that move down my neck to my collar bone, his body heating my skin as he moves, thumbs tracing the underside of my bra.

"I need you," I blurt, my face flaming at my outburst. *But who am I kidding? If this doesn't end the way I want it to, I may combust.*

A low moan leaves Niall's throat. He stops kissing and lays his forehead against my chest. "*Mo ghrá*, I never expected to meet you, never expected for this . . ."

"It's okay. This is okay," I reply, my heart racing in my chest.

"Are you sure?" Niall asks, his eyes searching mine. "I would never want to make you uncomfortable."

"If you leave me like this much longer, I will be uncomfortable but for an entirely different reason."

A needy growl surges up from his throat. I have only a moment to register how sexy that sound is before Niall lifts me up. I wrap my legs around him, and he carries me into my room and closes the balcony door.

"Now that was sexy," I say in a whisper.

His eyes pierce me, a fire of need raging in them. I pull closer to him and adjust my legs around his waist. The hardness of him is evident with each movement.

He sets me down gently on the bed, and his hungry gaze roams my body. Kneeling down, he moves his hands up my thighs. Within moments, we are both devoid of our clothes, the cold of the comforter a drastic contrast to the warmth of our bodies against each other.

The feel of his hands causes me to shiver as he massages my inner thighs. My breath catches as his hands move inward. His thumb leisurely strokes me as, clearly, he is in no rush. My body jolts at the sensations coursing through me, my breathing getting more erratic the longer he goes on.

After what feels like an eternity, he pauses, and I move to sit up. He adjusts lower on the bed, and I immediately fall back again as his mouth begins exploring and sucking on the same spot his thumb just vacated.

Holding my thighs down with his hands, he continues as I writhe beneath him. I'm close, oh so close, and he knows it. He doesn't let up, and soon, I hit my limit, coming so hard I see stars.

Oh my God, that was amazing.

I try to calm my breathing, but my body is buzzing. Glancing up, I see his eyes still roaming my body, and fuck if he's not the sexiest man I've ever seen. I reach up and pull him down on top of me, kissing him with a passion I've never felt before.

We move in an intimate dance transcending reality, our two hearts finding rhythm of connection. We move in harmony, each touch a thrilling promise, every glance an affirmation of our souls pulling toward each other. There is nothing but the two of us. The room and world beyond fades into a blur. In our heated embrace, we discover a language of our own, surpassing the need for words with heated gazes and a passion so overwhelming that time seems to stand still.

I wake up tucked in comfortably next to Niall, his arm wrapped over me, holding me close while he gently strokes my cheek. Opening my eyes, I turn my head to face him.

"Good morning," I say softly.

He pulls me in tighter, and kisses my hair. "Good morning, *mo ghrá*. You looked so peaceful, so I didn't want to wake you."

"It was a good night," I say.

"It was," he says, stroking my cheek, "but unless you changed your mind about telling people about us, I need to get up and meet Greg and Trent. They're waiting on me for an early game of basketball."

"I understand," I say, lightly trailing my fingers along his arm.

"Mmm . . . I'd love nothing more than to stay and enjoy the morning with you. Last night was like something out of a dream, and I don't want it to end."

"It's okay, really," I say as he gets out of bed to grab his things.

Then, he turns back around and sits on the side of the bed. He leans forward and gently cups my face. "*Mo ghrá*, you're important. I haven't even left yet and I'm already wishing I was back here with you. I'll be thinking about your beautiful smile until I see you again."

He gives me a soft kiss before heading over to his room.

Smiling, I lie back against the headboard. I'm important to Niall.

The thought causes a happy thrill to weave through me. Memories of last night flash through my mind. Niall and I exploring each other with each passionate embrace. The memory of kisses I still feel on my lips.

A happy sigh leaves me as I snuggle into the bed a bit longer.

When I wake up again, I take a quick shower, drink two cups of coffee, and dress in my bathing suit and wrap. Grabbing a floppy hat, some sandals, and a book, I look over my schedule. First, I have a meeting with Courtney, then I'll meet up with Holly and Margot at the pool.

"Hi, Gwen," says Courtney as I walk into her office.

"Hi, Courtney," I say. I'm happy I scheduled some time to check in with her. Everything has been so busy I haven't had the chance before now. "How's everything looking for the wedding?"

"Funny you should ask. I wanted to run something by you," she says.

Oh no, dread fills my stomach. Something is wrong and I've not been on top of everything like I should be.

"Is everything okay?" I ask hesitantly.

"Oh, of course, sorry, I didn't mean to worry you. I just wanted to confirm a few things about the rehearsal attendees and the SkyDeck for the wedding."

"Oh, thank goodness. Yes, so the rehearsal will just have the wedding party and our parents. So that's thirteen, because Gillian and Miles will be there to help Maggie with her cues. What about the SkyDeck?" I ask.

"Well, we were thinking, because it's going to be dusk when they get married, it would be nice to have lights hanging around the SkyDeck to give off a sort of fairytale glow."

"Holly would love that!" I say. "Yes, please do add them. And thank you for all your help with the wedding. I haven't had to do nearly what I normally would for an event, and as unnerving as that is, it's also nice being able to just take part in the wedding itinerary with my friends and family."

"That's what we are here to help with," says Courtney. "Everyone in the wedding party, including you, should be able to have a great time without worrying about a thing."

"Thank you, Courtney. I'm off to the pool to meet up with Holly and Margot," I say.

"Have a great time," Courtney says.

Sitting in the lounge chair beside one of the many pools, I read my book, and a feeling of calm washes over me, the warmth of the sun warming my skin. Holly and Margot sit next to me reading and drinking piña coladas, having joined me about an hour ago.

Turning the page of my book, I take in the people around me, all of us on the same ship but all with different lives. Even my life is different from what it was when I first boarded this cruise ship.

Laying my head back, I smile to myself. This is definitely the life. The gentle breeze lightly moves the pages of my book as I read.

"Gwen," I hear from an unknown location.

Looking around, I try to place the source.

"Gwen!" I hear again.

I glance up at the second level and see Niall waving to me from one of the hot tubs. I give him a small wave.

The grin that spreads across his face brings a smile to mine. As unpredictable as this whole thing has been since we first bumped into each other, I can always count on him to find me. And now, he's someone I have developed strong feelings for. Someone who has developed strong feelings for me as well.

Niall steps out of the hot tub, and the water glistens as he shakes off the excess and reaches for his towel. The sight of his bare chest brings a flood of memories from the night before.

"What's caught your attention?" Holly asks teasingly.

"It's Mr. Hottie with the accent," says Margot. Then they both break out into giggles.

"Hush, you two," I scold.

"He definitely has a crush on you," says Holly.

"Yeah . . ." I say dreamily.

"Seems like you might have one too," says Holly, pulling her sunglasses down to look at me, her eyebrow raised at my tone. "Does that mean you two are . . ."

She waits for me to answer.

But I can't bring myself to tell them yet that he's mine, and I'm his. I want it to be our secret for just a little longer.

As if my thoughts conjure him, Niall walks over to us, saving me from having to answer Holly's question. The sight of him with a plate piled high with chips, guacamole, and sour cream causes me to smile.

"For you, ladies," Niall says.

"Thank you," I say.

"You look breathtaking," he whispers into my ear as he hands over the nacho plate.

"Nachos!" exclaims Holly. "I would kill for some nachos." Laughing, Niall says, "Well, thankfully you won't have to go to that extreme. We wouldn't want the bride to end up in jail right before her wedding."

"Why is Holly ending up in jail?" asks Greg, coming over and giving his bride-to-be a kiss on her head.

"Well, for nachos, of course," says Holly. Greg just shakes his head like he should have known.

"Sounds about right," says Trent, who just arrived.

After we've about finished the nachos, Trent says, "Anyone up for a game of ping pong?"

"Are you ready to get beat?" I ask.

"Ha! Just because you beat me years ago doesn't mean you'll beat me again," says Trent teasingly.

"My money is on Gwen," says Niall, eating a nacho as we follow Trent to an open ping pong table.

"I'll bet it is," murmurs Margot next to me, smirking.

"Hurtful," says Trent, bouncing the ping pong ball to test it before sending it over to my side.

CHAPTER 30
Niall

We take turns playing increasingly competitive games of ping pong, each person stepping up to take on the prior round's winner.

After taking out all three of us guys as well as Margot, Gwen stands tall, twirling her ping pong paddle in her hand. "Alright, you ready to take on the ping pong champion, Hols?" she asks.

Holly steps up to the table to take the paddle from Margot. "Prepare to be taken down, G."

Laughter and friendly banter fill the air as the girls go head-to-head for the final round. The score is ten to nine, Holly in the lead by one. With a quick return of the ball, Gwen sends it to the edge of Holly's side. Holly manages to barely save the ball and sends it back over to Gwen in an equally tricky shot. Gwen misses, making Holly the winner.

"I didn't see that coming," says Trent in between laughter.

"Hey, I'm not that unathletic," says Holly.

With the scorching sun beating down, everyone is eager to cool down on the waterslides.

As we get in line, Greg pats me on the back and whispers, "You and Gwen should pair up for the two-person tubes."

Having overheard Greg, Trent says, "Margot, you're with me." Then he gives me a not-so-subtle thumbs up.

I laugh as I hurry along after them. A rush of excitement sweeps over us as we speed down the waterslides, our voices shouting out in joyful cries that echo and follow us down the slides. After a few rounds of sliding, I ask, "Anyone up for the WaveRider?"

"I've wanted to try that," says Trent. "It looks fun."

"Let's do it," Gwen agrees. "Oh wait, give me a minute. Becca is calling." She steps to the side of the stands near the WaveRider viewing area.

Trent gives me a little shrug before getting in line. I wonder if Gwen realizes her friends notice her absence. Just as the thought crosses my mind, Gwen locks eyes with me and pauses. "Becca, I'm actually supposed to be doing something right now. I trust you and know you can handle this." She hangs up her phone and says to me, "Sorry about that."

"No need to apologize. Work is important," I shrug.

"Not as important as spending time with my friends. Becca can handle it." Gwen puts her phone in her bag before joining the others in line.

"You've got this, Hols!" Gwen cheers Holly on as Holly steps on to the WaveRider. I can tell Gwen's fully in the moment now, no thoughts or cares about whatever Becca had called about. She's showing signs of change, and her friends notice. Greg gives me an almost imperceptible nod acknowledging the same thing.

CHAPTER 31
Gwen

After more time on the WaveRider and a round of ice cream, we find ourselves on the Grand Promenade. Gillian and Miles have joined our small group, and all the guys have each signed up for the bellyflop competition.

Well, this should be entertaining.

As the cruise director calls the bellyflop participants up, the guys are joined by about ten other men. The rules are pretty simple. Basically, when the participant is called up, there's music for them to dance to as they walk up the steps of the diving board, then they have to perform their best bellyflop, and the crowd will score them.

There are a few guys ahead of Niall, Trent, Greg, and Miles. They do decent but nothing amazing. Miles is up next, and we cheer him on as he struts steps in rhythm to the music, but his flop is a flop.

"Oh no! That looks like it hurt," laughs Holly.

"Yeah," agrees Gillian with an eye roll, "he's going to be sore after that awful flop."

Laughing, I turn to see Trent up next. He is a big goofball, playing to the crowd with his dance moves. His bellyflop gets a huge round of applause and is the highest score so far.

Niall, preparing for his turn, looks over at me and cocks his brow at me. Why that look makes me all hot and bothered is beyond me. He takes off his shirt and the crowd murmurs in appreciation.

Yeah, I know, folks, and it's even better up close.

I give him a thumbs up as music begins. And damn, is he sexy. He swings his hips, playing to the crowd to get them to cheer louder.

As he stands at the top of the steps, he cups his hands to his ear as if he can't hear the crowd cheering.

I know I'm grinning like a fool, but he does put on a good show. Now let's just hope his bellyflop isn't a dud like Miles' was.

We count him down just like every competitor before him with a "three, two, one, bellyflop!" and he leaps into the air, pulling his knees and arms in tight. Just before he starts to descend, he extends both arms and hands out in the perfect pose, belly slightly lower than the rest of him. He hits the water belly first with a loud bang and a splash that sends water over the edge of the pool, hitting people in the first row.

Well damn, that was good.

"Woohoo, go Sully!" Trent yells after his friend. Niall's bellyflop comes in at the closest score to Trent's.

As he breaks through the water, his gaze meets mine and I'm smiling from ear to ear. Why does he have to be so infuriatingly perfect? I clap along with the others and give him a slight nod.

As he makes his way out of the pool, the activities director walks over to Niall. "Before you go, Niall, come here, come here. We have to point this out, folks. Niall, do a little pirouette here. Look at this, folks," the director says, motioning toward Niall's stomach. "Look at the redness already set in. Look at this!" The crowd is clapping and laughing.

Niall joins us as we watch Greg jump. It's not as impressive as Trent or Niall's bellyflops, but still not bad.

After everyone has their turn, the cruise activities director tallies up the scores and announces, "We have a close enough top two that we need to have a jump off. Our two top-scoring contestants are going to be Trent from Tennessee and Niall from Massachusetts! It's down to the two of you. You'll each have a chance to do one more flop for first and second place."

Trent and Niall make their way up and prepare for one final jump.

The cruise activities director continues, "Alright we have Trent from Tennessee going first. Trent, are you ready?"

Trent nods, then gives Niall a fist bump before heading up the stairs to the song "Who Let the Dogs Out" as the director announces, "Alright, same rules as before apply, folks. We'll be watching for the same things, but this one has to be even more discerning. We are looking for the perfect flop. So, when you are giving your scores, keep that in mind. Give it up for Trent from Tennessee. Let's see it in three, two, one, bellyflop!"

Trent's flop is near perfection. And we all cheer for him along with the rest of the crowd.

Niall, up next, turns at the top of the stairs to shake his butt at the crowd. The crowd goes wild. Niall's bellyflop is also near perfection.

Both guys had different techniques, but both managed to soak the first row of people closest to the pool.

We cheer like crazy for both our friends, whose stomachs are now an even brighter red than before. That's going to be so uncomfortable in the fancy dress clothes tonight for our formal dinner.

The cruise activities director gives a final tally. "Now for the flop off winner, we are going to crown our Silver medal winner . . . Trent from Tennessee. Let's hear it for Trent! You had some beautiful flopping."

"Woohoo, go Trent!" I yell along with Margot, Holly, and Greg.

"Alright, and then for the Grand Champion medal we have Niall from Massachusetts! And our winner has agreed to give us one more bellyflop! Let's see it one more time, folks," says the activities director.

Niall turns and looks straight at me. He points, and mouths, "This one's for you."

I blush. Margot and Holly both give me a look and a mischievous grin. Greg and Trent also notice. *Oh no*, I think, *I'm sure they're going to say something to me.* But instead, they give each other a look before turning back to cheer on Niall as he jumps into the air to give another spectacular bellyflop.

Odd, I wonder what that look was for? I'm sure Greg will give me an earful about it later.

CHAPTER 32
Niall

My stomach itches as I put on my suit for tonight's dinner. That third bellyflop really did me in, exacerbating my redness and discomfort.

I slip on my dress shoes after kicking my flipflops out of the way and straighten my tie as a knock comes at my balcony door.

Turning, my breath catches in my throat. Out on my balcony is the most beautiful *beore* I've ever seen.

The curls in her hair blow lightly in the wind along with the bottom of her dress. My gaze travels down her toned body and back up to see her eyes narrowing at me, though the side of her mouth quirks like she's trying not to smile.

Ah yes, there's my feisty Rose.

Even her feistiness has me turned on and, feeling the increasing tightness in my pants, I adjust as I walk over to let her in. I'm trying hard to remember how to breathe.

I slide the door open. She's still narrowing her eyes at me but now the smile has broken through. "I'm not an object to be ogled, Niall," she says, trying to sound angry but not quite pulling it off.

"Can I help it if a beautiful goddess suddenly appears on my balcony making me forget how to breathe?"

Her gaze softens as a blush of red creeps over her cheeks. "Well, when you put it that way . . ."

"You look stunning, Gwendolyn."

Her dress hugs her in all the right places, then flows out at the bottom with a slit up to her thigh showing off her long legs. The dress is sleeveless and exposes her toned arms but wraps around her neck like a thick necklace. I know I'm staring again, but I want to run my hands all over her soft feminine features. Knowing her gorgeous body is hiding under that dress is killing me.

My gaze heats as I lock eyes with her. "Absolutely fecking stunning."

Reaching out, I pull her in close to me, her lips searing against mine.

I break apart from her slightly, resting my forehead to hers. "If we keep this up, we're going to be late for dinner," I say.

"Mmhmm," she replies breathlessly.

I kiss her forehead gently before backing up a few steps to let her in my room.

She follows, adjusting her hair in the mirror and checking her makeup. "Good, you didn't mess anything up," she says.

"Me?" I ask, picking up my discarded swimsuit and hanging it in the bathroom.

"Yes, you. I spent a lot of time getting ready."

"Do you regret me kissing you?" I ask, walking back toward her, and the urge to kiss her again overwhelms me.

Shaking her head, she says, "I'm definitely not complaining, just stating a point."

"Right, well, I'll leave you be, for now." I come up behind her, wrapping one hand around her waist and pulling her against me. My hardness presses up against the soft curves of her arse as she startles. Gently I move her hair as I whisper, "When I get you to myself later, that dress is going to be the first thing to go." I kiss along her exposed shoulder and up to her neck.

She swallows, looking at me through the mirror with wanting eyes. "Is that a promise?" she whispers.

"A guarantee," I say, locking eyes with her.

As we join the others in the Grand Promenade, there are people in all levels of attire. A majority dressed up for the formal night in various gowns, suits, and even a few tuxedos. It's like walking into a prom but there are people of all ages.

Even little Maggie has on a princess ballgown.

"Why, princess, I didn't know there'd be royalty here tonight!" I say in awe, reaching my hand out to her to twirl her around.

"Thank you," Maggie says, then giggles. "You look pretty too!"

"Thank you, Maggie," I say, seeing Gwen grinning out of the corner of my eye.

At dinner, we're seated closely together at a large, rounded table. After ordering our meals, we chat about our days. Trent and Greg fill in the rest of the group on the WaveRider fun and the bellyflop competition.

My thoughts are all on Gwen though. How she looked in her bathing suit. Seeing her cheer me on at the bellyflop competition. And now, all dressed up in this gorgeous dress.

She shifts in her seat, and her dress falls away at the slit, exposing her leg to me. I'm immediately overcome with the urge to touch her. I slip my hand under the table-cloth so no one can see and then place my hand gently on her exposed thigh.

She jolts slightly at my touch, coughing as she inhales some water.

"You okay?" Gillian asks her.

"Mmhmm," she responds. Then she gives me a look that screams at me to behave.

Chuckling, I turn back to the conversation, my hand never leaving her leg. Instead, I rub my thumb up and down her thigh. Her skin is so soft, so luxurious. It's only when our meal comes that I move my hand off her so I can eat. Her face, pouting slightly at the loss, makes me grin.

"Is everything alright, G?" asks Holly, "Is something wrong with your meal?"

I chuckle lightly beside her, and she looks at me as if to scold me before looking over at her friend. Shaking her head, she replies, "No, everything is good. It's just a little cold in here is all."

"Tell me about it," says Margot, who is wearing a short strapless dress. "I should have worn a long-sleeve dress. It's freezing in this dining room!"

Holly agrees, and the group chimes in about the temperature of the room.

Leaning over to Gwen, I whisper, "You won't be cold for long, *mo ghrá*. I'll warm you up later tonight."

She swats my side, shushing me, but the slight rose coloring of her cheeks tells me she won't mind being warmed up at all.

As our desserts come out, Gwen tells the group, "As you all know, tomorrow night is the rehearsal dinner. We have planned activities for the bachelor and bachelorette "party" days. After breakfast in the morning, we will all split off for the day and won't meet back up until the rehearsal at five o'clock on the Sun Deck, followed by a rehearsal dinner at Kings' Grille, one of the ship's specialty steakhouses. You'll all find your activities list for anything that is prescheduled on your apps in the morning. If you have any questions for me, I'll be just a text away."

Everyone acknowledges the plans for tomorrow, then we split up, some people heading back to their rooms, like myself and Gwen, and others heading back to the Grand Prominade for some professional pictures.

After saying goodnight to the others, we go into our separate rooms. I tug at my tie to loosen it up, then swiftly kick off my shoes and knock on the adjoining door. Hearing her shuffling around in the room, I lean against the frame to wait.

"Hi," Gwen says breathlessly as she swings open the door.

"Hello," I say, my gaze landing on her bare feet. She's kicked off her heels, and even though they looked sexy on her, the sight of her bare feet makes me swallow hard.

"Would you like to—" she starts, but I pull her into my room and against me in the span of a heartbeat.

Kissing her feels like heaven. I've been in agony watching her talk all evening, knowing how her lips feel against mine. My hands roam over her body, landing on the open back of the dress, and I moan into her as I trace my hand over her soft skin.

She presses against me harder, our mouths opening slightly to deepen the kiss as we taste each other again. Matching me with every kiss, every touch, every taste, she starts to unbutton my shirt, making my heart race in my chest.

I kiss her mouth, then move toward her neck, my hands roaming all over her. I want to touch everything, from her silky hair flowing down her shoulders to her soft skin. The exposed parts of her call to me and remind me of the gloriousness underneath that dress.

She undoes the last button on my shirt, leaving my loosened tie against my bare chest. I pull my shirt off as

I continue to kiss her. Without hesitation, she begins to unbutton my pants, letting them fall to the floor before I step out of them completely, tripping slightly over the flipflops I'd left on the ground. I'm left in nothing but my boxer briefs and my tie.

She grabs a hold of the tie and pulls me tighter against her mouth like she can't stand the thought of even a centimeter of space separating us. I reach up to unbuckle the top of her dress, but she swats my hand away. She pulls on my tie, leading me to the bed before spinning us around and pinning my legs against the side of the mattress. With a grin, she pushes me back, but I reach out and grab her waist, pulling her down with me.

Gwen is above me, the light like a halo around her, making her look like a beautiful angel with her dress billowing over me. The slit in her dress rides up higher to show she's wearing nothing underneath.

I let out a growl, my breath catching in my throat at the knowledge.

She has a smirk on her face as she traces her hands over my bare chest, about to have her way with me. And I want nothing more.

The thin fabric of my boxer briefs is the only barrier between us. Gwen's hands glide down my stomach toward the top of them, and my stomach jolts at the chill it sends through me. Her touch is maddening playing at the edges of what I want, and I groan with need, causing her to pause and glance up at me.

A wicked smile breaks across her face as she scoots back off my legs, pulling down my boxer briefs, then sitting back atop my legs once more as she takes me in her hands. I buck at the touch, unable to control myself. Her hands are soft and smooth against me, a drastic difference to how hard I've become. After torturing myself with being in her presence but unable to have her, I'm almost in pain with want, with need.

I take in the sight of her holding me, watching as her hands move up and down in a gentle rhythm. I'm mesmerized by her. A slip of her tongue stroking against her lips almost has me losing control. I give her a questioning look as if to ask permission and she nods slightly, it's all the answer I need.

I sit up quickly, and she lets go of me as I take her waist in my hands and pull her on top of me, then pull the dress off over her head. She's so wet that she slides onto my length easily. I feel her around every inch of me and it's achingly perfect. We fit together like we were made for each other, satisfaction overcoming me.

Her skin flushing, the intensity of her gaze meets mine. Her back arches as we move in a synchronized rhythm. I'm hyperaware of every slight movement she makes.

She's in control now, feeling the power of that control as she grows more confident. Circling her hips, her lips part as she sucks in a breath of air. She likes the friction her new movement is causing, and so do I. I push harder into her, matching her every movement. Pushing in deep as she circles forward and out as she circles back, I find an exhilarating rhythm with her. She doesn't stop circling her hips as pleasure radiates from her, her eyes closing as she lives in this moment. I reach up and brush back her hair, her head instinctively leaning into my touch.

"*Mo ghrá*, you are breathtaking," I murmur.

"Mmmm," she says.

I clench my jaw at the noise she makes, trying to keep it together. Our eyes locking as she glances down at me, a slow smile building as we move faster against each other. Our movements turn a little more erratic as we both start to lose control. I fight against my desires. She is the most important, and I need her to hit her release first. This right now is about her. I will do everything in my power to let her know that.

The joy on her face as we move in harmony causes me to reach between us, circling my thumb against her. She arches and moans, pressing harder against my thumb. As we reach the precipice of our desires, I only let myself lose control after she has hit her max.

After tossing a pair of sunglasses out of the way, I pull her down on the bed to lie beside me, sweeping the hair from her face. She smiles up at me and leans in to kiss me sweetly.

I love you.

I kiss her back, floored at how so much could change for me in just a week.

We fall asleep in each other's arms.

Not too long after, I awake to Gwen kissing me softly. What a perfect way to wake up. As I kiss her back, our kiss changes, growing deeper, harder by the second. *My little firecracker.*

I smile into her kisses, and turn so I'm hovering over her, my breath catching at the sight of her under me. She moans into my mouth, hands roving over my chest and arms as I slide myself once more into her perfect body. She feels exquisite and tight around me as we move in sync with each other in an ebb and flow.

This time, I'm in control, and I let her know how much I want her, how much I need her. How I desire her in every way. I'm rough with need, but she meets me every step of the way, scraping her nails down my back and my arms, even leaning up to playfully bite at my lips. It drives me mad with want, my eyes closing at the feeling.

Still inside her, I bend down and kiss her lips, then her cheek, trailing down her neck and nipping at her collar. She moans in pleasure, and I almost lose it. I want her to lose herself in ecstasy, need her too, her pleasure before my need always.

I trail my lips down to her chest and take the tip of her breast in my mouth, and she jerks at the feeling. Her fingernails scrape into my scalp, pulling my head closer to her. She tastes exquisite, sweet like strawberries and cream.

I can feel a change in her movements, a whimper escaping her lips as I continue to lick and suck on her breast. *Yes, do it.* She sighs with pleasure as I feel her reach her max, clenching around me and causing my movements to grow faster, harder. *This woman will be the death of me.* The arm holding me up starts to shake from the effort but the look on her face is worth it and I find my release just after.

CHAPTER 33
Gwen

I awaken to soft kisses on my temple. Yawning, I open my eyes and see the most brilliant blue eyes. Niall.

Last night was amazing. As he continues to trail kisses from my temple to my stomach, I'm giddy from everything happening between us.

How comforting and nice is it to sleep in his arms. To be woken up not by an alarm, but from his soft, sweet kisses.

"Time to get up, Gwendolyn," he says, though his eyes are playful as if he wants more. I'm sore from last night, but he looks like he could go again. He was insatiable. We ended up going multiple rounds, and I turned to putty in his hands.

Thank goodness we have a spa day today because I don't know if I'll be good for much else.

"Mmm," I reply, "but this is more ideal."

"You're right, but we have some friends who will be awfully upset if we miss the bachelor and bachelorette parties, don't you think?"

"I guess so," I grumble.

"Hey, none of that. No being Ms. Grumpypants today," he says playfully.

"Are you always this sunshine-and-rainbows in the morning?" I ask.

"Only when I have *mo ghrá* here in my bed looking so soft and kissable," he says, bending down to kiss my neck again.

"What's that? *Mo ghrá*, you've said that multiple times now, but I haven't asked what it means."

"Hmm . . . It's an endearment. I guess the translation would be 'my love.'"

I startle, my jaw dropping at his answer. Chuckling, he reaches over and takes my chin in his hand as he closes my jaw then leans in to kiss me.

"Let's get cleaned up, and then we can meet up with the others at breakfast."

I nod, watching him as he gets out of bed. My cheeks instantly flush and my mouth runs dry. Damn, is he a fine specimen of a man. How the heck does he look so delicious first thing in the morning? His hair is askew, so different from the toned features of the rest of his body. I've never been much of a morning person, but honestly, Niall might turn me into one if I keep getting to wake up to this view. After turning on the shower, he walks back to the bed and leans over me. "You coming?" he asks.

"Yes," I reply, moving the covers off and taking his hand in mine.

To start off the bachelor and bachelorette party days, we have a combined escape game before the two groups split up for the rest of the day. Niall and I make our way to the escape room lobby to find the others already there, including Bradley and Tammy.

Seeing everyone grouped together has me thinking about the predicament I've put Niall and myself in. Bradley and Tammy think we're a couple (and now we actually are), but no one else knows. I've filled Holly and Margot in a bit, but they don't know the full extent of our relationship.

Now we have to pretend to be a couple in front of Bradley and Tammy, while at the same time making it so that the others don't find out that we are a couple. I can't have Greg finding out about us before I have the chance to tell him we're together. He'd go all older brother on us, and everything would be a mess right before his wedding.

Gwen, how do you plan to pull this off?

CHAPTER 34
Niall

We fill out our waivers as Melvin, the escape room instructor, starts his pre-game spiel: "You've got a great game ahead of you. You have to escape from the designated room in sixty minutes or less to successfully escape. While in the room, you'll be looking for clues and solving puzzles. Anything with the 'do not touch' sign is not part of the game, and we ask that you don't try to use it. Alright, any questions?" Melvin looks around at our group as we shake our heads.

"This is going to be so much fun," says Holly, bouncing up and down on her feet.

"Definitely," exclaims Margot. "It was a great idea to start off our bachelor and bachelorette parties this way."

Melvin leads us into what looks like a mission control room at NASA. After we watch a brief intro video, Melvin releases us and the countdown to escape is on.

"Look, here's a lock with a four-digit number code. Does anyone see anything that could give a number?" Margot asks.

"I don't see any numbers," I say, "but the writing on this whiteboard looks like we're supposed to figure out a word from it."

"Gwen," says Greg, "why don't you go over and see if you can help Niall with that, and Holly and I'll look for the number with Margot." Greg gives me a wink as he not so subtly pushes Gwen in my direction.

"On it," Gwen says. Bradley looks in our direction, and Gwen quickly takes my hand in hers. I'm surprised she's feeling open enough about our relationship to hold my hand in front of all her friends, but then I remember that Bradley and Tammy think we're together.

Right, the boyfriend thing, not that it's fake anymore, but still, have to hold up pretenses. *Oh man, what did you get yourself into, Niall?*

Greg is trying to push Gwen to spend time with me, not knowing that I have spent a lot more time with her than he would probably like. I'm not sure how he's going to handle me being with his sister. Sure, we'd made a pact that I would spend time with her, but Greg made it pretty clear that he didn't want me crossing any lines. Too late for that. . . .

"You two figure anything out yet?" asks Trent, moving over next to us. Gwen quickly lets go of my hand, and I notice Bradley furrowing his brow. *I hope he didn't catch that.* How are we going to get through this game with so many different people knowing, or at least thinking they know, what is going on between Gwen and me? This is going to be a long sixty minutes. . . .

"The word is Galaxy!" says Gwen excitedly, punching the letters into the keyboard. A buzzing sounds, and a hidden wall opens up to a small space.

"Great job," says Vivian.

"Gwen," says Greg, "you, Niall, Gillian, and Miles crawl through and tell us what you find. I think we've almost got this code."

"Yeah," agrees Holly, "we're just missing this one number here."

I get down on all fours and crawl through a secret passage, Gwen, Miles, and Gillian following behind me. Once on the other side, I reach out my hand to help Gwen up. She takes it, lingering a bit longer than she needs to until Miles pops his head out. Noticing our intertwined fingers, Miles looks at us quizzically. I quickly drop Gwen's hand and reach for a lever. When I pull it, a part of the wall the size of a door opens up, and the others walk through with ease.

Bradley and Tammy are the first through. I put my hand on Gwen's waist, guiding her out of the way of the door.

"Looks like there's a formula over here," says Trent, who followed Bradley and Tammy through. Gwen steps to the side before Trent notices my hand on her and makes her way over with Bradley to try to work out the formula.

"Four, the number is four," says Bradley. Gillian runs back over to Holly and Greg through the open part of the wall and tells them the number.

"Great job," Gwen tells Bradley. He nods before looking for the next puzzle to solve.

We finish after fifty-nine minutes and twenty-three seconds and have one clue left to spare. When the door unlocks and the television announces that we've escaped, I wrap Gwen's hand in mine. I'm so ecstatic at winning and wrecked from all the secretiveness that I'm not thinking straight. I twirl her around to face me and pick her up. She reaches her arms around my neck and gives me a not-so-friends-only kiss. My heart races as I kiss her back.

"Gwen?" Greg says, his voice stern, sharp. "Niall? What is going on?"

We both freeze then break apart as we remember the rest of the group standing all around us. I close my eyes and squeeze her hand in mine, not able to let go of her.

"I guess it's no longer our secret," I say.

"I think you're right," she says softly.

"I knew there was something going on with you two," says Miles.

I take in the rest of the group. Margot is giving me a huge grin, while Holly wears a soft smile. Trent seems happily surprised, and Bradley and Tammy's faces are etched with confusion. Everyone else seems not too phased, but my heart drops to the floor when I see the look on Greg's face. It's the one I had been dreading seeing. And on the bachelor party day of all days. *Feck, Niall, way to pick the most inopportune time to forget yourself and blow your secret.*

Gwen, silent, glances up at me, and I turn and give her a lopsided grin.

"Well, this should make for an interesting day," I say.

CHAPTER 35
Gwen

"Gwen?" Greg says again, his voice even more stern than before. "Will you please explain what the hell is going on?"

I turn to face him, but Holly grabs my arm, pulling me away from Niall and toward her. "Oh, would you look at that, we're going to be late for the spa if we don't go now."

"Yep," Margot says, taking my other arm in hers. "Come on, ladies, we have to leave. See you all later!" Margot waves to the guys as we turn away and head toward the elevators.

I glance back just in time to see Greg glaring at Niall and Trent smiling and patting Greg on the back.

I hope Niall will be okay back there.

After the three of us get on an elevator, Holly says, "I know I just saved your butt, but I also want to know what is going on."

"I was going to tell you both," I say. "I really was, but I didn't want to take away from the wedding."

"So?" says Margot, gesturing for me to continue.

"Niall and I decided to give it a go."

Margot squeals. "I knew it!"

"I'm happy for you," says Holly, giving me a wide smile. "You deserve it."

"Thank you," I say. "I just hope I haven't ruined Greg's bachelor party."

"No way," says Holly. "He's going to be a grumpy over-protective brother for like five minutes, then he will see how amazing you two are for each other, and things will go back to normal. Plus, there is no way your joy could take away from our wedding. We love you and only want good things for you. Your happiness makes us happy."

"Thanks, Holly," I say as tears brim in my eyes. "You two are the best."

Margot waves her hand at me. "Yeah, I know we are. I'm so happy for you too. I've been rooting for you two to get together since this cruise started."

"You have?" I ask.

"Of course!" she says. "Anyone could see your chemistry a mile away. The real question, though, is what's the plan for after the cruise."

"After the cruise?" I ask.

"Yeah," says Holly, "how are you guys going to make the long-distance thing work?" The elevator comes to a stop, and we all shuffle out.

"I haven't . . ." I say, "we haven't talked about it."

Niall is such a good man. He's so good to me. I can't help but smile just thinking about him. McHottie isn't just a flirt with an accent and a nice body. He's the whole package. And I get him all to myself.

Well, at least for this cruise anyway. I have no idea what is going to happen after, and that scares me.

We greet the other women outside the spa. I take a deep breath and release the tension of not knowing what will happen between me and Niall when the cruise is over. For now, it's my best friend's bachelorette party, and I'll focus on pampering her.

"You ready for this, Holly?" Margot asks.

"More than ready!" Holly says.

I open the door to the spa and say, "Welcome to your bachelorette party spa day!"

As we step into the tranquil spa, we are greeted with the soothing ambiance. Soft, calming music floats through the speakers, and a gentle floral fragrance hangs in the air.

Our day of pampering begins with rejuvenating massages, pulling us into a state of bliss. The skilled hands of the masseuses work their magic, melting away my wedding-planning and long-distance-dating stress. By the end of the massage, there isn't an ounce of tension left in my body.

Following our massages, we move on to manicures and pedicures. Here we are treated like royalty, the manicurists offering us champagne in beautiful crystal flutes. All of us are seated side by side in plush massage chairs as we sink our feet into the warm, bubbling water with flower petals.

A ding has me glancing at my phone. Gillian, who is seated next to me on one side, glances over and teasingly asks, "Is that who I think it is?"

I unlock my phone and open up the cruise app. It's Niall. "Yes," I say. I can't help the wide smile that spreads across my face.

NIALL

How's your spa day going?

GWEN

Great, and your bachelor party? Is Greg upset about earlier?

NIALL

Good, just finished our second round of basketball with some other guys who were on the course. Heading off to the sports bar for some billiards and beer in a bit. And honestly, he hasn't said anything to me yet. I just wanted to check in on you.

GWEN

That's sweet. I'm doing fine here Holly and Margot were happy to hear we are together. And now that we're at the spa, I've been calming down and relaxing.

NIALL

Didn't I do a pretty good job of that myself last night?

I blush at the memories.

GWEN

You're so bad. I'm going now, they're about to start on my nails.

NIALL

Until later Mo Ghra.

The manicurists and pedicurists meticulously shape, buff, and paint our nails to perfection. Laughter and lively chatter fill the air as Mom and Mrs. Palmer go on and on about how they knew one day Holly and Greg would be together.

"Well, I wish you would have told me," says Holly. "It could have saved me years of trouble."

Mrs. Palmer laughs too. "Yes, but honey, if I did, would you have listened?"

Margot and I both chuckle at that. "No," we answer in unison.

"Hey!" says Holly with a laugh.

"Well," says Vivian, "you never did listen to me about him liking you."

"I guess that's true," says Holly.

"It all worked out in the end though," says Mom with a nod.

Between treatments, we lounge in plush robes in the most comfortable chairs imaginable. Our view is breathtaking as the spa overlooks the bow; we see panoramic views of endless ocean in front of us. The natural beauty is a perfect backdrop to our spa day.

"I could just fall asleep here," says Gillian.

"Same," I agree.

Lunch is catered to us, and we dine on a buffet of delicious gourmet food. This is perfect.

CHAPTER 36
Niall

Greg hasn't said a word to me since he caught Gwen and I kissing. I'm relieved to know the girls are on Gwen's side and not giving her a hard time, but the unease between Greg and me is making my nerves shot.

Grabbing a couple beers, we head over to the billiards table. I thought playing basketball would release some of the tension Greg feels toward me, but from the way Greg is looking at me, it clearly hasn't done the trick.

Greg's and Holly's dads sit over at the bar watching one of the games on the television. I look over at Greg, and he's throwing daggers at me with his eyes.

"Please just say what you need to. This silent glaring is killing me, mate," I say.

"Don't give me that 'mate' crap, man," he says angrily, roughly applying the chalk to the cue tip. "I saw you kiss Gwen. We all did." He points to himself, Trent, and Miles.

Trent and Miles both snap their eyes between Greg and me. *Shit's about to hit the fan, mates.*

Gwen and I had been so careful, but then I had to let my emotions overcome my common sense.

"You mean at the escape room?" I ask, trying to make light of things but then quickly realizing my mistake. I don't even know why that came out of my mouth. Clearly, he saw us this morning. Everyone did, and now I've alluded to more. *Why can't a black hole just open up on the floor and swallow me whole?*

"Of course at the escape room!" Then, Greg's eyes grow wide. "What is that supposed to mean? Have you kissed her before then?" He sets the chalk and stick down and leans his arms on the side of the table, quiet and breathing slowly, clearly trying to reign in his temper.

"Dude," says Trent, shaking his head at my daftness. *Yeah, I definitely put my foot in my mouth. Thank you, Trent, for noticing.*

"Well, alright then, this day just got a little more interesting," says Miles before taking a sip of his beer.

Breathing in deeply, Greg raises his head and looks me square in the eyes. "What part about 'not too friendly because she is my little sister' did you not understand?"

I sigh, rubbing my hand over my face. How do I even explain this without giving away the fake-dating agreement I made with Gwen?

"Look—" I start.

"Don't," interrupts Greg.

"Dude," Trent says, patting Greg on the back, "let the man explain. This is Sully, remember?"

Greg nods.

I swallow, giving a grateful look to Trent, who steps back and leans against the pool table waiting for my explanation. He gives me a small smile, letting me know to continue.

"Look, you asked me to be friendly with Gwen. Well, I was," I say, holding up a finger as Greg opens his mouth to say something.

"Please let me explain. You're like brothers to me. I would never intentionally do anything to ruin that. But please trust me when I say I never intended for anything to happen with Gwen. She's just . . . remarkable. She's funny and witty, grumpy and sweet, feisty and caring, and feck is she beautiful. It wasn't hard for me to fall in love with her."

All three of them snap their eyes to me.

"Love?" asks Trent.

"Did you just say you fell in love with her?" asks Greg.

Even though I'm admitting it for the first time out loud, nothing I have ever said before has felt this right.

I love Gwen.

She's everything and more than I even have words for. I've never felt so much for someone as I do for her. I crave her smile. Her grumpiness makes me laugh. She's everything to me.

"I did," I answer honestly.

"Wow," says Miles.

"Dude, that's huge," says Trent. "Greg, go easy on him. Remember how hard it was for you to tell Gwen how you felt about Holly."

Greg sighs, placing his hands behind his head. "Does she feel the same way?" he asks, a little of his anger dissipating.

"She's not said the words. Hell, I've only just said it out loud for the first time. But I can tell you that we are officially together."

Greg nods, then asks, "And after the cruise? What happens then?"

"I don't know. We haven't discussed past the end of the trip yet, but I want more with her. A few days just isn't enough."

"Long distance is hard," says Greg.

"I know."

"You have a career and a home in Boston. And Gwen has hers in Chessie Valley. She's not just going to up and leave her business, you know. She's becoming one of the most sought-after event planners in Middle Tennessee."

"I'd never ask her to leave or to change," I say adamantly.

"So," says Trent, "where does that leave things?"

"I have no idea," I admit. The question settles like a weight on my heart.

"You better figure it out soon," says Greg. "And you better not break her heart."

The guys nod in agreement.

After we shoot a few rounds of billiards, Greg's and Holly's dads join us for darts. The older men smoke us almost embarrassingly. We have burgers and beers for lunch, and Greg seems to have recovered from the shock of seeing Gwen and I kiss. He's back to his normal self in no time

"Man, I'm getting married to Holly tomorrow," Greg says. "Somebody pinch me."

Trent happily pinches Greg's arm.

Greg yelps. "What the hell, man!"

"You said to pinch you." Trent shrugs. "So I did."

"Believe it, mate," I say. "you're marrying your childhood crush tomorrow on a beautiful cruise ship overlooking endless seas of blue, with your best mates by your side cheering you on." I hold up my beer in salute, and we all cheer.

But there is a heavy feeling in my chest the rest of the afternoon. What's going to happen with Gwen and me once this cruise is over?

CHAPTER 37
Gwen

I'm relaxing in my room going over last-minute items with Courtney on the phone when a knock sounds at my door. Hope at seeing Niall surges through me before I realize the knocking is coming from the hallway door, not our shared door.

"One moment, Courtney, let me get this," I say into the phone, then hold it against my chest as I open the door to see Trent.

"Hey, Gwen," Trent says, looking sheepish. "How are you?"

"What's wrong, Trent? What's happened?"

"Well, you know how I was responsible for holding onto the rings?"

"Yes. . . ." I say, my nerves spiking.

"Well, I seem to have misplaced them."

"Excuse me? You. Lost. Them?" I ask through gritted teeth. "As in *the* wedding rings? As in the rings that Greg and Holly need to get married tomorrow?"

"Well," he says, taking a step back, "I misplaced them."

"Then I suggest you un-misplace them. The wedding is tomorrow, Trent. Tomorrow!!"

"Right, okay, I will go recheck my things," he says, stepping back into the hallway just as I register the sound of Courtney's voice coming through my phone.

"Gwen?" she says. "Can you hear me?"

I had completely forgotten she was still waiting on me. I pick up the phone and say, "One minute, Courtney."

Then turning my focus back to Trent, I say, "I suggest you turn your room inside out. Check everything and everywhere even if it doesn't make sense. And please tell me the moment you find them, and not a word to anyone in the meantime, got it? I'll figure something out as a backup plan."

"Gwen?" asks Courtney through the phone. "What's happened? Anything I can help with?" I put my phone back up to my ear, Trent eyeing me warily.

"Actually, yes, we do have a problem. Trent is here and has just informed me that he's lost the engraved wedding rings." I send another glare in Trent's direction.

"Oh," says Courtney, "that is a bit of a situation. How about I help him look for those rings?"

"That would be great," I say. "I'll help you look too."

"And," says Courtney, "there are a few places on the ship where we can get backup rings if we don't end up finding the original ones."

"Okay, good," I say. "The rings are engraved though. If we do have to get new rings, we'd need to make sure they're engraved too."

"That shouldn't be a problem," says Courtney. "Would you text me what the engravings are in case we have to go that route?"

"Yes, I'll send you a text right now." After sending the text, I say, "Thank you, Courtney. I appreciate your help with this."

"My pleasure," says Courtney. "Tell Trent I'll be over there shortly."

I shut the door after relaying the message and hanging up with Courtney. Ugh, please let this be the only thing that goes wrong today.

I'm just about to leave with Trent to search for the rings when Gillian rounds the corner looking a little worried.

"Hey, Gwen. Hey, Trent," she says. "Gwen, do you have a second?"

"Yes," I say. Then I turn to Trent. "You go ahead and meet up with Courtney. I'll be there in a minute."

Trent nods and heads to his room.

"What's going on?" I ask Gillian.

"I have some bad news," she says.

"Are you feeling okay?" I ask, worried that something is wrong with the baby.

"Oh yes, I'm fine, but Maggie isn't. She isn't feeling well. She's laying down in our room now, but I'm pretty sure she has a fever, and she's as pale as a ghost."

"Oh no, poor Maggie. Okay, one moment, I think I have something you can try." I leave the door to my room open as I rush and grab my emergency bag.

"Thanks, Gwen," says Gillian. "I'm hoping it's just a bug and she'll be good for the wedding tomorrow, but there is no way she'll be able to make it to the rehearsal dinner tonight."

I pause momentarily at her statement. It hadn't even occurred to me that Maggie wouldn't make the rehearsal dinner. And if she doesn't feel better soon, that would mean that she'd miss the wedding too.

"No worries," I tell Gillian, trying to hide the tension in my voice. *What are we going to do if there's no flower girl at the wedding?* "Here is some Tylenol and Ibuprofen, as well as a thermometer. You can order room service and get some apple juice or Powerade. I believe they have it in those little drink dispensers in Duke's Diner and outside the pizzeria."

"I'll keep you updated," says Gillian. "Either Miles or me will come to the rehearsal dinner to see what Maggie needs to do during the wedding, in case she does feel up to going, but the other is going to stay with her."

"Of course," I say, leaning in to give her a hug. "Let me know if you all need anything else."

She nods then heads back to her room.

Well, all the relaxation I felt at the spa is now gone. Now I need to figure out a backup plan in case there is no flower girl. I pull out my phone and text Courtney.

GWEN

> Something else came up. Are you and Trent ok to look for the rings?

My stress level is through the roof as I pace around my room trying to think. After a few minutes, my phone vibrates, and I check my texts.

COURTNEY

> Of course, I can handle the rings. You take care of whatever you need to.

I'm taking a few breaths trying to calm myself when another knock sounds at my door. If someone else is coming with more bad news, I might just lose it.

I swing open the door, almost hitting Niall with it.

"Whoa, you're going to take someone out with that swing," Niall says. Then, seeing my face, he asks, "What's wrong? Talk to me."

"It's nothing I can't handle," I say as I turn away from the door.

Niall follows me inside, and we both sit on the couch.

His warm hands tilt my head in his direction.

"Gwendolyn, whatever it is, I'm not going to leave you alone. You're clearly in bits about something and I'd like to help you."

"You don't even know what's wrong," I say. "Everything's just falling apart."

"Why don't you tell me what's going on? Then we will figure out how to fix it, together. Come here, *mo ghrá.*"

I turn from Niall, my shoulders slumping as my eyes well up with tears. I should have focused more on the wedding. I should have been double-checking everything. No, triple-checking.

Before I can stop him, Niall scoops me up and pulls me into his lap. I curl in against his chest and allow myself to be held. Niall, who was a stranger to me only a handful of days ago, now feels like such an important part of my life.

He hugs me, and it's a hug that makes me feel cared for, so full of warmth and understanding, a sanctuary amidst the chaos of my emotions.

His strong hands stroke up and down my back, providing me with a sense of security, a sense of calm. He's so tender, not saying anything and just letting me feel.

Time seems to stand still as we stay like this. There are things I need to get done, things that need to be fixed, but in this moment with this amazing man, I am safe to just be.

As my tears begin to dry and my breathing settles, Niall asks, "Gwendolyn, how can I help you?"

"I don't know. Holly and Greg's wedding is all messed up." I wipe the tears from my cheeks.

"What do you mean? Surely, they are still getting married."

"Hopefully," I say, then mumble, "no thanks to me."

"Rose, look at me," he says sternly.

I look up at him and blurt, "It's true. Their wedding isn't going to be perfect, and it's all my fault."

"Why don't you start with filling me in on what is meant to be your fault?" he asks, his eyes softening.

"Well for starters, Maggie is sick and may not be able to come to the wedding, which means that either Gillian or Miles may not be able to come. Then there's freaking Trent, who has somehow managed to freaking lose the freaking wedding rings."

"Well, those don't sound too bad," Niall says through soft chuckles.

"Excuse me?" I shoot up off his lap. "This is a nightmare. I should have kept Maggie with me instead of letting her stay at kids club all day. That's probably where she got sick. And I should have kept hold of the rings. I never would have lost them. Holly and Greg had these rings specially made, and they had quotes engraved on them. They aren't something that can easily be replaced."

I start pacing around the room. How can Niall think this isn't a big deal?

It's Holly and Greg. They deserve the best.

"I've spent too much time with you," I tell Niall. "And I've let myself get distracted. I should have just focused on the wedding and made sure everything was perfect for Holly and Greg."

"Now, Rose—"

"Don't 'Rose' me," I say angrily. "You don't understand."

"I didn't say that it didn't sound too bad to make you upset. I simply meant that as long as Holly and Greg still get married, then that is the most important thing. Everything else we can fix. It may not be perfect according to the original plans, but it will still be a perfect day."

I stop pacing. He's right. Of course, he's right. I just like things to be perfect. For things to go according to plan. If I have everything figured out and all possible issues planned for, then nothing bad can ever happen.

Niall sits on the couch calmly, his eyes full of hope and happiness.

The look stops me in my tracks.

"Okay." I sigh. "Help me figure out how to fix this?"

"Well, for starters, I can be the flower girl," he says happily.

I let out a laugh. "No really, what is your plan?" I ask.

"I am serious. Haven't you seen those videos where the groom's brothers or someone like that are the flower girls, and they have these bum bags with flower petals and sunglasses on? I could definitely do that."

I pinch the bridge of my nose. This is not helping, and while that sounds hilarious, it's annoying because it cannot be the best option we have. "No."

"Okay, what if Vivian stands in for the flower girl? She's not a bridesmaid, but she could be a flower lady?" Niall offers.

"It's not the worst suggestion you've given," I agree. "I'll have to talk to her about it. Now for the rings, Courtney is meeting up with Trent to try and help him find them."

"*Cúla búla*, for the rings, then, that one is resolved. Courtney won't let Greg and Holly get married without rings. With her on this task, you don't have to worry, right?" He looks up at me hopefully.

"That . . . that is true."

"And you told her about the engravings, right?"

"Yes."

"Okay, then rest easy knowing Courtney is on it. It's literally her job to make sure cruise weddings go off without a hitch. I'm sure this isn't the first time something like this has happened. She's got it."

I smile, starting to feel a little better about the situation and also a little bad about biting Trent's head off, though I'm sure he understands.

Considering it is just the rehearsal dinner tonight, we don't have to have either the flower girl or the rings with us. We still have some time before the wedding.

When it's finally time for the rehearsal, I'm feeling much calmer. I am still hoping that Maggie feels better and Trent finds the rings, but I know we have backup plans. For now, I'll just focus on the rehearsal.

The rest of the evening goes off without a hitch. The bridesmaids and groomsmen don't actually walk in, so we stand at the front near the alter. The flower girl would enter first; Gillian is filling in for this part. She said Maggie is asleep and seems to have broken her fever, so that's a good sign.

Mr. Kenton and Holly walk in, and even though it's just the rehearsal, I'm tearing up along with our parents.

Knowing everything Holly went through, I couldn't be happier for her.

As much as I love to tease him, Greg is such a good guy and loves her with his whole heart. Holly deserves nothing less.

I look at the groomsmen and catch Niall looking at me. His gaze is heated, even though the night air is cool, and a shiver goes through me as goosebumps race up my arms. A bump from my right has me glancing over at Margot.

"That is the look of someone who is head over heels for you," she says.

"You think so?" I whisper to Margot.

"I do."

"We haven't talked about what will happen with us after the cruise," I tell her, "and after Bradley, I'm not getting my hopes up. Not again."

She nods and whispers back, "Well, don't let the mistakes of the past keep you from potentially great things in the future. You deserve all this too."

I nod in agreement. I do deserve happiness and a man who loves me for all of me. I just don't know how we are going to make this work when I live in Tennessee and he lives hours away in Boston. What would we do about our jobs, our homes, our friends? Would we be too busy to even spend time together?

Nope, not going to think about it right now. Focus on the wedding, then after that, you can have a mini freakout.

CHAPTER 38
Niall

After the rehearsal, it's late. It looks like everyone is heading to their rooms. But I notice Gwen head another direction.

Catching up to her, I ask, "You're not heading to bed?"

"No, not yet. My nerves are still a little on edge, so I thought I'd go to the piano bar and listen to them play." She taps her phone and turns it for me to see. "They should start in less than thirty minutes according to the events list."

I nod. "Care for a bite of pizza? I could pick some up and meet you at the piano bar?"

"I'm always up for some pizza."

After picking up a couple slices for each of us, I meet up with Gwen at a table a few feet away from the piano.

I sit next to her and hand her a plate full of pizza. "Hope this helps," I say. The fact that she was in bits when things started to go wrong for her best friend and brother shows a lot about the type of person she is. She would do anything for the people she cares about.

But who takes care of her? *I am going to.*

"Pizza always helps," Gwen says, picking up a particularly cheesy slice.

"And," I add, "I hope it helps to know that Greg isn't upset anymore."

"Really?" she asks, surprised.

"Yeah, Greg, Trent, and I talked."

"Oh," she says, eyeing me tentatively.

"I had to tell him we were officially together, but he was understanding after that."

"That's sounds like it went better than I thought it would. When I found out about him and Holly, I lashed out at him; I was pretty angry. I'm surprised he didn't act similarly."

I wince a little at her comment but decide not to give her the full details of Greg's reaction.

"Well, at least they know about us now," she says.

"Yeah, no more secrets," I agree.

A man starts playing the piano as Gwen and I finish our pizzas. "I love listening to the piano," says Gwen.

"Maybe I could play you something," I offer.

"You play the piano?"

"I do. My mam always loved the piano, so she had me take lessons growing up. I still fiddle around with it every now and again."

"I'd love that."

I stand and walk over to ask the man playing the piano if I could play a song.

After he agrees, I glance over at Gwen and adjust the piano bench to sit. Her eyes are as round as saucers, watching my every move.

Before I know which song I'm going to play, my fingers make up their own mind and begin playing "Kiss from a Rose" by Seal. As I play, I start humming along.

Gwen's eyes are locked on mine and I only have eyes for her. Continuing to play, I sing to her. She's my rose, my everything, *mo anam cara.*

As the song ends, the bar erupts in applause. I smile, shake the hand of the original piano player, and make my way over to Gwen.

"That was beautiful," she says as I sit down next to her.

At the start of the next song, Gwen leans in close to me, and I wrap my hand over her shoulder.

"Thank you for how kind you've been to me this week," she says. "I know I've mostly been a jerk and get frustrated so easily."

"You don't have to thank me, and you haven't been a jerk," I reply.

"Yeah right."

Shaking my head, I say, "No really, it's a stressful week. Anyone would be flustered under the same circumstances. I just hope you've had a bit of *craic* this week, because I know I have. I'm not looking forward to the cruise being over."

"I've had fun. Honestly, I think this is the most fun I've had in a long time."

I grasp her hand in mine. She stills slightly, but after a moment, she gives my hand a slight squeeze. That squeeze has my heart doing the same. I don't know what it is with this beautiful lass, but she means so much to me.

So much that you're willing to uproot your life?

I think about what all I'd be giving up if I decided to leave Boston so we didn't have to date long distance. And if this is going where I hope it's going, I wouldn't want to be far apart from her for long. I'd have to leave the firehouse I've come to know as family. It would be difficult, but they'd understand. After all, they'd been rooting for me to find someone on this cruise, and I did. With my occupation, I'd be able to find a job in Tennessee fairly easily. The only other thing I'd be leaving behind is my childhood home. It's the only thing I have left of my mam. Leaving that home would be one of the hardest things I'd have to do.

I glance over at Gwen then give her a kiss on the head. She looks up at me and smiles, her features softening as her eyes sparkle.

"Come with me?" she asks, biting her lip and looking down at our entwined hands.

We walk back to our rooms, and as soon as we are outside our doors, I back her up against the wall. With my free hand, I lift her chin, holding her face in the palm of my hand while rubbing my thumb over the side of her face. As a rush of need courses through me, I press my lips to hers. She immediately kisses back, and I let out a groan at her passion.

She starts undoing the buttons of my shirt. Voices down the hall remind me that we should go in one of our rooms. Never letting go of her, I gently pull us through my doorway and onto my bed.

CHAPTER 39
Gwen

The stars twinkle outside as I lie on the bed next to a sleeping Niall. How is this man so perfect? Why couldn't we have met when we weren't on a time crunch? Once the cruise is over, he is going back to Boston, and I'll be heading back home to Chessie Valley. He has a home, a life, in Boston, and I have my business to run back in Tennessee.

I can't settle my mind. What's going to happen with Niall and me once the cruise is over? At the thought of us going our own ways, I am engulfed with so many emotions: sadness, hope, worry, anticipation, confusion, a lightness I can't describe. Could this be love?

No, this is too fast. I must be feeling something else. I'm not going to let myself fall for someone this fast.

Who am I kidding? I am in love with Niall.

I toss and turn all night, watching as the midnight blue of the sky retreats with the stars. The sun crests over the horizon, a new day bringing fresh beginnings.

Glancing over at Niall, so serene in sleep, I reach over and gently move his hair out of his face.

"Morning, *mo ghrá*," he murmurs, even before opening his eyes.

My heart skips a beat at his use of the Irish word *love*. It's just an Irish thing, right? He can't possibly love me so soon too.

Rolling over, Niall kisses me gently on the lips, a hint of desire in his eyes. A sweeping tornado of need suddenly passes through me, shocking me to my core. I kiss him back, setting aside my thoughts and swirling emotions about what will happen to us after the cruise. Right now, I am cared for. Right now, I am his.

The day seems to pass by in one breath. It's late afternoon, and I'm dressed in my bridesmaid dress and checking on some last-minute features in the reception room.

We have one hour until the wedding is set to begin.

Gillian and Maggie walk up to me. Maggie shows no sign of the sickness that kept her down half the day yesterday. "Feeling better?" I ask.

"Yes, thank goodness," says Gillian.

"Auntie Gwen, look at my beautiful dress!" Maggie spins around, her dress twirling around her. She is an adorable flower girl, dressed up in a puffy white dress with a pink ribbon around her waist and a matching one in her hair.

"You look so pretty, Maggie. You're going to be the most beautiful flower girl ever."

"I know," she replies.

"Come on, honey," Gillian says as she takes Maggie's hand in hers. "Auntie Gwen has to finish making sure everything is ready."

One problem solved. We have a flower girl. Check. Now, if only we could find the rings.

"Gwen!" Trent shouts my name from across the room. My stomach drops for a moment, unsure if it's good news or bad. I brace for the worst.

As I turn around, I'm greeted by Trent's smile. A smiling Trent can only mean . . .

"We found the rings!" Trent announces as he jogs up to me.

Overcome with happiness, I fling my arms around his neck and kiss his cheek. "That's excellent news," I exclaim, excitement pouring out of me as Trent spins me around, his smile stretching all the way up to his eyes.

Setting me down, he says, "I know, I was so stressed out yesterday, but Courtney helped me tear my room apart. She found them in my dress shoes. I forgot I'd put the ring boxes in there so I wouldn't forget them when I got dressed this morning."

I'm not sure if I want to hug him again or smack him. I'm just so relieved they found the rings. "Courtney saved the day!" I say.

"She sure did," agrees Trent.

"Thank you. Now go finish getting dressed. We've got a wedding to put on."

I find Courtney and thank her for finding the rings. Then, we go over more last-minute details. After, I make a final lap around the wedding space. It's one of my simpler designs, but even so, it's magical.

As I walk into Holly's room, the sound of crying immediately hits me. I rush in to find Holly in tears.

"What's wrong?" I ask, looking over at Margot and Mrs. Palmer, who've been helping Holly get ready.

"I can't find it. Everything is ruined," she sobs.

I scan the room trying to figure out what is missing. I see her dress, a gorgeous Oleg Cassini, off-the-shoulder, beaded lace mermaid wedding dress hanging up on a hook on the wall. Her ballet flats and bouquet sit waiting for her on the side table.

Kneeling down in front of her, I take her hands in mine. "Hols, what can't you find??"

"My wedding vows, G. I wrote them down, and I know I packed them, but I can't find them. And I was too nervous that I would forget them if I tried to memorize them that I didn't even try."

"Oh, well Holly, no worries. Remember when I made you and Greg send me your vows?"

She nods, wiping a tear from her eye, "Well, I always make a copy of the vows for my brides and grooms just in case this type of thing happens. You can use my copy."

"Really?" she squeaks, tears of happiness now falling like waterfalls down her face.

"Yes, now let's freshen up your makeup, get you into that gorgeous dress over there, and then get you married to my brother. How does that sound?"

"That sounds amazing. Thank you, G. I don't know what I'd do without you!" I give her one more hug and step back as Margot comes armed with makeup.

Finally, the evening arrives. The deck is lit up in strings of lights with a spotlight shining down the aisle. Greg and the groomsmen look dashing in their tuxes—Greg with a dark pink tie and boutonniere, and the groomsmen with matching pink vests. Niall looks handsome, and it's hard to keep my eyes off him, but he's not my main focus right now.

After the bridesmaids walk in, the music changes, preparing for the bride. The anticipation in the air is palpable, a mix of excitement and nerves. Glancing over at Greg, he's fidgeting, waiting for the moment he gets to see his bride.

I'm filled with a sense of rightness. I'm so happy for my brother, who deserves someone amazing, and for Holly, who deserves the love and respect of a real man, someone who will treat her right and show his love for her in every interaction they share. Plus, I'm excited that my best friend, who has always felt like a sister, will actually be my sister in a few minutes.

Finally, it's time. Holly walks around the corner with her dad.

Greg gasps at his beautiful bride. Her gown is a masterpiece of beaded lace, her long train flowing elegantly behind her. Her veil, delicately held in place by a simple tiara, adds an air of timeless beauty to her look.

In all my years of knowing Holly, I've never seen her as happy as she is in this moment. Her eyes, sparkling with joy and love, are locked on Greg's. A quick glance at Greg allows me to catch the moment a tear rolls down his cheek. The same joy and adoration echoes off his face. The rest of the world seems to fade away, leaving only the two of them in an eternal moment of connection.

Holly continues her slow approach, each step sure and graceful, deliberate with every second of her walk. The gentle sea breeze plays with her veil and train. The light catches on the beads, the shimmering adding a touch of magic to this moment. The ocean behind her has a gorgeous array of colors, the sunset appearing like a painting on a canvas. The moment couldn't have been more perfect.

As Mr. Palmer puts Holly's hand in Greg's and steps back, I glance at Niall and find him watching me. The smile on his lips causes my face to heat. Turning my attention back to the bride and groom, I watch as their two lives become one. As they start their life as husband and wife.

CHAPTER 40
Niall

As Gwen first walked in, I was left speechless—not that I'm the one who will need to be talking anytime soon, but she's a vision. Her dress, with a lace cutout and one shoulder bare, shows off her midriff and toned arms. She's beautiful in the dark pink that matches the groomsmen vest that I'm wearing. One look at her and my worry about what I need to do after this cruise is long gone. I'd do anything for Gwen. And now that I've fulfilled my mam's promise of finding someone I want to be with, she'd kick my arse if I didn't follow through with it.

Yes, Holly is a beautiful bride, but I can't keep my eyes off Gwen during the whole ceremony. Afterward, she's hard to get a hold of, as she's making sure everything is set for the small wedding reception that we're having in a banquet room.

Following the rest of the wedding party, I make my way through the buffet. With my food in hand, I look around for Gwen. She's sitting at a table looking a bit melancholy.

"Hey, Rose," I say as I set my plate down to sit in the seat next to her. "The wedding was class."

"Hmm? Oh, yeah. It was beautiful. Holly is gorgeous, isn't she? And Greg, did you see he teared up when Holly walked in?"

The words Gwen is saying make it seem like everything is fine, but something is off with her. Not even me using my nickname for her is riling her up.

"It was a beautiful wedding. So, why are you not yourself?"

Her eyes search mine. I don't know what she's looking for but whatever it is, I hope she finds it.

She's quiet for a moment, then says, "I'm not ready to get back to real life."

"What do you mean get back to real life? This is real life."

"No, I mean, yes, it is real life, but it's not at the same time, you know? I mean, when the cruise is over, we have to go back to our homes, back to our jobs and life as . . . normal, like before."

Holly and Greg start off the dancing with their first dance. Seeing my mate happy makes me happy. After years of loving Holly, he can finally call her his wife. But I don't know how he waited for so long.

One week with Gwen has me seeing life in a whole new perspective.

"Want to dance?" I ask Gwen, putting my hand out to her.

A small smile lights up her face. "Sure."

As others fill in on the dance floor and the songs change between romantic and fast-paced, I keep Gwen laughing song after song. The happiness radiating from her makes my soul feel full.

The band takes a break, and it's announced that Holly is going to throw the bouquet and all the single women need to stand on the dance floor. Even though she's the event planner, Gwen's also part of the wedding, so she cannot skirt this tradition no matter how hard she tries to convince me.

"Nope," I say. "It's tradition and you wouldn't want to break tradition."

She mumbles as she makes her way to the dance floor.

Holly stands in front of the group. There are about ten women out there including little Maggie. With a light toss, the bouquet lands directly in Gwen's hands. Everyone cheers and many women congratulate Gwen.

Well alright then, another sign from Mam.

CHAPTER 41
Gwen

Catching the bouquet doesn't mean anything. Right? It's not like these flowers can tell Niall and me how to make us work after the cruise.

Tammy walks up to me. "Looks like a good sign for you and Niall's future," she says, nodding to the flowers.

"Umm, thanks, Tammy," I reply.

"Hey, Gwen," she continues. "I know things have been a bit weird with, well, me and Bradley being here, but I just wanted to let you know he thinks highly of you, even after how things ended. And personally, I think you are an amazing event planner, I saw the wedding from a distance, and it was beautiful, and this reception is just so magical."

"Thank you, that was very kind."

"I will be sure to tell all my friends and coworkers about your event-planning business," Tammy says cheerily.

"Thank you, Tammy."

Bradley walks over to us and whispers something to Tammy. She nods then heads off, leaving Bradley alone with me.

"Gwen?" Bradley asks.

"Yeah?" I say.

"I wonder if I could have a word?"

I notice that Niall is immediately on alert, but I give him a small smile letting him know I'm okay.

"Sure."

"You really do have a knack for event planning," Bradley starts.

"Oh, umm. Thank you?" I say. *Is this really what he wants to talk to me about?*

"Look I know me being here with Tammy is so crazy, but I wanted to say thank you for letting us join in on the activities this week. I'm sorry if me being here upset you. But I'm glad that it's given me a chance to say something I should have said a long time ago, I'm sorry for the way I handled everything when we broke up. I wasn't a supportive boyfriend, and my communication skills were definitely lacking."

"Thank you," I say. "That means a lot. And I want to let you know that you were right. I did put my job before our relationship. I'm sorry I didn't see what was happening and played a part in letting things get out of control. You're a good guy, Bradley. Not the guy for me, but a good guy, and seeing you with Tammy this week has opened my eyes to the fact that we were better off as friends. You seem to really love her."

"I do," he agrees. "And he seems to really love you." He motions over to Niall.

"Yeah," I say, unsure how to respond.

We both nod to each other, happy to have the closure, before we go our separate ways. A content sigh escapes me as I watch him walk away. *I really am happy for them.*

Reaching Niall and gesturing to the bouquet, I say, "Not a word about this."

CHAPTER 42
Niall

"Wouldn't dare," I reply, smiling at her.

Gwen sets the bouquet on the table then heads off to let the DJ know it's time to announce the cake cutting. Holly and Greg make their way over to a beautiful two-tier wedding cake with white roses and pink ribbon spiraling around the cake like a waterfall.

Gwen hands over the knife and cake server to the couple.

"You ready?" asks Holly.

"Definitely," replies Greg as he places his hand over Holly's and they cut their slice of cake.

Greg nicely places a piece of the cake in Holly's mouth, but Holly smashes her piece into Gregs face. They laugh and then Greg pulls her in for a kiss, rubbing cake all over her face. The crowd cheers and whistles at the kiss.

The rest of the reception goes by in a blur. After the DJ finishes the last song, we line up with our bubbles and send off the bride and groom. Holly and Greg race through the bubbles, everyone cheering and congratulating them. Once everyone starts to trickle out, I spot Gwen chatting with Courtney.

"Thank you, Courtney," she says. "Everything was beautifully done."

I lightly touch Gwen's side to let her know I'm next to her.

"I couldn't have pulled this wedding off without you," Gwen continues.

"It was beautiful," says Courtney. "You have a great vision, Gwen. It was a pleasure to work with you. I will be sure to email you the itemized invoice and receipt once the cruise is over. If you need anything else, please don't hesitate to reach out to me."

"Thanks again, Courtney."

Once Courtney is out of sight, I grab Gwen's hand. "Let's walk."

We end up at the Imperial SkyDeck, a quiet place that will give Gwen time to unwind after pulling off a beautiful wedding. We find a big circular chair and scoot in together. I wrap my arms around her, the night air blowing softly around us, a slight chill to it causing Gwen to shiver slightly. The front of the ship gives a 180-degree view of the ocean beyond. Tonight, the ocean is calm, and the moonlight illuminates the water around us.

"These past few days," I say, wrapping around Gwen more tightly, "have been remarkable."

"They have," says Gwen.

"I don't want them to end."

"Me either." She turns to face me. "But what are we going to do? After the cruise, I mean. How are we going to make this work?"

"We'll travel to visit each other."

"My work is event-based, so it's hard to know when I have time off. I don't want to be a burden if you end up being the one who has to travel the most."

I adjust in our seat slightly, so I'm facing her. "Gwendolyn, look at me. I want you to hear me when I say this. You never have been, nor never will be a burden. Ever. I'd travel every single day if it meant that I could see you if only for a moment."

A soft gasp escapes her parting her lips, and a tear begins to fall slowly down her cheek.

I reach out and wipe away the tear, then stroke the side of her cheek with my thumb. "I know it will be hard, but we are going to figure out a way to make this work."

Another tear slips from her eye, and I lean in to kiss it away. "I want you to come to Boston with me."

CHAPTER 43
Gwen

"What?" I say. "Come to—"

"Boston," Niall finishes. "With me." His eyes shine with something, is that hope? Anticipation?

"When?" I ask, still dumbstruck by what he's asking.

"This weekend," he says. "Take the weekend, come with me to Boston. I'll show you around, and we'll make a trip out of it. You'll see that we can make this last in the 'real world,' as you put it."

"But I can't just up and fly to Boston."

"Why not?"

"I . . ." I start, but what real reason is there? I don't have another event until mid-week next week. I have no plans for when I get home. Do I actually have a reason? No, no I don't. "Okay," I say, finally meeting his eyes.

"Okay?" he asks cautiously.

"Yes, I'll go to Boston with you."

The happiness rolls off him in waves and it brings a smile to my face.

"I want to make this work too," I continue. "I care about you. I can figure out how to run my business and have a relationship. There are others who have done it before me, and surely I can do it if they can. Maybe I can hire an office manager or promote one of my other event planners to a senior role. Something to give me more time to visit with you."

"You've just made me the happiest man, *mo ghrá*." He kisses my head. "You'll see, everything will work out."

There he goes calling me *mo ghrá* again, it sends a thrill through me. Hope floods my senses. *Maybe we can make this work.*

CHAPTER 44
Niall

The next morning's debarkation is a whirlwind of activity. We all leave at the same time, breaking off into groups. Greg and Holly head to the airport for an early flight. They are going up to Vermont to the Kenton family cabin for their honeymoon.

Mr. and Mrs. Kenton leave in their vehicle, as they are driving back to Chessie Valley. Mr. and Mrs. Palmer accompany them after deciding to cancel their flight home in lieu of a road trip.

Everyone else goes to the airport, but at a less hectic pace than Greg and Holly. I'm as happy as a kid on Christmas morning that Gwen is coming back to Boston with me, as my girlfriend.

After arriving in Boston, I don't waste a minute. We load our luggage into my vehicle and go right over to the Revere Beach. The drive into downtown Boston would take too much time, and I want to do as much as possible with Gwen while she's here.

"Where is your favorite spot?" she asks as we walk onto the beach.

"It's just down this path," I say, pointing ahead of us.

"Oh, it's perfect. Let's take a picture," she says, motioning for me to come closer.

I've not done any proper sightseeing in years, and experiencing it through Gwen's eyes keeps a permanent smile on my face.

We grab a bite of clam chowder for an early dinner and then stop by a bakery for one of their delicious cannoli.

"This is seriously the best cannoli I have ever eaten," Gwen says, licking some of the icing off her lips. "Any chance they deliver?"

Laughing, I reach over and help her get the icing she missed. "It is the best. My mam and I would come down here to get a cannoli for every special occasion."

"I would have liked to meet her," Gwen says.

A soft smile spreads across my face. "She would have loved you, *mo ghrá*."

When we walk out of the bakery a few minutes later, Gwen says, "Alright, tour guide, what's next on our list?"

"The firehouse," I say.

"Oh," she says, eyes big as saucers.

"If that's okay?" I ask.

"No, I mean, yes, it's more than okay. I just didn't think, I mean I just thought . . ." she trails off.

"They're going to love you," I say, interlocking our fingers together as I take her hand and bring it to my lips.

Johnny sees us first and practically knocks me over getting to Gwen. "And who is this lovely thing?" he asks.

"Hi, Johnny," I say, trying to hide my grin at his reaction. "This is Gwen. She's my . . . well, she is my girlfriend."

Gwen's eyes meet mine at my statement. It's the first time either of us have said the title aloud, and it feels right.

"Your girlfriend, well hot damn," says Johnny, "that must have been some cruise and some wedding. Lovely to meet you, Gwen."

Some more of the guys and gals on the crew make their way over to us. Gwen gets swept up in a warm welcome from each person. I stand back and greet my brothers and sisters, each one offering me their whispered advice.

"That one's a keeper, Sully," Johnny says, clapping me on the shoulder.

"Don't let her go, man," adds Mitchell.

"She's so sweet, probably too good for you," says Brianna.

"She is too class for me, that is for sure," I agree with her. "And I don't plan on letting her go."

"Is it serious?" asks Mitchell. "I don't think you've ever brought someone to meet us. We were beginning to think you were embarrassed of us or something."

"I've never had someone that makes me feel the way Gwen does," I say. Looking over to where she stands talking to Captain Frank, I add, "I'm hoping it will be serious. But we've got some things to figure out, seeing as she lives in Tennessee and, well, I'm here."

A mixture of shock and sadness fill the faces of my brothers and sisters. A mirror of my own nerves.

Will Gwen want to continue what we have and try things between us long distance? Or is all of this too much? I don't know what will happen between Gwen and me long term, but something in my gut is telling me not to give up.

One thing I know for sure is I'll do just about anything to convince her to stay with me.

CHAPTER 45
Gwen

As we leave the firehouse hand in hand, whistles and catcalls follow us out. Niall shakes his head at the antics of the members at his firehouse crew.

Now, we're heading to his home. The house Niall grew up in. Suddenly, I'm full of nerves. I'd be lying if I said I wasn't excited to see the place he's called home since childhood, but I recognize how important it must be for Niall to share this intimate space with me, the place he shared the last few memories with his mom. Seeing Niall in this house will bring out an aspect of him that I don't think I've seen yet.

Niall leads the way in to his childhood home. Ever the gentleman, he holds the door out for me, allowing me to walk in first.

His home is a charming bungalow-style home, a huge front porch leading into an open concept interior. There are built-in bookshelves on the wall off to the side of the living room holding a myriad of books, pictures, and knick-knacks that have been gathered over the years. The house is quaint, with natural wood accents and exposed rafters. Large windows give it a cozy, natural feel.

"This house is adorable," I say.

"Thanks, not much has changed in it since my childhood except maybe some updated technology and appliances," he says, standing off to the side with his hands in his pockets as he watches me walk around the room.

I smile at him. "Well, it's perfect. I especially love all the pictures of you and your mom here," I say, gesturing to the shelves of framed photos.

He stands next to me and takes a more recent picture of him and his mom off the shelf. "My mam was an amazing woman," he says. "Losing her was like losing my best friend; she was my everything. Since her passing, I've become a shell of myself."

"I can't even imagine how hard that had to be," I say, leaning in to give him a side hug as we both look at the photo.

After setting the picture down on the shelf, Niall walks over to the couch to sit down. I follow and sit next to him.

"Tell me more about her," I say.

"She was amazing. She loved to cook food for anyone who was in need. She was constantly feeding the neighborhood. She was a very observant woman and wise beyond measure. No matter the problem, my mam would have a solution or the right words to say. And she was brilliant. Never have I met someone who could solve the *Wheel of Fortune* puzzle so quickly or answer most of the *Jeopardy!* questions. We'd have weekly picnics at the beach. In the colder months, she'd bring warm Irish potato soup or Dublin Coddle soup. We'd pack it in a thermos and sit wrapped in blankets."

"That sounds amazing."

"Maybe this fall when you come up, we can head over to the beach and have ourselves a picnic," he offers.

"Yes, please. I'd love that." I smile. "Did your mom ever get to meet Greg and Trent?" I ask.

"She did, many times. I'd tell her I was bringing my mates home for the weekend, and she'd cook up a feast."

"Oh, I bet Trent loved that. That man can eat." I laugh, scooting closer to Niall as he pulls a blanket over us.

"He can, but my mam didn't mind. She loved that I brought home friends and loved cooking for them even more. She'd harp on about how they weren't eating enough and told them they were welcome to come over anytime." Niall sighs happily, his expression softening at the memory.

"Seeing your house," I say, "gives me a glimpse into who she was, and she seems like someone I'd have loved to spend time with."

"I'd have loved that," Niall says, then kisses the top of my head.

We lie there on the couch talking, Niall sharing memories of his mom, funny antics from his childhood through college, and life at the firehouse. I look up at another picture of his mom, the woman who raised him to be the man he is today. *You'd be proud of him*, I tell her.

I nod off during a lull in the conversation, and Niall kisses me lightly.

"Come on sleepyhead, let's get you to bed," he teases.

He scoops me up in his arms, blanket included, and I lay my head against his chest. He takes me into his room and lays me on the bed. Moments later, he snuggles in next to me and pulls me in close.

"Sleep well, *mo ghrá*. I love that you're here."

"Me too," I say before drifting off, safe and warm in his arms.

In the morning, I wake up to the bed empty next to me and the smell of coffee. Niall must've gotten up already. I slip out of bed and head to the bathroom. After washing my hands, I splash water on my face in the sink. Something to help wake me up until I've had some of that coffee. I turn off the water to hear Niall moving around downstairs. This all feels so domestic, so easy.

That's how it's been the whole time with Niall and I— easy. We get along really well. He's the happy to my grumpy, always trying to make me laugh and succeeding most of the time. He truly cares about me, and that thought makes my heartbeat quicken in my chest. I want to make this long-distance relationship work. I want to be with him, no matter what that means or where we live or who is traveling where.

When I enter the kitchen, Niall is glancing through the mail on the counter while listening to some voicemails on his phone. He's shirtless with grey sweatpants, and they ride his hips like a model's.

"Morning," I say, giving him a peck on the cheek.

"Morning, beautiful," he says, handing me a steaming mug of coffee.

I take it and slowly sip it while I walk into the other room to look at the pictures on the bookshelves.

Then I recognize Greg's voice coming from Niall's phone.

". . . she seemed so much more herself on the cruise. I'm hoping our little deal did the trick to get her out of her funk. . . ."

What deal? What is Greg talking about? Did Niall tell Greg about our pact, our fake relationship? I walk into the kitchen, closer to Niall. He looks up at me from the island where he is sitting, shock on his face.

". . . Thank you for not telling her. She'd be furious with me if she knew I'd asked you to spend time with her. . . ."

I can feel the blood drain from my face, while the beating of my heart simultaneously thumps loudly in my ears. I feel as if I'm going to pass out or explode.

Hundreds of memories flash through my mind, from our initial meeting to laser tag, jumping in the water, talking on the balcony, intimate moments between us, and my heart stops beating.

None of it was real.

He was just pretending to like me because Greg asked him to. *How ironic when pretending to like me was exactly what I'd asked him to do.* No wonder it was so easy for him to agree. He'd already agreed to pretend for Greg.

Niall quickly presses stop on Greg's voicemail.

"Gwen, I—"

"Don't say a word!" I snap.

"Listen, *mo ghrá*, I can explain," Niall says, reaching for my hand.

I step back and say forcefully, "No."

Niall stops, worry in his eyes. "Please—"

I hold up my hand to silence him and shake my head. "It was all a game to you. Nothing was real."

"But it was real."

"Not based on that voicemail it wasn't. You just pretended to like me this whole time—for Greg! And I fell for it like some fool."

"Gwendolyn, it's not like that—"

"Would you ever had told me Greg asked you to date me if I hadn't heard his voicemail? You had so many chances to clue me in on the whole charade. But you chose not to because this is all fake, some game to you."

I swiftly turn my eyes on him, glaring.

"That's not true."

"Don't. Don't lie to me, Niall. All you've done is lie. I heard what Greg said, clear as day. I just can't believe I fell for your lies. I can't believe I was blindsided again by, by these secrets." I say the last word through clenched teeth. I'm angry at myself for trusting that Niall wouldn't hurt me, wouldn't keep things from me.

"Gwen, please let me explain. It's not like that at all. What I feel for you is real. It may have started off—"

"What was the deal with Greg? Was it to stop me from being a workaholic? For your information, I love my job," I spit out.

"It wasn't like that," Niall says. "Greg and Trent both thought—"

"Trent was in on it too?" Now I'm furious. "How many people knew about this favor? Were Margot and Holly in on it also?"

"They didn't know anything about it. Gwen, please—"

"I'm sick of everyone deciding they know what is best for me. Everyone just needs to get over the fact that I have a successful business. I hate that everyone keeps trying to change me. That they keep things from me, like I can't handle the truth. You know what . . . I'm done."

"What are you talking about?" Niall asks, pain evident in his eyes.

"I'm done with us."

I have to get out of here. I have to leave this place. I hurry to the bedroom to pack my things. Niall didn't love me for me. He just wanted to change me. And stupidly, I fell for it. I fell for another man who wants to keep me from my job.

With a packed suitcase, I take out my phone and order a rideshare to the airport. From there, I can be home in a few hours. Back where I should be, to the safety and solitude that won't hurt me. I won't be made to look like an idiot, not again.

Then I head for the front door.

"Gwen," says Niall, who had followed me to the door. Tears fill his eyes. "I need you to hear me. It wasn't like that. I wanted to tell you, but I didn't want you to take it the wrong way. I thought we'd grown real feelings for each other so it wouldn't even matter. A funny story to tell later," he says.

"Do I look like I'm laughing? No. No part of this was funny. This is so different from the pact we made. No one could have gotten hurt with our pact. But your pact with Greg, how did you think I wouldn't get hurt by that? I thought I knew you better, but I guess I never knew you at all."

My phone pings, letting me know that my ride is here. "Well, that's my ride," I say.

Niall's eyes go wide. "Gwen, please don't go."

"I won't deny that we had fun on the cruise," I say, ignoring his pleas. "And I don't want to ruin Greg's post-marriage bliss, so I won't tell him that I found out about your deal." The words drip from my mouth with contempt.

"Goodbye, Niall," I say, then leave through the front door, tears rolling down my cheeks.

The next day, I wake up late, feeling like a freight truck hit me. I glance at my clock and notice it's one o'clock in the afternoon. My face is puffy from crying myself to sleep. My phone rings, and I flip it over to see Niall is calling. I send him to voicemail, noticing I have four missed calls and nine missed texts from him. I read the most recent text.

NIALL

Gwen, please call me, we should talk.

I silence my phone. I can't do this. I can't handle the calls and messages right now.

I can't just sit around all day, because I might be tempted to answer one of his calls or read more of his texts. So, I do what I do best. I take a quick shower, drink some coffee, and head to my office.

The quiet of the office on the weekend and going through next week's events will help me clear my head of the Irish hottie. No, the Irish liar.

Even though I still have feelings for him, I have to remember that he lied to me. everything was fake, just a favor for my brother. I want to strangle Greg for interfering.

When I had been with Bradley, he had hid his true feelings from me for months. Then hearing that Niall had lied about our entire relationship makes me wonder if he ever had genuine feelings for me. Did he even like me for me? Or was he just spending time with me for my brother's sake?

How is a relationship supposed to work when one person withholds vital information?

Answer: it doesn't.

Which is why it can't work out for Niall and I. And if Niall was lying to me from the start of our relationship, what would that mean for the rest of it? And if you add on the fact that we don't even live in the same state, it's too much for me to take.

Shaking my head to clear away unwanted memories and thoughts of the past week, I pull out next week's contracts to review. I'll just dedicate my life to my work and making other people's dreams come true. Having my friends and family will be enough.

I don't need a man; all they do is cause heartbreak.

CHAPTER 46
Niall

I'm in bits. Looking at my reflection in the mirror the day after Gwen left, it's clear that I haven't been myself. Other than call and text Gwen, I've sat on my couch or in my bed staring at my phone, willing her to answer my calls or message me back.

It's been radio silence.

I made such a hames of things. I should have told her about the favor. The moment I realized Greg had been talking about Gwen was the moment I should have gone to her and explained everything.

I found someone perfect for me, *mo anam cara*, and then I lost her. Mam was right. I do need someone in my life. It's Gwen. I fulfilled the promise to my mam and really tried, but now I've ruined everything. She'd be so disappointed.

I should have told Gwen I love her. I need to get a hold of her, explain everything, and profusely apologize. But if she won't answer my calls or texts, I have no way of reaching her.

Wait, I do. I quickly grab my phone and dial as I pace around my living room.

"Hey, dude!" Trent's cheerful voice comes across the line. "Miss me already?"

My heart aches, and I try to clear my throat. "Hey." It's all I can get out.

"Sully, dude, what's wrong?" Trent asks. I can hear water in the background. He must be at the marina. I hear some muffled voices before Trent says, "I didn't think I'd hear from you so soon. I thought you'd be busy with Gwen, showing her around Boston."

"I'm not. . . . I've screwed everything up." I say, running my hand through my hair.

"I'm sure it's not all that bad. What happened?"

I tell Trent everything starting after the cruise, how everything was going perfectly, then everything fell apart.

"Wow, so she's been back home since yesterday?" he asks.

"She has. So, you haven't seen her?"

"She didn't call me. I figured she'd be in Boston for another day from what you all had planned. I'll get a hold of Margot and see if she's heard from her. Don't worry. I'm sure everything will work out."

"I don't see how."

"Sully, I saw you two together. She cares about you a lot. Listen, I'll check in on her and get back to you."

"Thanks, mate," I say, clicking off my phone and sinking down into the couch.

CHAPTER 47
Gwen

The next day, I'm still immersed in work. I'm thinking about what kind of decorations to use for next week's fundraiser gala when I turn and almost run into Margot and Trent. Both are staring at me, Margot with her hands on her hips.

"What?" I ask, not in the mood to talk to either of them. I have a feeling I know exactly why they are here.

"What do you mean 'what?'" says Margot. "What happened?"

"Why don't you ask Trent?" I motion next to her. "I'm sure he can fill you in on the little deal Greg struck with Niall."

"That's not what you think it is, G," says Trent calmly.

I snap a cold glare at him. "Don't. Don't try and defend them. Either of you. You both know how hard the breakup with Bradley was for me. You know how much his poor communication blindsided me. And then you," I turn to Trent and continue, "You and Greg had Niall lie to me. It wasn't even bad communication; our relationship was just a full-blown lie! You all lied to me." Angry tears fall down my face. I wipe my cheek with the back of my hand. "You all are supposed to be my best friends. And Niall . . . Niall didn't mean anything to me. So, there's nothing more to talk about."

Both Margot and Trent have pained expressions on their faces.

"I'm so sorry," says Trent. "I didn't mean . . ."

"Gwen . . ." Margot starts, but I walk away from them.

Reaching the hallway and turning the corner, I sag against the wall and lower myself to the floor. Tears run down my face, but I don't brush them away this time.

Niall hadn't meant anything to me; he'd meant everything to me. How that man had weaseled his way into my heart was beyond me. Now, I need to figure out a way to get him out or live my life regretting what could have been.

CHAPTER 48
Niall

I'm thankful for my shift the next day. It's good for me to be around others and not be alone. When I'm alone, I have too much time to relive every moment. To think about what I could have done differently so things wouldn't have ended up like they did.

"You look awful," says Johnny as I put my things in my locker. "Here, take a cookie."

"Thanks," I say, reaching over and taking one. Not that I feel like a cookie, but in no way am I going to have him report back to his wife that I refused one of her desserts. The first bite takes me back to the day Gwen first popped her head into my rental car and her sweet strawberries-and-cream scent flooded my senses. The reminder of her brings a fresh wave of grief. I've never felt this strongly for someone in my entire life, and the sadness is drowning me.

"Oh no, I know that look," says Brianna, joining us near the lockers as she ties the laces on one of her boots.

"What?" asks Mitchell. "What did I miss?"

"It's the girl, isn't it?" asks Brianna softly.

"Did you already mess things up with her?" asks Mitchell. "Man, I told you not to let her go."

"Let's leave the poor guy alone," says Johnny. "He doesn't need us making him feel worse than he already is."

I tip my head at him in thanks as I pretend to rummage around in my locker, avoiding eye contact with my crew.

They all trickle out, and I'm left alone. Taking a deep breath, I square my shoulders and prepare myself for the shift. At home, I can wallow as much as I want, but when I'm on duty, it's no longer about me. It's about keeping the community and my crew safe. I join the rest of the crew in the kitchen and pour myself a cup of coffee.

The rest of the day goes as normal. No one brings up Gwen, which I'm grateful for. Before long, we get a call.

The days go by in a mix of working at the firehouse and wallowing at home trying to see a way to make things better. And even though Gwen had visited my home only briefly, it feels so empty without her, like she was meant to be there with me, a part of my life.

My calls to Trent are pretty much the same. Gwen is working all the time, doesn't come hang out with anyone, and when they try to talk to her, she snaps at them to leave.

On Sunday, as I'm getting ready to head to bed before my next twenty-four-hour shift begins, my phone rings. I quickly answer, hoping it will be Gwen, but it's not.

"Hey, man," says Greg. "How are you?"

"Miserable, mate," I say.

"Look, Trent and Margot filled Holly and me in on what happened. And trust me, I got an earful from both Holly and Margot. I'm sorry I ever asked you to spend time with my sister. If I'd had any clue that you two would have hit it off, I never would have suggested anythi—ouch!" Muffled voices on the other end cause him to stop.

Greg continues, "As Holly not so subtly just reminded me, I shouldn't have ever asked you to begin with, whether I thought you'd hit it off or not," he finishes, then adds, "I'm going to get a bruise from that."

"Look, mate, it's okay. I should have just come clean to her. It's my fault for agreeing and my fault for not telling her the truth."

"Sully, you're a good man, one of the best. I'm going to talk to Gwen, explain to her that it was all my fault, that she should give you a chance to say your piece."

"Thanks, but I doubt she will," I say. One thing I learned about Gwen is she can be stubborn. She's adorable when she is, but no one can force her to do something she doesn't want to do.

"We'll see about that," he says. "Don't give up on her. Deep down, Gwen cares about you. We all saw it. She wouldn't be so upset otherwise."

"Well then, I wish you luck." I'm quiet for a moment before I add, "I miss her, Greg. I'd do anything for a second chance."

The next day, Captain Frank pulls me into his office. "Sit down, Niall, I want to talk with you."

"Yes, sir, is something wrong?" I ask.

"That's exactly what I was going to ask you. For the past week, you've been coming into work, doing your job, and heading home."

"Am I not doing a good job?"

"You're doing a fine job. You always do. But you're not yourself lately and I'm curious, why is that? I need my firehouse to run in tip-top shape. Lives are on the line."

"Yes, sir. I understand. I've been dealing with something, but it's over, and I just need to let it go."

"Is it that gal you brought in to meet us a week ago?" he asks.

"Sir?"

"I saw the way you two were, reminded me of when my wife and I first met. It was clear you're head over heels for that gal. And if I were to guess, I'd say that you messed something up between the two of you."

"How did you . . ."

"I've been around a long time, son, and have learned a thing or two. You need to go after her. Tell her how you really feel."

"I want to, but I just don't think—"

"Doesn't sound like you are thinking at all."

I snap my head up at his comment, and he chuckles.

"Go after her," he says matter-of-factly.

"But what if she doesn't want me? It hurts too much," I admit.

"But it'll hurt more if you don't. You've had a lot of heartache this past year, and I know that can't be easy. Love can hurt, but when you find the right person, it's worth going all in. What would your mam say?"

I picture my mam. Mam would have loved Gwen. Gwen is spunky and loves fiercely. My mam would say that is just the person her son needs: someone who can make me laugh, keep me on my toes, and feel like home. She'd be appalled I'd been moping around the house and not fighting for who I love.

I smile a genuine smile, the first in a few days, before I reply to the captain, "She'd tell me to get my head out of my arse and go marry her before someone else does."

"Then what are you waiting for?" he asks.

CHAPTER 49
Gwen

The following Wednesday, I'm back at my office bright and early. I decided to get a head start on the day's to-do list before the rest of the staff arrive. It's not like I can sleep anyway. Last night, we held an alumni event at one of the historic mansions in Donelson, and there's still a lot that needs to be cleaned and put away.

"Hi, Gwennie," a voice startles me. I spin around to see my brother looking sheepish.

"Hi, G," adds Holly warmly from behind him, then she glares at her husband. I walk past Greg, practically ignoring him, and give Holly a big hug.

"How was Vermont?" I ask, forcing a smile for my best friend, now sister-in-law.

"It was perfect, but that is not the point of why we dropped in unannounced, is it, Greg?"

Greg nods.

"Greg has something he wants to say to you," Holly continues. "I'm going to For The Love of Sugar. When you two are done, come over and I'll have your favorites ready for you."

Greg and I watch as Holly leaves out the door. "Marriage has made her fierce," I say.

Greg laughs. "Yeah," he agrees, "but I wouldn't have it any other way."

"I'm guessing I know what you want to speak about, and while I don't really want to hear anything you say, I know Holly will know if we've had this talk or not, so let's just get it over with." I pull out two stools for us to sit on.

"First, I want to say I'm sorry," Greg says, looking sincere. "What I did was with good intentions. I never meant for you to get hurt. I wanted the opposite actually."

"Go on," I say.

"The morning we boarded the cruise, I ran into Niall at breakfast. I asked him to spend time with you during the cruise to help you have a good time like Trent, Niall, and I had in college together. You've just been so distant and sad lately, not like yourself at all. I've been worried about you and got the not-so-brilliant idea that you could benefit from some of Sully's energy. And for the record, I just want to say it worked. You came out of your shell on the cruise."

I glare at him, my arms crossed over my chest.

"But that's beside the point," he continues. "Niall was hesitant to agree to it at first. It took some convincing on my end. And then you two seemed to be having a good time, maybe more than a good time." Greg gives me a wink, but I remain stoic.

"Anyway," Greg continues, "I didn't find out about your pact until much later. Then I saw Niall kiss you, and I confronted him about it because that definitely wasn't part of the favor I asked him. I mean, I practically pulled a you, when you yelled at me about Holly. I was going to kill him for playing with you like that."

Then Greg says something that shocks me to my core. Something I never saw coming.

"But, Gwennie, the sincerity in his eyes and the tone of his voice when he told me how it wasn't pretend and it had never been pretend. I just, I saw a little bit of me in him.

How I felt about Holly, I mean. He truly cares for you; I'd say he even loves you."

My eyes shoot up at his use of the word love. My breath halts. It can't be, he couldn't.

"If he cared that much," I say, "he wouldn't have kept a secret like this from me. I can't be in a relationship that is based on a lie. I need someone who is going to be open and honest with me."

"Yes, Gwennie, but Niall is a good guy, a great one even. Did he maybe make a bad decision in listening to me? Yes. But I don't think he'd ever purposely try to hurt you. And I'd bet if you gave him a chance, he wouldn't ever do anything like that again."

"I'm still angry," I say.

"As you have every right to be," Greg says. "But give Niall another chance."

"I can't promise anything, but I can think about what you said."

"Thank you. I think you'll see that giving him a chance, even just hearing him out, will be worth it." He stands and pulls me into a hug. "And for what it's worth, I'm sorry for meddling and giving him a reason to lie to you in the first place."

I hug Greg back, then thump him on the head. "I know you were doing this with the best intentions, but please never meddle in my life again."

The next two days, I'm a mess. I work long hours during the day and toss and turn all night. I can't get what Greg said out of my head.

Were Niall's feelings always genuine? Does Niall truly love me?

My mind flashes back to the look on his face when I left him. Was it true sorrow and heartbreak I'd seen on his face? Not just anguish from being caught?

Taking a deep breath, I pull up my voicemails. They've gone down in number over the past few days, but he hasn't missed a day yet trying to get in touch with me. The realization makes my heart thump loudly in my chest.

I pick a random voicemail from the long list and hit play. Just hearing Niall's voice causes tears to well in my eyes. It's a simple voicemail, asking for a chance to explain everything when I'm ready to talk. I can't take hearing his voice again. It hurts too much, so I look through a few of the texts.

NIALL

Gwendolyn, I'm sorry for hurting you. That was never my intention. Please let me explain.

NIALL

Please let me know you made it home ok. I just want to make sure you are safe.

NIALL

Gwen, I heard from Trent and he says you are working a lot and avoiding them. Please know this was not their fault. The fault is fully mine. I should have been open and honest with you.

NIALL

Rose, I'm sorry.

NIALL

I miss you, Rose, I care about you. Call me anytime, day or night. I just want the chance to talk.

After reading through the rest of the texts and even listening to a few more voicemails, I put my phone down, tears falling from my eyes like a dam has broken and nothing can stop the downpour of emotions flooding my system. Never once was he angry or mad with me. Each text and voicemail was calm, caring, sincere.

I feel so confused. I'm hurt that he didn't open up to me. I mean what I said to Greg about a relationship not being able to start on a lie, but my gut is telling me that I need to forgive Niall, that I should give us another chance. But how do I do that? How do I move past what happened?

I have another sleepless night, unable to get these thoughts out of my head. I'm so confused. I need to talk to Holly.

Early the next morning, I go to see Holly before she opens up her bakery for the day, a strong cup of coffee in my hands.

The sweet smells of pastries baking overwhelm my senses as I walk in the back entrance. "Hols, you close by?" I yell out after not seeing her in the kitchen.

"I'm up front."

Walking to the front of the shop, it's like walking into a fairy garden. Display cases, grass, and flowers cover the walls in a beautiful mural. Plants hang from the ceiling as well as strands of lights giving off a magical glow. Outdoor-style tables and chairs dot the floor, making it feel like you've entered an actual garden. No matter what mood I'm in, the moment I walk into her bakery, it brings a smile to my face.

"What brings you in this early?" Holly asks, not even looking up from where she's loading some baked goods into the display cases.

"I . . ." I start, but then stop immediately.

I don't know what to say.

"G, what is it?" she looks over at me, worry creasing her brow.

"I . . . I think I messed up, and I don't know how to fix it," I admit, sinking into a bench by the wall.

"About Niall?" she offers.

I nod.

"Okay, how can I help?" Holly asks, wiping her hands on her apron and then heading around the display cases toward me.

"Can you just tell me what to do?" I laugh meekly.

"Afraid not, G. But I can tell you that Niall is an amazing guy. Probably one of the best."

"He lied to me."

"Yes, he lied. And while that's not okay, you can't really put the whole blame on him. I mean, you asked him to do the same lie, to spend time with you with your little fake relationship thing. So really, if you both had that pact going on, and Niall agreed to do the same favor for Greg, did Niall even really lie?"

"You've got a point," I admit.

"Niall really cares about you, G. Even now, after everything."

I snap up at her admission. "You think so?"

"I know so," she says so matter-of-factly that I can't not believe her.

"Then I think I know what I need to do," I say, pulling out my phone. "I need to book a plane ticket."

I hop in a rideshare and head to the Nashville airport. With traffic on I-24 always a nightmare, I have to leave three hours before my flight. In the blink of an eye, the normally forty-five-minute drive can take an hour and a half, and I'd rather not miss this flight.

Sending a quick text to my second-in-command, Becca, I explain that she'll be in charge for the weekend because I have to take care of something important immediately. And that, oh yeah, she's getting promoted to senior event planner effective immediately.

I have no clue if Niall will want anything to do with me after how I treated him, but I have to try.

I love him.

Thankfully, at ten o'clock on a Friday morning, the traffic isn't so bad. We actually make it to the airport in record time. Now, if I could just calm my beating heart.

Clyde, my rideshare driver, says, "If it's alright with you, miss, can I drop you off at the rideshare pickup spot so I don't have to drive all the way around to pick up my next passenger?"

I need all the good karma I can get, so I tell him, "I have no problem with that."

"Thank you, miss," he responds, driving toward the pickup area.

Clyde parks and hops out to meet his next passenger as I lean down to pick up my backpack. Reaching for the door, my hand misses as the door is opened from the outside.

"*Mo ghrá?*" says a male voice, one that makes my heart stop.

It can't be.

There's no way. It's not possible.

I look up, and sure enough, it's Niall.

"What are you doing here?" We both say in unison.

A single tear rolls down my cheek. Stupid emotions taking over. Niall reaches out a hand to me, and I take it. Then, he wipes the tear from my face.

"Why are you crying, Gwen?" he asks, his voice cracking with emotion.

"Niall, I'm so sorry," I manage to say on a sob, as more tears begin to fall.

"Oh, *mo ghrá*, so am I. More than I could ever describe." He pulls me into a soul-crushing hug. I feel the hug throughout my entire body. Fifty years from now, I will remember this hug, the way it feels to be held by him.

"You two know each other then?" Clyde asks.

"You could say that." Niall laughs. "If you could give us a minute, please?" Clyde nods and gets back in the car.

"Look," says Niall, pulling back from me slightly. "I should have told you about the favor I agreed to do for Greg. It was daft of me to keep it to myself."

"I was just so hurt and confused that you didn't tell me about the pact you made with Greg. And it made me think that you were just spending time with me because he asked you to, not that you really wanted to be with me. I was afraid you didn't really like me for me. And I was scared you'd want me to change, be someone else."

"Gwen, that's just not true. From the first moment we'd met, there was something about you that called to me, and I wanted to get to know you more, so when Greg asked me, I went along with it. I was happy he was, in a way, giving me his stamp of approval. I was hoping it would keep Greg from acting like an overly protective, angry older brother if things between us went somewhere. And I really wanted them to go somewhere."

"You did?"

"Of course I did. Why else would I agree to fake date you if I didn't already want to date you in the first place?"

More tears stream down my face, and I wrap my arms around Niall.

"Though I was totally wrong about Greg's reaction," Niall says, shaking his head. "He was not thrilled when he found out I was being more than friendly with you."

"Overprotection and hot-headedness do seem to be a family trait of ours," I say, then laugh.

"I'm so sorry for lying to you," says Niall, "and I promise to never knowingly do so again. But as for making daft decisions, I'm sure I'll make plenty of those in the future. But hopefully you can be patient with me. Maybe even give me a second chance? That's why I'm here. I had to give this one more shot. A life without you isn't a life at all."

"I was coming to you," I say, "to ask you to give *me* a second chance. I'm so sorry I let my emotions and fears get the best of me and that I didn't give you a chance to explain. I can't promise that won't happen again, but I can promise that I will work on hearing you out. I just need you to be patient with me while I work on it."

"Were you really going to fly up to Boston to see me?" he asks.

"Yes, but seems like you beat me to it by coming here." I chuckle lightly.

"Gwendolyn, even though we've only known each other for a few weeks, and some of those days we've spent apart—by the way, those were some of the worst days of my life—" he admits, "I've been a shell of myself without you. I've felt empty and so lost. Because I want us to give this a real chance. I realized I was falling for you. No," he stops himself.

"No?" I ask.

"Correction, I was not falling for you. I have fallen for you. To be more specific, I've fallen in love with you."

"Oh," I say timidly, letting out a small hiccup sob.

"Being without you made me feel like I had lost a part of myself. You make me happy. You make me whole. I don't ever want to lose you again."

And then his mouth is on mine, not soft, but fierce. A kiss filled with a desperate longing from both of us.

We pull apart to take a breath, and he leans his forehead against mine. "I want to be with you, Gwendolyn. I don't want to be apart from you ever again."

Nodding, I say, "I would love nothing more. I love you, Niall."

TEN MONTHS
Later . . . .

EPILOGUE
Niall

After a whirlwind ten months, I've finally moved the last of my things to Tennessee. It was an easy decision to move. While leaving my crew at the firehouse was difficult, a spot opened up for a lieutenant in Chessie Valley, and having passed my lieutenant exam, I was able to get the position. The crew at the Chessie Valley firehouse welcomed me with open arms.

Gwen and I decided not to sell my house in Boston but to fix it up and rent it out for part of the year. It took us a little more time than anticipated to renovate it, but now it will not only remind me of my mam but also be a home to Gwen and me when we spend a few weeks there during the summers or holidays. Boston will always be home to me and have a place in my heart. It's where I grew up and where the memories of my mam are the strongest.

But just as my mam made me promise I'd find someone after her passing, she'd also want me go out and live my life. My life now is in Chessie Valley with Gwen, and Greg and Trent, who've always been like brothers to me. I may not have a family of my own, but I've found *mo thaeghlach* with them.

Gwen left her apartment, and we found the perfect house that we just moved into about two months ago. She has also been making changes at work. After promoting

Becca, her second-in-command, to senior event planner, she also hired two additional event planners and an office manager. With those changes, she has more freedom to pick the jobs she wants to work and has a great work-life balance. It's a decision she said was a long time coming and completely worth it if it means we get to spend more time together. She's decidedly less grumpy but still a little fire-cracker full of life and happiness.

Deciding to propose to Gwen was easier than deciding to breathe. She'd come up to Boston for a weekend, and I planned a picnic at Revere Beach, where I used to go with my mam. I wanted a spot where I felt close to my mam because I know she would have loved Gwen. I remember the look on Gwen's face when she realized what I was up to and will never forget the smile that broke out as she agreed to be my wife.

If I had to guess, I'd say that my face was a mirror of hers in that moment.

Tonight, we are celebrating our engagement with a housewarming party.

We decorated our backyard with string lights and set up tables and chairs. We've invited everyone—friends, family, coworkers—because we have a surprise to share with them all.

Walking into our master bedroom, I look over at Gwen, who is watching as friends and family mingle out back. She is gorgeous with her hair down and a crown of flowers in her hair. Her whimsical off-white dress with long flowy sleeves hits just above her knees and shows off her lovely, sculpted legs. That plus the plunging neckline takes my breath away.

"Wow, *mo ghrá*, you are a vision," I say, coming up behind her and kissing her neck.

She twirls around to face me. "You look pretty dapper yourself," she says, admiring me in my white button-down shirt and khaki pants. She kisses me gently.

"Are you ready to do this?" she asks.

"Not having second thoughts, are you?" I counter.

"Never." Her eyes sparkle with mischief.

Tonight is not only our engagement-plus-housewarming party, but also our wedding. And only the two of us and the pastor we've sworn to secrecy know.

"And you're sound with not having a huge wedding?" I ask, checking for what is probably the hundredth time.

"Of course I am," she says. "I've had to plan too many big, over-the-top weddings. I just want something simple, where I have you, and we are surrounded by the people we care about most. I love that we get to start our life together in the backyard of our new house. The first of so many memories." She reaches into her dresser drawer and pulls out a box. "I have something for you."

"What is it, *mo ghrá*?"

"I know your mom can't be here, though she will be in our hearts, but I wanted her to be a part of this wedding too," she says, placing the box in my hand.

I open the box, and inside is a beautiful pocket watch.

"Open it," she urges.

Inside, I find two pictures, one of my mam and me when I was little, and one of my mam smiling that had been taken just before she passed.

"It's perfect," I say, kissing her once more before adding, "That means more to me than you know." Placing the watch in my pocket and then taking her hand in mine, I lead her down the stairs and out to our friends and family.

When we step out onto the back porch, I say, gesturing to Gwen, "We have an announcement to make."

"I know you all are here to celebrate our engagement and housewarming," says Gwen, "and while that is true, it's not the full truth."

"We've been keeping a secret from you," I add.

Taking a deep breath, she looks at me, then turns back to the crowd. "We invite you all to stay and celebrate our wedding."

Stunned murmurs echo around us before everyone converges on us in a euphoric happiness. We lock eyes for a moment before Gwen is quickly ushered inside by her mom, Holly, and Margot.

"See you in a minute," she says as I leave with Greg and Trent.

The ceremony doesn't last long. Gwen is glowing as she walks out of the house and down the makeshift aisle. The pastor says his part, and then it's our turn.

"Niall," says Gwen, "I vow not to be too grumpy when you wake me up in the mornings. I promise to be your sanctuary, a place of love and support. A place of security and calm. When you first met me, I'd been lost in the dark, but you brought a light to my life and helped me see that the future holds amazing opportunity when we are together. Once, you asked me if I trusted you before we took a leap off a cliff. Now I'm telling you I trust you as we take this leap into our new life together. I look forward to creating a lifetime of memories together. I love you." A tear rolls down Gwen's face, and her smile is so full of light and happiness that it makes me weak at the knees.

Then it's my turn, and a grin breaks across my face. Never have I ever been more ready for something in my life. "Gwen, I stand here today, my heart overflowing with love for you. You are exactly the woman my mam would have wanted me to be with, feisty and full of life. You also brought me out of my darkness from her loss. You showed me that there is still light, happiness, and love in this life. You've given me a family, something I never thought I'd have again. I promise to be patient, to listen, and more importantly, to communicate openly with you each and every day. And I vow to always have a pot of coffee ready for you when you wake each morning."

After everyone's laughter dissipates, I continue. "From the moment we first met, I knew there was something about you that called to me, and I choose you, today and every day forward, *mo ghrá*. With you, my life is complete."

By the end of my vows, we are both in tears, and thankfully, the pastor doesn't skip a beat telling me to kiss my bride.

I pull her close to me and kiss her to the whooping and hollering of those around us. After we break apart, I whisper to her, "You are *mo anam cara*, my soul mate, and now *mo theaghlach*, my family."

She leans in and kisses me softly again before we turn to the crowd and are announced as husband and wife, Mr. and Mrs. O'Sullivan.

As I look around our backyard, I realize that less than a year ago, I was feeling so alone after the passing of my mam, worried I would never have this feeling of being home, of having a family who loved me.

I smile, looking around at our friends and my newfound family and chuckle.

"What is it?" Gwen asks, curiosity in her starburst eyes.

"Just thinking, there was a time when I thought I would never be happy again, but now . . . after bumping into you, I have found my happiness. Now I get forever with you."

The End

Your Reviews Matter.

No matter what version of this book you've read, a review can help other fabulous readers like yourself find their way to my books. If you loved, or even just liked, *Bumping into You*, please consider leaving a review.

Thank you so much for your reviews and support, as well as for taking a chance on a new author and reading one of my novels!

ACKNOWLEDGMENTS

Thank you to all my readers and those of you who follow me on social media. Without your support and taking a chance on a new author, my second book would never have found its way into the amazing world of romance readers. You are making my dreams come true!

I loved getting to build out Gwen and Niall's story. Gwen holds a special place in my heart because a piece of me went into building her character, like her obsessive need to fix everything for everyone else and the way she cares fiercely for her friends and family.

I can't believe I've now written two novels and have a third on the way. Every day that I get to sit down at my computer and write, and every positive review I read, it's like a dream come true.

To the Bookish Babes, April, Bella, Courtney, Kate-lynne, Mallory, and Sara, I love that I've found you all. Going through this indie author experience is not for the faint of heart, and you make it easier to keep going when things get tough. Y'all are the best!

I want to send a special thank you to my brilliant cover designer, Melody Jeffries. Your talent blows me away every time, and I love how you bring my characters to life.

Another special thank you to my amazing team of editors at Ever Editing. Thank you for guiding me through the editing process and making this task seem manageable. Thank you to Breanna for helping me develop the story and character arcs to really bring this story to life!

To Wendy, my sensitivity reader and new friend who found me through the crazy world of social media. Thank you for helping me make sure I did this book justice by portraying the loss, anxiety and Irish culture to the best of my ability.

To my official *affect* versus *effect* helper and marketing guru, Chanel, thank you. I don't think I will ever grasp the difference between the two, even though you've been so patient in trying to help me—not only with that but with my marketing. I may not always listen to you, but I'm trying little by little.

To Rachael, thank you for answering all my random and sometimes late-night texts with my off-the-wall questions and helping me get this book just right!

To Abbey, Denise, and Elizabeth, thank you for being my first try at having beta readers. I am still learning, and you all were patient and willing to give feedback on the first draft of *Bumping into You*. It wouldn't be where it is today without you all.

Finally, to my husband and kids, thank you for allowing me the time to write and edit my stories. It's a dream come true to be sending another book of mine into the world, and I couldn't do it without your support and love.

Lastly, to my readers, thank you for taking a chance on a new author. You are making my dreams come true!

JESS JEFFERIES

Jess currently lives in Tennessee with her husband, three kids, and their dogs. She has a bubbly personality and can almost always be found with a smile on her face.

While reading has always been a passion of hers, she has also dabbled in writing short stories and poems since she was a little girl. *Thirteen-Year Crush* is her debut novel, a romcom that released in March 2023.

When Jess is not writing, you can find her swimming with her kids, playing board games, or snuggling up with a book and comfy blanket.

Follow her on Instagram and TikTok:
@jessjefferieswrites

www.jessjefferieswrites.com